THREE DAYS
on
MIMOSA LANE

ALSO BY ANNA DESTEFANO

CONTEMPORARY ROMANCE

Christmas on Mimosa Lane (A Seasons of the Heart Novel)
A Sweetbrook Family (previously available as *A Family for Daniel*)
All-American Father
The Perfect Daughter (Daughter Series)
The Prodigal's Return
The Runaway Daughter (Daughter Series)
A Family for Daniel
The Unknown Daughter (Daughter Series)

SCIENCE FICTION/FANTASY

Secret Legacy
Dark Legacy

ROMANTIC SUSPENSE

Her Forgotten Betrayal
The Firefighter's Secret Baby (Atlanta Heroes series)
To Save a Family (Atlanta Heroes series)
To Protect the Child (Atlanta Heroes series)
Because of a Boy (Atlanta Heroes series)

NOVELLAS/ANTHOLOGIES

"Weekend Meltdown" in *Winter Heat*
"Baby Steps" in *Mother of the Year*
A Small-Town Sheriff (Daughter Series)

THREE DAYS
— on —
MIMOSA LANE

—A Seasons of the Heart Novel—

Anna DeStefano

Montlake
Romance

Published by Montlake Romance
PO Box 400818
Las Vegas, NV 89140

ISBN-13: 9781477807330
ISBN-10: 1477807330

To families and survivors and heroes of all ages.
You inspire me beyond words.
May your dreams bloom into vivid reality.

DAY ONE

Chapter One

January 14, 2013

On a scale from nervous to freaked out, Samantha Perry had been having a silent meltdown all weekend. Somewhere during the night, she'd risen from beside her sleeping husband, showered and dressed, and bundled into the lightweight coat that only a few North Georgia months required each year. Then, heading downstairs and through her cozy kitchen's French doors, she'd escaped into the peace of being outside.

She'd been night walking ever since.

It was nearly dawn now in her winter world. Yet midnight felt closer than morning. And amidst what would be a flowering garden in a few months, she was wandering the edges of her community's park. It was just another day, like any other in suburban Atlanta, full of harmless moments that would carelessly string themselves together. She'd soon be getting her family ready for their Mimosa Lane Monday. Life was good. Nothing was amiss. It should be so easy to believe that nothing bad could happen in this silent, nurturing place, even as her nerves rattled onward and her mind braced for an invisible collision.

Outdoors, distanced from the memories that had spoiled her sleep, she longed to believe that today of all days she wouldn't crawl back beneath the covers and disappoint her family by not coming out again until tomorrow. Or the next day. Or even the day after that. Maybe not until spring. Sam was tired of the drama. They all were. It had been an exhausting twelve years of ups and downs and never moving forward, and she refused to let today be about hiding. Her boys and her husband would see that she was finally well. *She* would see.

Chandlerville had been her home for more than a decade. It was past time for her to begin living the kind of life she and Brian had transplanted here to build. Their two boys were getting older, their young worlds expanding. If Sam didn't tunnel out of the protective cocoon her endlessly patient husband had helped her construct on their secluded cul-de-sac, she'd miss even more of the precious growing-up moments that had passed her by already.

With waning moonlight illuminating her path, she retraced her steps, leaving the park and its playground behind and returning to her own pampered gardens. Sunrise silvered the distant horizon, promising every bright, hopeful thing she craved. She took the turn where the lane curved into a cluster of homes owned by her family and cul-de-sac neighbors. Kneeling beside the bed of sleeping bulbs she'd planted around her mailbox, she brushed away leaves that had tumbled into the yard from the oaks next door.

Sulky pansies rimmed the bed, shifting in breezy shadow. Their tattered blooms were flags of hope that the colder weather wouldn't last forever. Smiling, Sam headed around the house until she reached her roses. Delicate and regal, they inspired her like nothing else she grew. Not that she was anyone's idea of a master gardener. Friends who'd known her before she'd moved here would have been shocked to learn that she no longer killed everything she planted. She had at first, when she'd taken up the solitary pastime as she and Brian awaited the arrival of their secondborn. Over the years gardening had become a much-needed escape, and it was the roses that had first befriended her.

They spent most of their lives as prickly, ruthlessly pruned vines twisting around the wooden trellis Brian had built—a jumble of leaves and thorns, little more than overgrown weeds. But when it was a rose's turn to thrive, its beauty reigned supreme. Sam's bloomed twice a year, including in January. She cradled one of the hearty flowers. It was a splash of deep crimson, a promise against her palm that Sam could handle heading back inside in a few minutes. That she could handle anything, as long as she kept growing and thriving and leaning on the unconditional support of her family.

Being indoors made her feel trapped sometimes, even in her own home. And there'd be kids and teachers swarming around her later at school. She'd want to run. Literally. But when the panic came, today she would stay. Today was the fresh start she and the people she loved deserved.

Her and Brian's long-ago move from Manhattan was supposed to have been their do-over. Her husband's bright blue eyes and devilish grin flashed through her mind. She felt again the exhilaration of being in his arms last night, and practically every night of their fifteen-year marriage. She thought of each thumbs-up of encouragement he'd given her since she'd decided this New Year's Eve to make today happen. He'd been so proud that she felt strong enough to try again.

She thought of Cade, her eldest son who'd barely been a toddler when they'd first arrived on Mimosa Lane, and his surprise that she wouldn't simply be sending in her gourmet brownies to Chandler Elementary's PTA bake sale. She was delivering them herself, and staying to sell them to his classmates. Today Cade would see that she was there for him. Her sixth grader wouldn't head to junior high school next year without her ever having made it through a single school function.

Thank goodness their school district was pilot-testing a "shorter" middle school model, where kids stayed in elementary for an extra year, with junior high truncated into two years spent on the high school campus. Without the extra time, Cade would have already graduated from Chandler, and likely wouldn't have wanted Sam volunteering at the high school at all, even *if* she'd been up to it.

Cade.

Her sensitive boy.

Her writer.

He felt everything and watched every move people made. And more than anyone else, he watched Sam, forever aware and worried and waiting for her to need him and his dad's help in desperate ways that no mother should.

"Mom?" a young voice asked, making her jump, though she shouldn't have been surprised to find him waiting on the patio.

She turned slowly. Her smile was a believable, motherly façade.

"Hey, buddy," she said to her eleven-year-old, who was blond and blue-eyed and already lanky, just like his father. Cade was sprawled in the wooden swing next to the house. "What are you doing up this early?"

"Couldn't sleep. I figured I'd wait for you to come back."

She woke up halfway through most nights, and everyone in the house knew that outside felt better than inside when she couldn't shut her thoughts off. So they left her to her wandering when she needed to, as if it were no big deal. But Cade always seemed to sense when she was having a particularly difficult time.

She sat on the swing's dark green cushions and curled him into the half hug that he still let her steal every now and again. All-out *smothering* mothering was no longer cool with her almost teenager, even at home. And on the few occasions when she went along as the boys and Brian did things with friends and neighbors, Cade insisted on an affection-free zone in the community.

He was such a big guy. Soon he might shy away completely from even these private moments. The little-boy things she and Brian had treasured with him were fading so fast, making room for who he'd become.

"Are you going to be okay?" he asked.

"Sure." It wasn't a lie. She couldn't, she absolutely *wouldn't*, disappoint him and Brian and her youngest, Joshua, again.

"I know you're scared." Cade scooted to the other side of his cushion. "I mean, I don't *know*, but . . ."

She reached for his hand. His skin was ice cold, even though he was wearing his navy blue winter coat over his flannel pajamas. She mentally clunked herself upside the head for dragging him out of bed. It was ludicrous, getting everyone this wound up about something so simple.

"I'm sorry," she said. "I wish . . ."

An awkward silence joined them on the swing.

"You don't have to talk about it," Cade said. "I know you and Dad don't like to, you know . . . remember what happened. It doesn't bother me. Being around a lot of people bugs you. It's no big deal. You don't have to come today. Not if you don't want to."

She squeezed his hand. "Honey, I want to be there for you and Joshua today more than I've wanted anything in a long time. I promise you," she insisted, even though she was a teacher who was terrified of being anywhere near a school. "Everything will be better after today. You'll see."

Cade nodded, but she could tell he wasn't convinced. The sun's first rays topped the ridge of pines at the back of their property. She stood and took a bracing breath.

"Want some breakfast?" she asked.

"Yeah."

He smiled his dad's smile. Her boys loved breakfast almost as much as Sam loved making it for them. Cade headed inside in front of her.

"Get your brother up," she called. "Take turns in the shower while I get things started."

This wasn't *just* another morning. It was going to be, hands down, the second-hardest school day of her life. But on this beautiful winter morning her family had the chance to bloom into something it had never been. Something *she'd* never been in her sons' lives—easy, open, and no longer afraid.

And that was exactly what she intended to become for them, whatever that took.

***

"Big day!" Brian Perry bounded down the back stairs to the kitchen, where his boys were munching on amazing-smelling muffins.

Orange juice sat before them on the granite island, in a pitcher and poured into two glasses. Sam would have freshly squeezed it, just as she'd have baked the pastry from scratch and set out the place mats she'd sewn herself. As difficult as this morning was, nurturing their boys came as second nature to her as breathing. A man couldn't ask for a better mother for his children.

The day-to-day details and demands of home took a lot out of his wife, energy she often didn't have to spare, though she'd once been able to outwork, outthink, and outparty him. But time with their boys in the mornings and afternoons—cooking for them and talking with them and working one-on-one with them on their schoolwork—never slipped down Sam's priority list.

"Everyone sleep well?" Brian asked.

Cade shrugged and kept eating.

Brian knew his oldest was stressing about today. He also knew Cade didn't want to talk about it. He just wanted this latest attempt by Sam to be a normal mom to end differently from all the rest. It was what they all wanted. And things had been going so well, Brian wasn't about to rock the boat.

Sam's improvement since the holidays had had a remarkable effect on their family. Particularly Cade, who was laughing louder with his friends and bickering with his brother more and good-naturedly harassing Sam most afternoons when Brian walked through the door at the end of a mind-numbing work-day. All typical kid stuff, and in their house *typical* was like ice cream on a blistering summer day.

But over the weekend Sam's fraying nerves had strained everyone's excitement. She hadn't withdrawn completely, the way she would have in the past. But Brian could sense his eldest bracing for another disappointment. That morning, when Brian hadn't found his wife sleeping beside him, he'd checked Cade's room next, discovered his son's bed empty, and had walked to the window at the end of the second floor to find Sam and Cade talking on the patio below. And even if Brian hadn't made out their conversation, his son had sounded worried.

"I always sleep good," Joshua chirped. Only eight and oblivious still to the ever-present tension in the house, he gave Brian a Perry family thumbs-up.

His red hair, so dark it was nearly brown, just like his mother's, curled in every possible direction, still wet from his shower. His crumb-covered smile spotlighted a gaping hole where his two front teeth used to be. In between bites of muffin, Joshua was tinkering with whatever LEGO creation he'd gone to bed building the night before.

Joshie, as Cade had dubbed him the week Joshua was born, was the family's happy center. Nothing fazed him. He was the ever-calm reminder that Sam and Brian's life in Chandlerville was a charmed one. As long as there was a new LEGO project to work on, there couldn't be too terribly much wrong with their youngest's world.

"Spaceship?" Brian asked, fingering whatever Joshua was building from the pieces perpetually strewn about his room.

"Transformer," Cade said for his brother, because Joshua was only halfway through chewing another mouthful of breakfast. "At least it's a Transformer until it comes out wrong and he says it's something else, so he doesn't look like a dork."

Joshua poked Cade with his elbow.

Cade downed a gulp of orange juice, ignoring him.

Chuckling, Brian headed for the coffeemaker. An oversize yellow Post-it note was stuck to the counter. Flowering loops and swirls of cursive writing smiled up to him from its surface.

Big day!
You're my HERO for putting up
with me all weekend. Feeling much
better.
Outside in the garden for just a few.
Love you like dark chocolate, S.

Sam and her garden. Her passion for chocolate so dark it was bitter. Her notes. It was endless, the list of things about her that still intrigued him.

His wife was both frailer and stronger than anyone he knew. Even when things were at their worst, she kept going. She never gave up, not completely. He'd married a crusader who'd longed to save the world one student at a time. And fifteen years later, he knew he'd only scratched the surface of what made her so remarkable. She was a survivor, tested and proven and unstoppable. Between the two of them, *she* was the hero. He'd never been more proud of her.

The back door swung open. A blast of frigid air sailed in along with the love of Brian's life: an auburn-haired, petite beauty with cornflower-blue eyes and a heart of gold. Sam's smile was instantaneous when she saw him, which took some of the sting out of waking up and finding her gone.

Their passion last night had rocked him. That had never changed for them. And it seemed to have steadied her, after she'd spent most of yesterday scattered and unable to sit still for more than a few minutes at a time. She'd fallen asleep in his arms, her long, soft hair covering his chest. Yet those perfect moments of closeness hadn't been enough to keep her with him.

She rushed to Brian now, smelling of shampoo, toothpaste, outdoors, and spices. Her lips clung to their kiss a little longer than normal, desperate, as if she still doubted that he'd always, always be waiting for her to find her way back to him.

"Apricots and cardamom?" he teased. She had no shame when it came to mixing and matching spices to create the home-made things she fed him and the boys.

"Apples and ginger." Her laughter at his gentle ribbing felt like old times—before the tragedy that had ripped away at so much of what they'd dreamed would be theirs.

He tucked his nose behind his wife's ear and breathed deeply, knowing he'd scatter goose bumps all over her body. He touched the tip of his tongue to the sweetest spot on earth, just beneath her earlobe, and gave himself permission to dabble, ruthlessly staying focused on now.

"You smell good enough to eat," he whispered. Even though their boys were watching, he nibbled a path down her neck and fantasized about carting her back to bed, the way he would have if they were still young and living in their one-room, fourth-story walk-up in New York.

Joshua groaned, clicking LEGOs either onto or off of his toy. "Get a room, you two."

"And give up the chance to humiliate our spawn?" Brian turned Sam until the curve of her back pressed against his middle. He linked his arms around her waist, leaving her the freedom to slip away if she needed more space. When she settled in, he kissed her temple, a lucky man with his entire world gathered around him. "What would be the fun in that?"

"Mom's already threatening to blow our whole day." Cade slouched in his high-backed stool. "She says she won't be able stop herself from *smothering* us when she sees us at school."

"Hugging?" Brian felt his wife tremble at the mention of what was ahead. He snuggled her closer.

"Kissing," the boys said in unison.

"I have to announce my presence with authority." Sam snagged a muffin from the hand-painted platter she loved and took an enthusiastic bite that made Brian wince. Her stomach didn't tolerate stress well. "If I don't do something to humiliate you, your friends will think I'm an impostor."

"Why not come dressed in a clown costume, and scar me for life?" Cade asked, playing along. But there was something in his gaze, something careful and worried, that Brian wished he could take away.

"A megaphone would be cool." Joshie received his own elbow jab from his brother. He returned it with enthusiasm. "You could shout that you love him across the cafeteria during his lunch period. Or over Ms. Hemmings's morning intercom message after we say the Pledge of Allegiance. 'Attention, students, *Cade Perry Is a Dork* Day has begun.'"

Everyone laughed on cue. Sam kept eating, the boys settled in again, and the easy, hopeful moment choked the air from Brian's lungs.

God, please let this work.

"Why don't I put you guys out of your misery?" He kissed the top of his wife's head. "I'll call in sick and ride with your mother to school. We'll make out in front of everyone at the bake sale. The rest of the day should be downhill from there."

Joshua made a hurling sound.

Cade snickered and poured himself more juice, his smile more relaxed.

He was destined to be a poet. Brian and Sam had known it years ago, when they'd first begun finding wondrous combinations of words and phrases randomly jotted into books and onto napkins and once even onto his chest of drawers in the corner near the head of his bed. Cade collected notebooks now, never completely filling any of them up, but always wanting another one when it was his birthday or Christmas or when they were in a store and discovered a stash of them on sale. He scribbled into something practically every day, whether it was for a composition assignment or just for fun.

"Our kids aren't sufficiently afraid of us." Sam set her muffin down and stepped to the sink, where she was soaking the pan. "Where did we go wrong?"

"They don't know how ruthless we were in our youth." Brian followed her, sensing a shift in her playful energy.

"They don't know a lot of things about who we used to be," she said under her breath.

It was her biggest regret, that their boys never got to see her strong and fearless and ready to take on the world.

"They'll know after today," Brian said. "After they see you rocking the bake sale. It all gets better from here."

She nodded at the promise they'd made each other so many times. She didn't look up from the sink. Had she heard it—the doubt in his rush to reassure her? He sensed her tears, her fear of disappointing everyone, but she'd turned her head so he wouldn't see her face. She never wanted anyone to see her struggle, even him. Maybe especially him.

He wanted to tell her that the dishes could wait. That he'd sit with her for as long as she needed after the boys left on the bus. And if that wasn't enough, he really would head to school with her and blow off a day's worth of important client meetings. Mostly, he wanted to hold her again, because it would go a long way toward reassuring *him* that he was doing the right thing, encouraging her to try one more time. But that wasn't what she'd wanted this morning. For two weeks, this morning had been their focus, her victory lap, and he wasn't going to take that away from her.

"You didn't come back to bed," he said instead, caressing her shoulder, because their love for each other was something they'd always been able to talk about. It had seen them through so much. "I missed you. I woke up dreaming about you."

She nodded again. "I went for a walk and then—"

"Hung out in the garden . . . You could have gotten me up."

Her hand moved back and forth, scouring the already-clean pan. "You've been so tired, with work kicking your butt so much lately."

"When hasn't work been kicking my ass? Still—"

"It was so early when I came back in to start the muffins. I'd already grabbed my clothes, so I could shower down here in the guest room. I didn't want to disturb you."

Sam never wanted to disturb anyone.

"You're amazing," he said, believing it for her. "You're going to be amazing today."

The pan slipped through her fingers and clattered to the sink, making them both jump. Soapy water sloshed onto the crisply ironed oxford shirt she'd paired with tailored khakis that showed off her maddening curves.

"Mom?" Cade asked.

"She's fine," Brian answered out of habit.

"I'd better go change this." Sam grabbed a dish towel and mopped at the worst of the mess. "I don't want to miss walking the boys to the bus."

"You've got time." Brian cursed himself for pushing too hard or getting too close or crowding her or whatever else had set off this latest burst of nerves.

She rushed up the kitchen stairs toward their bedroom. Both

boys stared after her. They turned to him in unison, synchronized by a lifetime of looking to Brian, as if he'd finally be able to explain what neither he nor Sam had found a way to share in detail—the never-ending aftermath of their life in New York.

"Big day," Brian said, smiling and repeating the mantra the family had adopted ever since Sam agreed to help with the bake sale. "Your mom's so excited to be there for you guys. You both mean so much to her."

So much more, he wanted to add, than the garden that never would have held her interest before. Or the debilitating depression and other PTSD symptoms that could swoop in so quickly and steal so much. He could try once again to help his sons understand, but Sam was so eager to finally move on. She wouldn't want him bringing up the past on a day like today. Plus, Cade and Joshua had dealt with mornings like this all their lives. And Brian . . .

He was tired.

He was bone-tired of always being the one left to deal with the boys' insecurities, when San upset them in unintentional ways that left scars he compensated for any way he could. Even with work consuming close to sixty hours of each week, he volunteered to coach every sports team and to chaperone every school trip and to be involved in any other activity he could get away for—while his wife hid at home. And all these years, he'd been happy too. He'd held up his part of their bargain, and now Sam had fought her way back to herself, just like they'd planned. There was no point in looking back now, right?

Cade and Joshua each grabbed another muffin. They didn't pepper Brian with questions. They'd learned to be careful, even if Joshua was more following his big brother's lead than understanding yet how fragile his mother could be. *Careful* was what kept their family going. So despite the fresh worry in Cade's too-wise expression, Brian shut down the nagging little voice in the back of his own mind that said he should be at the school today just in case, to minimize the damage if Sam had an episode.

Lighten up!

His wife was depending on him to help her make this work.

"You'll see," he said to his sons. "Everything's going to be okay."

Chapter Two

"You're really something, you know that?" Mallory Phillips said to Sam an hour later, as they walked in from the school parking lot.

She'd be Mallory *Lombard* soon, Sam corrected herself.

In five months her friend, who was today wearing cartoon frogs all over her pink nurse's scrubs, would technically become Mallory Lombard—once she wed the widowed father of the sweet little girl who'd charmed Mallory into putting down roots amidst the quaint chaos of Mimosa Lane. But Sam would always think of Chandler Elementary's school nurse as Mallory Phillips—the kindred spirit who'd slipped so easily into her solitary world this past Christmas, and helped coax Sam onto the precarious path that had led her to school today.

"Yep." Sam made her smile count, even if her confidence felt as crepey and thin as the winter sky above them. "I'm a bake sale warrior, reporting for duty."

She jostled the heaping platter of brownies she'd baked last night in one hand, saluted with the other, and held open the door to the school's front entrance for Mallory to lead the way. And then they were inside. Where there was less air. Where the walls were too close. Where the voices of the administrative assistants in the school office to the right were too loud and too near, and any minute now hordes of children would be streaming in from their buses to swarm the hallways.

The floor beneath Sam was suddenly mush, grabbing at her legs and trying to suck her to her knees. In a flash, her heartbeat rushed out of control. Heat flooded her body, making everything tingly and numb at the same time. Damn it! She was *not* going to lose it now.

Mallory glanced at her.

Her hand came up to grip Sam's forearm.

"Sure," she said, in response to absolutely nothing, covering for Sam's disintegrating composure. "You can stop by for a few minutes."

The tray of brownies began slipping from Sam's fingers. Mallory took them, her solid presence keeping Sam upright as they marched down the hall.

"The coffee should be ready in my office," Mallory said, for the benefit of whoever might be listening. "I program it before I leave at night so I have something bracing to get me through bus call. Why don't you have a cup before heading to the cafeteria to set up the bake sale?"

She kept talking and Sam kept walking, a zombie, stiff-legged and dazed beside her gorgeous, never-say-die neighbor, feeling less there, less real with each step, until she collapsed and found herself sitting on a crisply made cot in the school's clinic.

Mallory closed the door. She set the brownie platter on the low cabinet at her elbow, returned to Sam, and knelt in front of her.

"Deep breaths." She took Sam's hands and squeezed tightly, an anchor to reality, as if Mallory understood just how close Sam was to going under. "Keep taking deep breaths until your vision clears. This one hit fast."

This one.

Mallory had known Sam for less than a month, but of course the former social worker—one of the most intuitive women Sam had ever met—would understand how many panic attacks must have come before this one.

Sam managed a nod, swiping at the perspiration misting her face. Damn it! Her entire body was soaked in fear. A traitorous rumbling low in her belly sounded a different kind of warning. Mallory must have heard it, too. She hitched a thumb over her shoulder.

"Bathroom's behind my desk." She stood, and Sam rushed into the cool, darkened room just in time to skid to the floor, raise the thankfully sparkling clean toilet seat and lose her apple and ginger muffin in a way that ensured she'd never again bake with that particular spice blend.

She should have known better than to eat.

But having a normal morning with her family had meant so much to everyone. She'd wanted it to be perfect. And it had been. They'd all been laughing, and Brian had been holding her, and she'd felt secure enough in herself, even after her sleepless night, to share a bite or two with her boys. What was the harm, right? What could possibly go wrong? Then she'd run upstairs like a scared girl, and she'd barely made it to the bus stop to see her sons off. And she'd almost turned back twice on her drive to the school.

The spasms didn't stop until Sam's stomach was beyond empty. And still she stayed where she was, hugging the bowl like a long-lost friend, waiting for her spinning world to settle.

"Food poisoning?" Mallory asked from the other room, giving Sam an easy out.

She could hear Mallory moving around now, setting her domain to rights before the first wave of students began to trickle through her doorway.

"I wish." Sam grabbed the rim of the porcelain sink beside the toilet and hauled herself to her feet.

There was antibacterial soap for her to wash with, a caddy full of disposable, single-use toothbrushes, and a bottle of mint mouthwash. Dixie cups with SpongeBob emblazoned all over them rounded out her toiletry options. If you were going to hurl your self-esteem into the commode, this was definitely the place to do it.

"Late night of binging?" Mallory tried again.

Sam emerged back into the main clinic. "I wish."

Mallory offered a Diet Coke in one hand and a steaming mug of coffee in the other. Sam shook her head and stumbled across the room toward the cot. After two steps, she recalibrated and stopped at the desk, propping her backside against it. If she lay down, it would be too tempting to curl into a ball and wait for Brian to come to her rescue, swooping in and making excuses and explaining yet another setback.

She wiped a damp palm down her tragically wrinkled khakis and cast a rueful smile toward her friend. Mallory's raised eyebrow confirmed just how rough Sam must look.

"Don't forget," Sam said. "I'm *really something.*"

"You've been sweating today ever since you let yourself get cornered into doing this at that party Pete and I threw."

At the Mimosa Lane New Year's gathering two weeks ago, Mallory had tried to deflect their cul-de-sac neighbor Julia Davis's enthusiasm that Sam was ready to dive into school volunteer work. Sam had been talking to Mallory about helping a few hours a week with the kids in one of the assistance shelters Mallory donated clinic time to. Sam had mused out loud that after the first of the year, maybe she could do something small at the boys' school, too. And Julia, their community's volunteer queen, had been all over the idea in a flash.

It was time for Sam to stop hiding from the things that scared her, Julia had said. It was time for her to see that she didn't have to be so careful and worried and alone, just to get through her day. She'd see, Julia had promised. She would be fine.

Julia was a good friend, Sam's best friend in Chandlerville, and she always meant well. But her neighbor was always insisting on something. She was always certain she was right about what others needed. And she always believed in better things and places and people than reality could sometimes deliver. It was almost as if focusing on everyone else's lives and needs distracted Julia from her own increasingly quiet home, now that her boys were nearly grown and gone.

"It's just a bake sale." Sam felt ridiculous.

"If it's *just* a bake sale," Mallory asked, "why am I wishing I had the credentials to prescribe you some Xanax?"

"You know I don't take sedatives." Not anymore. Years of pharmaceutical intervention had convinced Sam that she'd rather be rattled or in pain than numb.

"I know you want today so badly, you're being reckless."

"Reckless?" Sam grabbed her purse from beside the desk. As she bent and straightened, she ignored how the room dipped and didn't quite right itself. "I'm helping out with a PTA fund-raiser."

"You're spending the day in a cafeteria that will look and smell and sound like the school where you heard planes rip apart two Manhattan skyscrapers, not to mention the safe world we all thought we were living in back then."

Her new friend's logic, though kind, was as blunt as always. Sam should be choking on the memories rushing through her. If anyone else had dared to bring up that horrible September day twelve years ago, she'd be curling into a fetal position or sprinting for the bathroom again. Instead, she took her first full breath in hours. Or had it been weeks? Mallory's unapologetic honesty and unconditional acceptance soothed her nerves better than any of the anxiety meds she'd tried.

Sam stared down at the new Keds she'd bought especially for today. She was terrified of embarrassing her boys in front of their friends, once everything was in full swing. But she also didn't want to disappoint Brian or Julia or her sons . . . or herself.

How was she going to pull this off?

"You don't have to talk about it," Mallory said.

Sam nodded, grateful and aware that Mallory knew just how isolating fear could become. She had grown up homeless. Before moving to Mimosa Lane, she'd let her own past hold her hostage. She'd only recently, after meeting and falling head over heels in love with Pete and Polly Lombard, found a way to conquer her personal demons. And then in the shortest of conversations, at Sam and Brian's Christmas party, Mallory had become one of the few people with whom Sam had ever shared anything about her life in New York.

She had recognized a kindred spirit on the spot.

They were both survivors—Sam and this former grief counselor whose nursing and psychology degrees made her overqualified to run a school clinic, but Mallory loved helping kids and families and was clearly thriving at Chandler. She and Sam were fighting to overcome pasts most of their friends couldn't fathom, and to hold on to what so many in a town like Chandlerville took for granted. Peace, with no aftertaste of panic or loss. Happiness that was blind to how quickly it could be lost. Closeness that felt safe and secure, rather than threatening. Real community and connection and belonging that would never fade.

"I think maybe I do need to talk, if you have a few minutes," Sam admitted. Mallory had called the house several times since New Year's, but Sam had avoided her for fear that talking more about today might be the same thing as talking herself out of it. "I'm a disaster."

"You're doing the best you can." Mallory checked the wall clock. "You're fighting your way through. And you're trying to do it on your own, because you want everyone to believe that you're already past all this. That's no way to live." She sat on the cot Sam had abandoned. "You've got to let the people in your life know what you're really going through, even if you don't want to still be going through it. Trust me. Otherwise, days like today will never get any better, no matter how much you love your family, or how confident people like Julia are that good wishes really can make dreams come true. Pretending, gritting through something you're not ready for . . . Sometimes that's the most dangerous thing you can do. So, start with me. We've got a few minutes. Spill. I'm listening."

And that was that.

It was all Sam could do not to throw her arms around the other woman and cling. Without the pressure of pretending today wasn't terrifying her, Sam's agitation was dissolving into the kind of calm that always seemed to surround Mallory.

"When I'm inside any building, especially a school or anywhere with a lot of people, it's all still there," Sam said. "I'm hearing the sounds and the feel and even the smells of that day, a split second before the first plane hit its tower, and then the second one. The other teachers and I were watching it all on TV by then, while our assistants monitored our classes. So many of our kids' parents worked in the towers just down the street and commuted with them back and forth every day, and we couldn't do anything but watch and listen and wonder how we were going to get our students through it. *If* any of us made it through at all. No one knew what would happen next, and at first the authorities wanted everyone to stay in their buildings, rather than being outdoors in the chaos on the street."

"Are the panic attacks about still not knowing whether you're going to make it through?" Mallory asked, zeroing straight to the meat of things, as usual.

"Maybe I'll never be able to go back to the way I was before," Sam answered, without really answering. Because she never knew what would cause the next attack, not really. Walking into a school. A plane flying over her house.

"Before 9/11 happened?"

Sam shrugged. She and Brian had spent a fortune on her therapy the first few years after the attack. And for what?

"It's like they're gone," she said, "all the things that I loved before that day. All the things I thought I'd always have. My social life and the friends Brian and I had in Manhattan. My dreams of what having kids would be like for us. Teaching, and where I wanted to go with my career. Hobbies I wanted to take up, anything besides cooking for my family and fussing with my yard. It's all changed. All of it's been gone for so long. Everyone else is so sure I can get that life back, but . . ."

"Everyone?"

"Brian. The doctors I've talked with. The boys. Julia."

"But not you? You don't think you can go back?"

Did she?

Did Sam even know, after all this time, who she wanted to be—besides *better*, somehow?

Sam wiped both hands across her face and ran her fingers through her bangs. "We'll see."

Longing to be home, in the park, in her garden, or in those few stolen moments at breakfast when her boys and husband had been so relaxed with her, she lugged her purse to the bathroom, flipped on the light over the sink, and began touching up her makeup.

A brush of powder.

A sweep of lip gloss.

Some concealer carefully applied to mask the dark slashes beneath both eyes.

"Mask complete?" Mallory asked as Sam rejoined her.

The bell rang before Sam could answer.

"Bus call." Her friend opened the door and lifted Sam's overflowing brownie tray. "You're going to get through this, you know. It doesn't have to be pretty. Just get through lunch any way you have to, and you've won. Now, let me drop these and you by the cafeteria on my way outside to help with the kids."

Mallory's gaze had softened with worry, but her voice was rock solid. There was no pretending. No strained laughter, the way Sam's family dealt with everything. There were none of Julia's forced smiles. But Mallory was just as firmly in Sam's corner. It was an amazing blessing.

"Let's do this." Sam stepped into the hallway, the walls not feeling quite so close this time. The second bell hurried them along. There was a ton of setup to do in the cafeteria. And whether things turned ugly or not, she wanted to be part of all of it. For Cade and Joshua, because they deserved to see their mother healthy for a change. For Brian, because he deserved better than pouring optimism down everyone's throats while he sacrificed so much of his life to pick up the pieces when she crumbled. And for herself, because she deserved not to be a burden to everyone who cared about her.

***

"Leave him alone!" Cade grabbed at smelly Bubba Dickerson. He pulled the bully away from Troy Wilmington.

Bubba stumbled. He tripped over his backpack and landed on his butt. The other boys who'd gotten off the bus with them laughed. Bubba made it to his feet, his belly hanging over the top of his pants, his fists balled up to hit somebody.

"You're going to pay for that," he yelled at Cade and Troy.

Troy pushed his glasses higher on his nose and stood taller. Except he was standing behind Cade.

"Pay for what?" Troy sounded so scared, he might wet his pants. "For you being so clumsy you can't keep your stupid butt off the sidewalk? I'd pay a week's allowance to see that happen again."

Bubba had been pushing Troy around the whole ride from Mimosa Lane. The whole school year. No one stopped him—not even the teachers, who *had* to hear some of the mean things he said. Only it hadn't gotten so bad that any of the adults really paid attention. Not yet. Except it really was bad—at least for Troy.

Cade and Troy talked a lot more than anyone knew. The other kids thought Cade was way cooler than skinny, pimply Troy. And it was better for Cade if no one made a big deal about him still hanging out with the wimpy kid he'd shared Twinkies with in preschool.

Sometimes it was like he was the only person Troy had to talk to. And Troy had been weirder than ever since Christmas, acting out in class and pissing the other kids off more and crying a lot when he and Cade were alone. Cade felt bad for him. When Troy had mouthed off to Bubba as they'd gotten off the bus, and Bubba had gotten angry, Cade had shoved the bully away, hoping Bubba wouldn't do something stupid like pushing back now that they were at school.

Not that hoping always worked out the way you wanted it to. Because now Bubba was shoving his way through the other kids, and everyone was laughing at what Troy had said. So far the teachers hadn't noticed. But that wouldn't last.

"Where's your money, you little shit?" Bubba snarled at Troy, his face all sweaty and red even though it was cold out. "'Cause I'll take that bet. Give me what you got. Or do I have to waste my time smacking you around for it? I can take it from you here, and you can cry like a girl. Or I can take it at lunch, and you can cry like a girl in front of the whole sixth grade."

When everyone laughed at Troy this time, Bubba puffed up like he was something big, when almost every day someone pushed Troy around at lunch. He was an easy target. He was a card-carrying dork, now that they were almost in junior high. Clumsy. Too shortsighted for sports without his glasses. And too easy to make cry. He never stood up to anyone.

Sure enough, he was about to cry now. But Troy stepped around Cade and stared Bubba down anyway, holding his backpack in front of him like that would protect him.

"My dad said not to let you take any more of my money, no matter what I have to do. Don't think I won't stop you this time."

Bubba towered over Troy. He was the tallest boy in their grade. He smiled when Troy gulped and shrank back. But when he didn't run like he always had before, Bubba stopped smiling. He pushed Troy toward Cade.

"You tellin' me you're not afraid of me anymore?" he bellowed.

"No." Troy pushed Bubba back for the first time Cade could remember, not that Bubba moved much. "I'm telling you that I'm more afraid of my dad than I'll ever be of you."

No one laughed this time.

They'd all seen Mr. Wilmington treat Troy like a loser. None of them wanted a guy like that for a dad. He seemed to enjoy it, making Troy feel like nothing, especially in front of the football team a few years back, before Troy had stopped playing. Having a dad who called you a sissy all the time because you couldn't keep up with the other boys must suck.

"Not afraid of me, huh?" Bubba swung one of his meaty fists.

Nate Turner grabbed the goon's arm before he made contact.

"Get off me!" Bubba rounded on Nate. But he was outmatched and he knew it.

Nate was almost as big as Bubba, and he was the best linebacker on the Chandlerville Chargers football team. With his muscles, he could beat blubbery Bubba to a pulp, and Nate wouldn't even be breathing hard. And unlike Troy, Nate wasn't afraid of anyone.

"Leave him alone," Nate said. "And stop being such an asshole at bus call. You're going to get us all in trouble. Ms. Hemmings is coming."

The assistant principal really was on her way over. She had a nose for trouble. She always knew what a kid had to hide, just when he was praying he wouldn't get caught. But Nate's glance to

Cade said that Ms. Hemmings wasn't the only reason Nate had gotten in the middle of Bubba and Troy's fight.

Nate and Cade talked a lot, too. Everyone knew they were best friends. They talked about everything. Nate was the one kid Cade felt like he could say anything to. They talked about their families, when they were at Nate's house and his parents were gone somewhere making all their killer money, and Cade needed to get out of his own place, where he couldn't think or feel or say anything that might worry his mom. And they talked about Troy, and how they were glad neither of them had Mr. Wilmington as a dad.

Nate's parents were so busy they didn't care what he did as long as he didn't get into too much trouble, and Cade's family was definitely warped, too. But they'd agreed that they had it great compared to Troy. So they kept standing up for him with kids like Bubba, even when Troy was being a jerk like today and blowing his chance to back down.

"You just wait until lunch." Bubba's smile made his threat extra ugly. He included Nate and Cade in his sneer. "You'll get yours, you stupid dorks."

"I'll be waiting, asshole," Troy said.

But Bubba was already stomping away, several boys following and patting him on the back for being so cool.

"Is there a problem, Mr. Turner?" Ms. Hemmings asked. She called them all by their last names, like they were going to the prep school on the other side of Chandlerville or something.

"No, ma'am," Nate answered.

Cade shoved his shoulder into Troy's, warning the kid to be cool.

"No, ma'am," they said together.

The AP stared down from what was like a mile above them. She was the tallest woman Cade had ever seen. All the boys were secretly dying to see her play basketball. They'd heard from someone on the staff that she'd been an all-conference MVP wherever she played in college. And even though she was tough and talked weird sometimes, she was nice to all the kids and had made some cool changes at the school since she came there when Cade was in third grade.

"I suggest you find your way to your homerooms," she said, "before a problem that I don't need to be dealing with this morning comes and finds you."

"Yes, ma'am." Cade grabbed the sleeve of Troy's winter jacket and hauled him away.

What was up with him today? Taking Bubba on was suicide. Did the kid have a death wish? Nate followed them. They stumbled into the bathroom across from the cafeteria.

"Leave me alone!" Troy yanked away.

He crashed into one of the stall doors and almost fell into the toilet. He was holding his backpack still, like he'd never let it go. Like Joshie had held his favorite stuffed animal when he was little.

"You mean," Nate asked, "like we should have left you alone outside? So you coulda kept on riling Bubba until he stomped you into little bits? The guy's twice your size. Stay away from him at lunch."

"No. I'm going to make him stop. My dad said if I didn't he'd . . ."

"He'd what?" Cade asked. "What does your dad have to do with this?"

"Everything! I have to make Bubba stop picking on me."

"Because your jerk of a dad says so?"

"Because if I don't, my dad won't stop."

"Won't stop what?" Nate looked as confused as Cade.

"Hitting me, okay?! When he hears about me taking Bubba's crap, he says he's going to show me how to toughen up, and then he . . ."

Troy's face twisted in an ugly way, like he was as shocked as Cade and Nate by what he'd just said.

"He hits you how?" Cade asked, but Troy just shook his head, looking like he was going to puke.

"How bad does he hit you, man?" Nate asked. "What does he think you can do about Bubba Dickerson? Your dad doesn't know what's going on. If he did—"

"He doesn't care!" Troy screamed. He was crying and shaking, spit flying out with every word. "He doesn't care if I get punched out. He told me that if I didn't stand up to Bubba today, I'd have to answer to him when he gets home from work. The more Bubba beats on me the better. Then my dad'll believe that I wasn't a sissy this time."

Cade stared at his friend, not wanting to believe it but knowing it was true.

"Then tell your mom," he said, thinking about his own parents and how they never did or thought or decided anything without talking to each other first. And they'd never, ever come close to hitting him or Joshua. "Tell her about Bubba, and get her to make your Dad stop, and then—"

"She can't do anything about it," Troy said, still crying. "She's afraid of him. She can't do nothin'."

"Because he hits her, too?" Nate asked. Now he was the one who sounded like he was going to cry. "That's just wrong, man. Why don't you tell somebody?"

"We don't tell anybody." Troy was quieter as he said that, like he hadn't just totally lost it, and they were talking about how much they hated their math homework or something stupid like that. "Mom says telling people will make things worse."

"You don't have to take a beating to make your dad leave you alone." Cade wanted to help somehow. Someone had to help. "Just tell one of the teachers about Bubba, and—"

"Don't you think I have?" Troy was being too loud again. Someone was going to hear them. "I told Mrs. Baxter on Friday." He and Nate and Cade were all in Mrs. Baxter's homeroom. "And what did she do? She called my parents and Bubba's parents. Bubba probably got a pat on the back. He and his dad probably went out in the woods over the weekend and shot something to-gether, to celebrate how cool he is. My dad beat me with his belt this time, and he said I'd get more tonight if I didn't keep my mouth shout and take care of this and stop making it his prob-lem because I'm too much of a sissy. I'm not a baby. He'll see. I'm not going home until Bubba's so afraid of me, he'll never bother me again. And he will be!"

Troy was totally freaked out, his voice bouncing off the bath-room's pasty-white walls. Cade shivered, thinking about how it would feel if his own dad were to hit him . . . with a belt. It made him feel like he was going to throw up.

"Why would Bubba Dickerson ever be afraid of you?" Nate's eyes squinted while he stared at Troy.

Troy edged around them toward the door. The warning bell rang. They were going to be late for homeroom. But something made Cade grab Troy's arm before he could get away.

"You can't take him on, man, no matter what your dad said." Cade had seen his mom like this, when she'd felt trapped somewhere, like she was afraid she'd never be able to get out.

Only no one else was afraid at all. When she was that scared, she'd do anything to get away, and that made him scared for Troy now. "Bubba's never going to be afraid of you. You're gonna get hurt."

Troy's shoulders slumped. He wiped his jacket sleeve across his wet face and the snot trailing from his nose. Then he smiled like Bubba, mean and awful. He started laughing in a really messed up way.

"You'll see, you stupid babies." Troy sneered as if he hated Cade and Nate as much as he did his dad and Bubba. "You'll see!"

He raced into the hallway. Cade and Nate ran after him. The late bell rang. They were officially tardy, with no excuse to give Mrs. Baxter without ratting out Troy.

"I don't care what kind of trouble he thinks he'll get into at home," Nate said. "We should tell somebody."

Cade glanced into the cafeteria. His mom and Ms. Hemmings were talking. His mom had actually made it to school. He stopped running, and Nate stumbled into him.

"What?" Nate asked.

Cade could only stare and point.

There she was, acting normal like all the other moms, instead of hiding at home so Cade couldn't go a day without some adult asking him how she was doing, or another kid thinking it was weird that she never showed for any sports events or neighborhood stuff. She laughed at something Ms. Hemmings said. It wasn't a real laugh. He could tell. It was a fake laugh like this morning, that meant she was nervous.

But she was there, when he'd bet Nate yesterday that she'd back out like all the other times she'd tried to do something like this.

"See?" his friend said. "Told you so."

Cade nodded. Then Ms. Hemmings looked their way, and he and Nate ducked behind the cafeteria door.

He should tell his mom—about everything. She'd know how to help Troy, at school and with Mr. Wilmington. And Ms. Hemmings was right there, too. They'd both know what to do.

"Do you think we should—" Nate started to ask.

"No," Cade cut him off, understanding a little why Troy had sounded so freaked when he'd talked about the stuff going on at home. "I don't want to tell anyone but you about my family, either. And . . ."

"And you don't want to mess things up for your mom today."

Cade nodded.

She looked so pretty, like she always did. Except now she was at school, so everyone else could see how pretty she was. Something in Cade's chest swelled up. He peeked back around the door. She was arranging her brownies and other people's stuff on the bake sale table, like she did things like that every day.

What if something he said scared her? Then everyone else would be watching them while she was upset, and she wouldn't like that. She hated when people stared at her like she was broken or something. She'd probably want to go home then.

He had a cool family, even if dealing with them was a pain sometimes. But not today. Today his mom was going to stay. She and Dad had promised she'd be there for him and Joshua. They'd promised everything was going to keep getting better.

"Let's get to class." He ran toward the stairway to the second floor.

"What about Troy?" Nate called after him. They took the steps together, two at a time.

"We'll stick close to him at lunch." Cade had been worried about lunch all morning. Now he couldn't wait—forget Troy's stupid plan to be Bubba's punching bag. This was going to be the best lunch ever, because his mom would be there. "Even if we have to sit on Troy the whole time, we'll keep him away from Bubba."

Chapter Three

"Let me help you," Kristen Hemmings said.

It was the second lunch period of the day, and Cade and Joshua Perry's mom was trying to set to right a bake sale serving dish that had fallen over, the one her extra-large, extra-fudgy brownies were on. Only Mrs. Perry's hands were shaking so badly, she'd knocked it over again. Sam had stayed all morning like a trouper, much longer than anyone had expected, and Kristen had stuck as close to her as possible. The other woman's nerves seemed to fray a bit more with each passing minute.

"If the noise is getting to be too much," Kristen said, helping re-sort the treats on the tray, "why don't you take a break for a few minutes?"

The sweet woman had had a smile ready for everyone who'd approached her, even the adults who'd nosily asked how she was doing and whether or not she thought she'd be able to participate in this or that volunteer activity next, now that she was out and about. But in the last half hour she'd started to fade. She'd begin sentences that skidded to a halt before she finished, with Sam turning her face away in embarrassment, as if she'd forgotten what she was talking about. Her hands shook each time she picked something up to serve to one of the kids, or to restock the ever-dwindling array of goodies the PTA was selling to raise money for the spring carnival.

Kristen had watched Sam brace herself for each boisterous wave of kids who swarmed the bake sale. The classes took turns buying treats at the beginning and end of their lunch periods. But the orderly process didn't dampen the students' enthusiasm to be first in line, and to inspect and ask questions about everything before they decided what to buy. And Sam seemed to have reached her limit. She clearly would be more at ease hiding beneath the folding table they'd dragged in from the storage closet than she was smiling across it at her next sugar-crazed customer.

"Really." Kristen looked around for another mother to fill in. "It's fine if—"

"No." Sam squared her shoulders and brushed at the crumbs she'd scattered across the lemon-yellow tablecloth. Then she handed a brownie to the next student in line, Sally Beaumont, the sixth grader rumor had it was wanting to be Cade Perry's steady, if the boy ever took it upon himself to notice. "Not today. No breaks today."

"Thanks, Mrs. Perry," Sally said. She gave Cade's mom her fifty cents and grinned extra wide. "It's great to see you here. I know Cade's excited about it."

Sam nodded and rearranged the treats on her platter, until Mrs. Baxter's class headed back to their table so another group could have their turn. Sally sat beside Cade, who hadn't yet come over to see his mom. He laughed at something Sally said, and then turned back to Troy Wilmington, who was sulking between Cade and Nate Turner. Nate leaned across Troy to say something to Cade, his mouth full of pizza.

Sam watched the exchange with obvious longing. She'd been trying to catch her son's eye ever since Mrs. Baxter's class had arrived a few minutes ago.

"Yeah," Sam said. "Cade is superexcited that I've crawled out of my cave and into the daylight. After everything I've put him through, it's a wonder he wants me here at all."

When Kristen glanced at her companion, she realized that Sam had been talking to herself. Kristen watched her press a hand to her chest, just above her heart, as she stared at her oldest son.

"Maybe he's trying not to make this any harder for you than it already is," Kristen said. Knowing what the other woman had fought her way back from, she couldn't imagine a child not being proud of having a mother like her.

"More likely"—Sam shot her a grateful if rueful look—"he's waiting for me to do something to embarrass him. His father and I were even teasing him about it this morning."

Kristen had caught Cade watching his mom a time or two, only to glance away before Sam saw him. Kristen hated that the Perry family was still struggling. This was none of her business, but she couldn't stop herself from at least trying to make things easier in some small way.

"I think he'll be proud of you one day, if he isn't already," she said. "Especially once he knows the whole story. I'm guessing he doesn't yet. Does he?"

"About me?" Sam shook her head, frowning. "He knows enough."

"You've talked with him about what you went through on 9/11, and why? All the young lives you protected that day, and why things have been so hard for you ever since?"

The other woman looked downright puzzled.

"Why would I burden him like that?" Sam asked. "He doesn't need to know that I spent that entire day trying to reassure terrified children that everything was all right, when I knew most of their parents were never coming home. Or that I and the teachers I worked with had to walk those babies out of Manhattan, through the dust and dirt and pieces of the World Trade Center that had crumbled down on top of the city, only to wait in Queens all night with them, wondering if they had family coming to pick them up. We wanted to run screaming from what happened and never look back . . ."

She looked around them, as if horrified that the memories that had been troubling her all morning had slipped free. When she realized no one but Kristen was listening, Sam shook her head at herself or Kristen or both of them, determination smoothing every other emotion from her expression.

"Cade has enough on his plate," she said, "dealing with having me for a mom. He doesn't need to know all the gory details about how brutal this world can be."

She walked away and another parent filled in, selling one of Sam's gourmet brownies to a sixth grader pulling a crumpled dollar bill from his jeans pocket. Kristen caught Cade watching his mother's sudden departure.

He watched until she disappeared into the kitchen, then stared down at his lap. Sally said something in his ear and he laughed again. He grinned at her in a way that looked more sad than happy.

Kristen followed Sam through the kitchen and out the back door to the parking lot, where the trucks pulled up each morning to deliver produce and other groceries in bulk. She had no idea whether she was making things better or worse. But she'd promised Mallory she'd do the best she could to keep an eye on Sam, amidst the rest of Kristen's daily responsibilities. And even if she hadn't talked with her clinic nurse, she wouldn't have been able to help herself after what she'd just seen.

She couldn't imagine how difficult it had been for Sam to be here this morning, after so many failed attempts in the past to be part of her children's lives. It was troubling to see such a gifted teacher and loving mother so isolated from the world. From the first moment Kristen had heard the Perrys' story, she'd vowed to help somehow.

She found Sam with her back to the building's redbrick façade, bent at the waist, her hands on her knees and her head down, breathing deeply. Someone passing by might think she was physically ill, rather than suffering from one of the panic attacks that rumors said she endured most every time she ventured out into their community.

"I don't think it would be a burden to Cade"—Kristen stepped to Sam's side—"to know all that happened that day and how it's still hurting you. It might help him understand how bravely you're fighting your way back. It might help all of you if you'd talk about it and—"

"All of us?" Her companion stood and braced a hand against the side of the building. "Have you noticed Cade having problems? Is he—"

"Cade's fine."

Get a grip, Kristen!

She was better with people than this. An ace. An MVP at relating and understanding and staying calm, no matter the situation or the players.

But this beautiful, brave, broken woman had rattled her from the first parent-teacher night Kristen had supervised at Chandler three years ago. Sam had tried to be there for Cade then, too. After only a half hour, the entire family had headed home amidst a flood of avid interest from other parents and kids. Kristen had watched Cade drag along behind his parents, confused and embarrassed.

Kristen had indulged in school gossip that night, when she normally shoved it away like the deadly virus it could be. She'd quickly realized who Sam was, and she'd been in awe of the woman ever since. Even before Mallory's request, Kristen had cleared as much of her schedule as she could to help with today's bake sale. Sam needed a successful experience at Chandler. Her sons and the entire school community needed her to have a good day—so she'd come back again and do even more next time.

"If Cade's fine . . ." Sam's voice cracked. She cleared it. "If my son is fine, why would talking to him help 'all of us'?"

"He . . . misses you when you don't make it to school activities." Kristen had felt for him with every flash of sadness she'd seen cross his normally happy expression, especially when some well-meaning adult would ask after his mother. "And I wonder whether he's more aware already of what you're going through than you and your husband give him credit for. Kids are alarmingly intuitive emotional barometers."

"Yeah, well . . ." Sam wiped at her eyes with the heels of each palm. The woman's porcelain complexion meant she didn't need to wear a stitch of makeup to enhance her natural beauty. Otherwise she'd have mascara smeared everywhere by now. "*Missing me* has been better for Cade than watching me come unglued in front of his friends every time we're in a crowd of people, or indoors somewhere besides our house. Or, God forbid, in his school, like today. Selling brownies. He can't even count on me to get through selling brownies . . . It's better, the less he knows about why his mom is so messed up."

"Is it?"

"Is it what?"

"Is it better for him not to have the chance to admire you for who you really are?"

"Ms. Hemmings . . ."

"Kristen, please."

"Kristen." Sam's voice was shaking, like the rest of her. "I'm sure you mean well, but you can't possibly understand what's going on, and—"

"You've been a hero for me for twelve years, Mrs. Perry." If nothing else, Kristen wanted to say what she'd longed to since that first parent-teacher night. "Before either one of us moved to Georgia. I was in school, thinking about what program to pursue with the master's degree I wanted, and I read the interview you gave after 9/11. From then on, I've committed myself to making the kind of difference in a child's life that you and the rest of those teachers did for your students at Ground Zero."

It felt like disappearing, Sam had said to the reporter. *Like the buildings were gone, and my students' families were gone, and the New York we'd all loved was gone. But we couldn't let our kids down. We had to keep them calm and get them off the island and give them hope . . . somehow. All day, all night. The teachers waited, desperate for good news. And each time it didn't come, whenever a family was reunited but it wasn't a parent who collected a child, we all disappeared just a little more . . .*

Sam straightened away from the building, as if Kristen's memories had slapped her across the face. Her eyes glistened, diamonds gathering. Demons. How long had it been since this woman had talked with anyone about that day?

"You . . ." She defiantly blinked her emotion away. "You read my interview with the *Times*?"

"Yes, ma'am." Kristen reached out her hand. "And you were my inspiration to become a primary school teacher."

Sam shook her hand briefly. She curled her arms around her petite body.

"Thank you," she said in a timid way that belied how utterly courageous she was.

"Thank *you*," Kristen replied, "on behalf of all those families. If there's ever anything I can do for you, Mrs. Perry, even if it's just sharing my story and your role in it with Cade, I'd be more than happy to. I'd be honored."

"Sam." A more genuine smile bloomed across the other woman's delicate features. "I'd be very pleased if you'd call me Sam."

"Cade and Joshua will know you're a hero one day, Sam. And that will make days like today disappear for them. You'll see."

Sam shook her head again, but she was still smiling a little. "Not if I can't stop being terrified of ridiculous things like brownies. Because you know how scary chocolate and kids eating lunch can be . . ."

Kristen chuckled. "I was ready to find somewhere to hide myself. They just keep coming. I don't know what we'd do if we ran out of treats to feed them. Sugar is a dangerous, dangerous drug."

Sam gazed at the door leading to the kitchen. "He's waiting for me to come back. Even if he pretends he's cool with whatever happens, I know he's watching and waiting and expecting me to bail again, to not be here for him."

Kristen motioned for Sam to precede her into the kitchen. "Then let's show him what you're made of. Just do what you need to, and we'll make it look good. Offense was my specialty in basketball. Still is in school. Otherwise the inmates will think they're running the asylum."

Sam laughed again. Kristen opened the door to the kitchen, and they were about to walk inside when the sound of angry shouting erupted from the direction of the cafeteria, followed by an earsplitting explosion. A loud bang. Then another.

They both froze.

Kristen had heard those sounds before. On TV. In movies.

But that wasn't possible here.

Not at Chandler.

"Was that . . ." Sam's hand flew to her mouth as kids and adults began screaming inside.

Kristen, momentarily paralyzed by the impossibility of what she knew had happened, released the door's handle and rushed inside.

"Stay here," she ordered without looking back. "You're safest in the parking lot."

But Sam was right behind her. Brushing past her. Running toward the sound of another gunshot.

***

Cade, was all Sam could think. *Where's Cade?*

This couldn't be happening. It couldn't be happening again— the world, her entire life, crumbling before her eyes.

She and Kristen raced through the kitchen. Sam reached the cafeteria first on legs she once more couldn't feel. Kristen stopped in front of her. Sam skidded to a halt behind the assistant principal.

"Oh my God," Kristen said.

"No . . ." Sam peered around the six-foot-two ex–college basketball star, refusing to accept the sight before her.

"Mom!" Cade cried from somewhere Sam couldn't see.

Troy Wilmington pivoted away from a crowd of terrified kids and aimed the pistol he was holding in Kristen and Sam's direction.

"Get down!" Sam tackled the taller woman.

They hit the ground hard. The sound of a gunshot ripped through the screams and sobs and mayhem around them. A bullet shattered the cinder block wall next to where they'd been standing. Her ears ringing, Sam fought the panic sucking her away from what was happening. She shook her head to clear it.

This wasn't happening. Not again. Not like this.

Cade.

She took off in a crawler's version of a sprint, slinking toward the freaked-out eleven-year-old who was screaming now, still waving a gun.

"Don't come any closer," Troy said, and she had no idea whether he was talking to her, to one of the other adults, or to thekids he was threatening. "I didn't mean to shoot again. I don't want to hurt anyone else. I mean it, Cade. Don't mess with me, man."

Cade!

Her son was still okay.

He had to be okay.

Sam crawled past crying, shaking kids and teachers and parents who'd plastered themselves to the floor.

"Get out of here," she whispered as she moved forward. "Behind me. Ms. Hemmings is back there. There's a door through the kitchen to the parking lot. Stay down, crawl, but go! Don't stop until you're outside. *Go!*" she whisper-yelled.

She was ranting and half shoving people behind her, not looking to see what the AP was doing, but hoping the younger woman was keeping her head about her and dragging parents and kids out of harm's way. It was what Sam should be doing. What she and all teachers in New York had been trained to do in a crisis, long before potential shootings had become a threat to the rest of the nation.

But all Sam could focus on now was her son.

Cade's name kept repeating in her mind. Images replayed of him as a baby and a toddler and then a young boy. Moments in time she'd never get back, then moments in the future that could be lost forever if she didn't do something to save him. His high school graduation. College. Marriage. Babies of his own.

God couldn't be that cruel. He wouldn't take all of that away from a life so young and innocent. Except Sam knew death could be just that random and merciless.

Well, not again.

Not this time.

Not to her family.

Where was Cade? Was he still with Troy? They'd been sitting together eating lunch when Sam left the bake sale. And now Troy was trying to hurt the other kids? Troy Wilmington—sweet, shy, awkward Troy—had a gun. What the hell was going on?

Please . . .

Cade had to be okay.

He had to be.

It was ripping open again, the place inside Sam that had been tied in knots for twelve years, forever seeping toxic memories and panic and loss. And in that place where she'd felt this helpless once before, she found her senses growing deadly calm. Because experience told her that she couldn't let the terror have her. Not yet.

We couldn't let our kids down . . . She remembered telling the *Times* reporter.

Just as she had to stay in the moment now. Panic and adrenaline would be her allies for a while. She could feel their familiar bite seeping through her, focusing her. For as long as she was needed today, she could do anything, handle anything, fight back against anything, as long as she kept going. Just as she had at Ground Zero. Otherwise people—children—were going to die. And this time one of those kids could be her son.

"You shot him, man!" Cade yelled. He was somewhere to her left, his voice shaking with a young man's fury and a little boy's tears.

She crawled closer. She scanned the part of the cafeteria where his class had been sitting. She saw Cade on the floor. He was crouching beneath the table he and Sally and Troy and Nate had been sitting at.

"Why'd ya shoot him?" Cade demanded.

"He shoved my face in my food!" Troy screamed.

Sam was just a table away and crawling like a bug—hugging the ground and inching toward the threat waiting to squash her, her son, and the other kids.

"So you shot him?" Cade yelled back.

"Shut up!"

Sally screamed.

Sam couldn't see why. She couldn't breathe. The desperation that had fed her so far was already wearing off. Her arms and legs were beginning to tremble. She couldn't exactly feel them yet, but the numbness was gone, enough for her to know that she soon wouldn't have the strength to get to her feet. She had to end this before that happened. No other adult was close enough to stop Troy.

"Put the gun down," Nate said next. "You're scaring Sally and everybody, and Bubba's hurt bad."

"I told him to leave me alone." Troy wasn't screaming anymore. He sounded like he was hyperventilating and struggling to understand what had happened, just like the rest of the kids. "You heard me. I told you I was going to make him leave me alone. 'Don't come home until you've settled this once and for all,' my dad said. And I did. I settled it."

"With a gun?" Sally sobbed, her words barely words at all.

Sam was at the edge of the table where all the kids but Troy were huddled together. She could see that her son had put his body between Sally's and the horrible-looking pistol that the Wilmington boy held.

"Put it down, Troy," Sally said. "Please." She was clinging to Cade, shaking so hard her words were slurred. "Stop being so stupid."

"I'm not stupid." Troy turned his gun on Sally—which meant he was aiming it right at Cade.

"Whoa!" Nate was kneeling beside someone. Oh, God. A boy was on the ground, bleeding. Badly. "Okay. You're not stupid. Leave her alone, man. No one else here is after you. You wanted Bubba off your ass. I think he's dead. You . . . You killed him," Nate said, wiping at his eyes. "He's dead. Are you happy now?"

"D-dead?" Troy stuttered, while Sally cried harder and the racket around them continued—the sound of everyone else running away. "Are you sure?" he squeaked out. "I didn't mean . . . I mean, I didn't want to—"

"Kill him?" Cade was crying, too, her son whom Sam had heard upset only a few times in his life, and never, ever this afraid. "You shot him. You stood right there and shot him. What did you think was going to happen?"

"I didn't know it would hurt him so bad." Each word Troy said sounded both sorry and defiant. He kept the awful gun aimed at Cade and Sally, no matter how shocked he clearly was by what he'd done. "You don't know. You don't know what it's like when my dad's after me. So shut up. Just shut up talking to me like we're still friends, or you care how much crap lands on me every day I go home and I haven't made Bubba stop. Just shut up!"

"Put it down, man." Nate stood up and away from Bubba, putting himself between the gun and the other kids who were now only an arm's length from Sam.

"Shut up!" Troy raged.

"It's over. Bubba's over." Nate raised both his hands. They were trembling. He glanced back at Cade and Sally, tears streaming down his face no matter how calm he sounded. His attention snagged on Sam next, his eyes widening as she slithered another inch closer, and then he was silently pleading with her to do something, anything, to make all of this go away. "Your dad will stop pounding on you now. Put the gun down. It's just us. Your friends. It's okay. It's over."

"Friends . . . ? Over?" Troy cried harder, the horrible thing he'd done destroying him right in front of them. The gun wobbled in his hand. "I didn't mean to shoot him. I just wanted to scare him. But they won't believe that. They're coming. I know what's going to happen. They'll have guns, and they won't believe what he did to me. Bubba deserved it, but I'll be the one in trouble. What will my dad do now?"

"Don't shoot us, too." Sally clutched at Cade's shoulders, the two of them still behind Nate.

"I don't want to," Troy whispered. "I never wanted to."

"Then don't." Cade glanced Sam's way, too, finally seeing her as she somehow managed to stand behind Troy, gripping a chair for support. "Don't shoot us, and we won't let anyone blame you."

"Like you care," Troy sneered through his tears.

"Put the stupid gun back in your backpack." Nate stepped closer.

"Don't call me stupid." Troy's voice dropped to something low and deadly. He was calmer now. Too calm.

"Then stop acting stupid." Nate sounded out of his mind with panic and fear now. All the kids were. As brave as everyone was being, they weren't equipped to handle this. How could they be? And sooner or later someone was going to say the wrong thing and set Troy off again.

"Shut up, man." Troy wrapped his other hand around the gun.

From opposite sides of Troy, Nate and Sam both inched closer.

Troy lifted the gun higher, aiming it at Nate's chest. He was going to shoot.

"No!" Sam screamed, tackling him from behind.

The gun went off with a deafening explosion. She landed hard, with Troy yelling beneath her.

"Mom!" Cade yelled.

"Nate!" Sally screamed.

The ringing from the gun firing so close to Sam's head streaked pain through her ears, making it impossible to hear anything else. All she knew for certain was that they were on the ground, she and Troy, her arms wrapped around the squirming kid, holding tight because that was all she could manage.

Where was the gun? If she let go, Troy might shoot again. Would he shoot anyway?

Was Cade hit?

Nate?

Sally?

The darkness wouldn't answer her—the darkness behind her closed eyelids, flashing like a strobe light with images of smoke and flames and tall, majestic buildings flying apart and falling. Lives ending. An innocent world was dying around her, while the most vulnerable of lives were depending on her to make everything safe again.

She had to keep moving. She had to take care of the kids. She had to keep Troy and his gun down. But the memories she fought daily to control were seething. The anxiety they fed was taking over, shaking through her, making her weak.

Let's go home, Brian had said, that morning after 9/11, once he'd finally found her in Queens and the last of her students had been claimed by their families. *It's all going to be okay.*

Only she couldn't forget the sound of the towers falling, while she and her colleagues had watched it on TV, wondering whether their building was next. Or the utter desolation of walking through the clouds of dust and grime coating the city and everyone's hearts.

Atlanta will be our fresh start, her husband had promised a year later, when they'd been talking about packing up their almost one-year-old and leaving forever. *Once we're away from New York, your nerves will settle down and everything will be better.*

Only it hadn't been. It *never* had been, no matter what they'd done or how they'd tried to make life be again what they'd dreamed it could be. And now . . .

Troy was still trying to get away. She lost her hold on him. Her arms weren't her own any longer. Footsteps scrambled toward them, appearing from every direction. Troy was yanked to his feet. She could hear him now, crying and screaming.

"Secure him and the weapon," a gruff voice commanded. "Get the paramedics in here for the kids. The ones who aren't shot, get them to the team outside . . . We're in lockdown. I want a target search for other shooters. Weapons. Booby traps. Get me the layout of the building and a master key. Ma'am, are you okay?"

"Cade," she croaked. *The ones who aren't shot . . .* "Is Cade okay?"

"Are you hurt, ma'am?"

Hands cradled her skull. The man knelt beside her. A knee, a navy pant leg, filled her fuzzy vision. His fingers found a sensitive spot near the base of her skull.

"Ah!" she cried.

"You're bleeding, ma'am," he said. "You've hit your head. Can you talk to me? Can you tell me your name?"

"Sam Perry," a familiar voice answered. Another pair of knees skidded to a halt beside her, covered in pink with frolicking frogs hopping all over them. "Her name's Sam. I'm the school nurse. Let me check her and the boys who've been shot."

Boys? More than one . . . Sam hadn't been fast enough. She hadn't stopped Troy in time.

The activity around them intensified. More voices and noise and bodies were coming and going. Sam couldn't keep up. Her swimming vision refused to make sense of any of it. She kept trying to collect her thoughts, to keep them focused on the only thing that mattered now . . .

"Cade?" she whispered.

Or maybe the words weren't coming out at all. That must be why no one was answering her. It had to be. The reason no one was telling her what had happened couldn't be that Cade was hurt or dead. It just couldn't be.

She was screaming his name now. Silently. She couldn't stop screaming for him.

Cade!

"Can you hear me, Sam?" Mallory asked. "Brian's on the way. Pete called him. Let me take a closer look at your head. Are you hurt anywhere else? Sam? Sam . . ."

Chapter Four

"Sam?" Brian whispered to his unconscious wife, worried that the sound of his voice alone might break her. Or him. "Sweetheart, can you hear me? It's okay. Cade's fine. You got to him in time. He's down the hall getting checked out, but there's not a scratch on him. Not like . . ."

Brian bit off the impulse to talk about Bubba and Nate. Or to tell his wife about his shock at Pete Lombard's call—another damn doomsday call on Brian's fucking cell—telling him that his life was disintegrating. And this time he could have lost both his boy and his wife.

Relax, son, his dad had said on the one-year anniversary of 9/11, when Brian had confided that Sam wasn't improving, she'd ditched her therapist, she wasn't going back to teaching, she was terrified of something happening to their infant son, and Brian was thinking about taking the job offer he'd just received from an Atlanta architecture firm that didn't do his kind of work. But moving might be what he and Sam both needed to make a fresh start. *Have a little faith, Brian. Give it time and things will get better. The worst is behind you. Stay positive, and time will fix everything.*

Everything but the reality of Sam's fear that nothing was safe or certain any longer. Her ever-present anticipation of another explosion, another tragic loss, had taken Brian's wife away from him, from herself. Maybe forever. What she'd been through had changed the kind of mother their boys would have. It had changed things about their lives that Brian rarely let himself dwell on. Looking to the future was what his family had needed from him for more than a decade.

He'd made the move south to help Sam. He'd given up his seniority at his Manhattan job, busting his ass again to pay his dues in yet another firm that had never quite fit him, when his dream since college had been to run his own shop. He'd shouldered the bulk of the parenting Cade and Joshua needed outside of the home. He'd stayed positive that everything would work out and he and Sam would eventually move forward the way they'd planned, even as the boys grew older and began to notice that their mom was different. He'd kept fighting, and so had Sam, and things had finally, *finally* been coming together for them . . .

Then a part of him had died when he'd answered Pete's call about the shooting at Chandler. Brian would look back on that moment forever and swear that his heart hadn't beaten again, that he hadn't taken a full breath until he'd arrived at the school and found his family.

Pete, a fire and rescue paramedic and first responder, had been on duty and was en route to the school. He'd had no details to share other than that an emergency call had come in about multiple shots fired, and multiple victims. Brian had dropped to his knees on his office carpet, his face in his hands. Then he'd

raced out the door and driven to the school like a man possessed, oblivious to whatever traffic laws and lights and signs he
passed, until he'd driven up to find every police and emergency
vehicle in town converged on the elementary school parking lot,
lights swirling like the midway of a demented carnival.

An EMT had been wheeling a stretcher out of the front
of the school. Relief had almost dropped Brian to the ground
again when he'd realized it was Nate Turner on top, not one of
his own boys. Cade's best friend had been unconscious and
bleeding from a gunshot wound in his shoulder. His mother,
Beverly, had been hysterical, jogging alongside the stretcher in
an altered state Brian knew all too well. And at that moment,
he'd wanted to turn tail and run. The cowardly compulsion to
escape had nearly sent him sprinting back to his car. He'd never
forget the shame of it.

He hadn't wanted to face whatever was waiting inside the
school. But he'd shoved down the panic, hearing his father's
voice again. *Relax, Brian . . . Have a little faith.* He had a wife and
children, a family and a future that he'd fight anything and anyone to keep. So he'd sprinted past the ring of ambulances in front
of the school, scanning the crowd of emergency responders and
parents and teachers and kids, looking for a familiar face. Someone had finally mentioned that his youngest son's class was out
back, near the track where the kids took PE.

"When Joshie ran up to me," he told his wife, "I couldn't
turn him loose. Holding him felt like holding all of you. No one
was telling me anything about you and Cade yet . . ."

Brian smoothed Sam's bangs away from her face, willing his
voice to sound confident and strong, the way she needed him to
be, while his entire body felt like it was crumbling. Everything
but his fingers. Sam deserved only the gentlest of touches. She'd

proved all over again just how brave and flat-out astonishing a human being she was. She'd run toward gunfire, toward a freaked-out kid, to save their son and his friends. Brian caressed his wife's bruised cheek.

"The police had evacuated the school," he said. "The cell lines were on overload. I couldn't get through to anyone the whole drive over. But Joshua had asked people. He told me right away that you and Cade were both fine. Then Ms. Hemmings took us to Cade, where he and Sally were talking to the police. That's when an EMT told us you'd been transported here. As a low-priority victim, thank God . . ."

His rambling ground to a halt. His voice failed him as thoughts of everything that could have happened took over.

How long had it taken after 9/11 before he could close his eyes and not see terrifying images of what might have been—his wife of only two years buried beneath tons of rubble? And each time, as the panic raced closer, he'd whispered, *Thank God,* over and over, until the nightmare faded, eventually for good.

But the fear and the hate had remained, somewhere deep and greedy inside him. Fear of the next time. Hate for the next stranger who'd take it upon himself to destroy Brian's peaceful world. He gazed down at Sam, whose eyes were still closed. It didn't matter whether she could hear him. He had to keep talking.

As long as he kept telling Sam that they could make it through this disaster, too, maybe he could believe himself that his wife would come back from yet another emotional spiral.

"Thank God you stopped Troy from doing even more damage. Thank God you were there to protect Cade." She'd saved Cade and Nate and Sally and countless other kids Troy could have turned on next. Just as she'd set aside her own well-being to be there for her students in New York. But at what cost? "You . . . You're amazing, sweetheart. It's okay. It's all going to be okay. Please come back to me. Please . . ."

He cleared his throat. He had to stop this. Sam and his boys deserved better than him falling apart when she'd found a way to be so brave.

"Wake up, sweetheart." He kissed her uninjured cheek, willing her eyes to open so he wouldn't feel so god-awful alone. "I'm here. You're here. Cade and Joshua are safe. Mallory and Pete and Julia and Walter are hanging out with them until you're awake. I'm right here for you, just like before. You can do this, Sam. Come back to me again. It's all going to be okay."

***

. . . going to be okay.

Sam swam toward her husband's voice, his promise, his insistence that they could both keep going.

"Everyone's waiting for you to wake up," Brian said. "I think all of Chandlerville is in the lounge down the hall, wanting to hear that you're fine and to tell you how proud they are of you. All of Mimosa Lane is here, for sure, not just our neighbors on the cul-de-sac. You're a hero, Sam. The way you helped Ms. Hemmings and then the kids, even though Troy was still . . . I'm so proud of y—"

"Stop," she croaked.

Hero?

Proud?

He had to stop. Kristen had said something like that at the school, before the shooting. How much she admired Sam. How

Sam was an inspiration. She was *really something*, Mallory had said. They all had to stop. Sam couldn't take it again. She couldn't.

Cade! her mind screamed, as it replayed for her all the new reasons why she wasn't okay, while her husband said that he was proud, so she'd smile and believe him and try to be okay because that's what she wanted to be, too. Didn't she?

Pretending . . . Mallory's voice echoed from the in-between place that still owned Sam's thoughts. *Sometimes that's the most dangerous thing you can do.*

"Sam?" Brian kissed her fingers, then her throbbing temple.

"Stop it," she whispered. She didn't have the strength to pull away, but she needed to. Far, far away.

His strong hand was soft against her fingers, as if he'd realized the simplest touch might be too much for her. But all she had to do was wake up, and everything would be fine again?

"Sam, sweetheart," he said. "You and Cade are safe. Nate is going to be okay, too. We're all going to be fine. We'll start over again, just like before. All you have to do is—"

"No. Stop it!" She made her eyes open. She pulled her fingers away. "It's not okay. We're not safe. I almost watched our son die!"

"Cade's fine. We're all fine, Sam." Her husband's encouraging smile broke her heart. Because his eyes were full of the doubt he didn't know she could see each time she really looked at him. "The doctor said you have a concussion, that you'd be confused. Don't try to talk too much. Don't worry about anything right now. Let me call the nurses' station and—"

"No." She grabbed for him and held on so hard, she thought her head would explode. "Not yet. Don't call anyone yet."

She couldn't handle anyone else. She couldn't stop feeling it: the hopelessness and the helplessness. She was breaking apart again, just like before. It was awful. And her husband didn't want to know. She could feel it in him, the desperation for them not to be these people again, devastated with no hope of moving forward, or back, to the lighter, brighter world they wanted so much.

"Please," she begged him, "talk to me, Brian."

"About the shooting?" He sat on the edge of her hospital bed, as steady and sure on the outside as always. "We don't have to do that, not until you're better. You don't—"

"I have to talk about it. Don't you see? About the shooting. About us. About me."

"Not right now." He sounded almost angry. Desperate. This wasn't what they'd agreed to be, this broken thing she could feel them becoming again. She was letting him down. "We don't have to do all of that right now, Sam."

"Yes, right now!"

She sounded half crazed. Cade was alive, and so was she, so she should be happy, right? Maybe she was crazy. Because instead of being grateful, she was screaming at her calm, reasonable husband for not freaking out like she was.

Brian never did.

"You weren't there," she said. "You didn't see it . . ."

A memory of Troy's angry face gobbled up the fuzziness still protecting her—his gun and his hatred aimed at Cade and Sally and Nate. Another boy was lying there, bleeding. Children were in danger, not safe in a world where people killed and destroyed and ripped lives to pieces without warning, without giving anyone a chance, without—

"I'm going to be sick." She shoved herself higher on her pillows, feeling all over again the powerlessness of both today and twelve years ago. Everything was surging upward, outward, refusing to remain buried.

Her husband wrapped his arm around her. A plastic tray appeared beneath her chin. She leaned against him, loving him and hating him at the same time, and became violently sick, raw emotion emptying from her, until she could finally ease away and lean back against the pillows.

"Don't try to talk right now, honey," he said, his voice once more loving and gentle. "You're not making any sense. Take your time. We'll find a way through this together, just like before."

Just like before.

Everything inside Sam froze.

Just like before . . .

Pretending, gritting through something you're not ready to do . . .

"No," she croaked, "I can't."

"Sam," her husband said, his patience wearing thin, "you need to calm down. You've had a shock. We both have. But we're going to be—"

"I thought our son was going to die! I am not going to be okay, not even for you. You can't ask me to do that again . . ."

Like when she'd tried therapy and medication in New York, and it hadn't done any good. Like when she'd tried to go back to teaching, and couldn't walk through the front door of her new school, or take calls from families of her former students or friends or colleagues. Like when they'd moved to this peaceful town and she couldn't *start over* like they'd planned, even though they had a beautiful little boy to dote on, or be the happy soccer mom her sons deserved, or even take part in a PTA bake sale without having a two-week-long panic attack leading up to it.

They'd been so certain through all of it that she'd be okay soon. All they had to do was keep believing in each other and having faith in their new life, and they'd make it, no matter how much of what they'd been through had to be shoved deep inside to keep going. Only . . .

"I can't handle this," she heard herself say.

"I know it was horrible." Her husband's voice was almost unrecognizable. "But—"

"Not the shooting. Us. I can't handle *us* anymore, not this way." What she was saying, what she was thinking, was terrifying. And it was setting her free. "Going home with you, going back to our life, pretending that I'm a hero, and that I'm not just as messed up as I was in New York, so we can get on with what's supposed to be making us happy. I love you, Brian, but I can't do it anymore. Avoiding the truth. Not trusting each other enough to face what's broken, even if what's broken is us."

I know you're scared, Cade had said. *You don't have to talk about it . . . I know you and Dad don't want to.*

"Sam . . ." Brian whispered, sounding betrayed and panicked and so very young and afraid. He stood and backed away from the bed. Her husband looked ready to run. "You don't know what you're saying."

"I want some time by myself," she blurted out, desperate to take the words back. Only she couldn't. "It's the only way, Brian. The only way to save us."

"Save us?" he demanded, devastated. "From what?"

"From ourselves." The truth kept tumbling out, no matter how awful. "I need time. So do you. We need to figure things out. We need to deal with ourselves and our sons and what's happened—apart for a while. Away from everything we've thought could fix us. And then . . ."

"And then what? We'll be a family again, whenever *you* decide you're ready to stop giving up?"

"I'm not giving up," she promised them both, while haunting memories tempted her to let him help her disappear again from her life and her family and the world that kept refusing to be *okay* for any of them. "All I know is that if I go home with you before we figure out a different way to handle what we're both going through, I'll never make it back this time. *We'll* never make it back. Please, Brian, try to understand . . ."

DAY TWO

Chapter Five

April 8, 2013

Darkness could be shot full with light, Sam reminded herself, each time she walked outside to greet the night, grateful for the freedom and the space and the time to think.

Beneath her feet, the road sparkled with spring rain, moonlight, and the glow of Mimosa Lane streetlamps. Her thoughts had been jumbled tonight, like most nights since the shooting. And late hours were still easier, somehow, when she was outside. On her walks up and down the lane, her frayed nerves knitted themselves back together, remixing into something brighter and cleaner—the way her garden at home had once soothed her.

Outdoors still felt free. In this hushed world, while others slept, she was separate but still belonged. Shadows transformed the community she'd retreated from once again into the non-threatening place that had embraced her and Brian and their boys. The night calmed her compulsion to run. It reminded her why she'd stayed so close, still living on Mimosa Lane, even though she'd moved across the cul-de-sac to Julia and Walter's house.

It had been three months since Bubba's death, since Troy had destroyed the peace Chandlerville families had taken for granted for so long, and since she, her son, and Nate Turner had been heralded as heroes for preventing Troy from killing anyone else. Yet Sam was no closer to resolving her issues with Brian than their town was to resolving the chaos that had consumed everything since the shooting.

She hadn't had a flashback to 9/11 since she'd regained consciousness at the hospital. So that was something. And she was trying her best not to shut down completely every time her thoughts strayed to that day at Chandler. But she couldn't go home. Not yet. And the more she heard from Julia about what was going on with the rest of their town, the more it seemed that no one else was getting back to normal either.

Troy's and Bubba's families had been the focus of the initial media swarm that had invaded their community. Bubba Dickerson's parents had been besieged by journalists and cameramen determined to chronicle every tear. Troy's had been hounded out of Chandlerville after his statement to the police confirmed that he'd used his dad's gun, and that his dad had pushed him to confront Bubba.

Within a week of the shooting, Troy was transferred to a juvenile detention center in Atlanta and placed on suicide watch. His parents relocated to a condo in the city, to be closer to him and to hide behind the security guards and cameras at the building's front desk. Nate had come home from the hospital after just a few days, with a shoulder wound that had since healed. But his parents' anger over what had happened might never be assuaged. And they'd been happy to share their grievances with whatever reporters were interested in listening to how Chandler and the school board were to blame for not protecting Nate and the other kids.

And all the while, the spectacle of media attention aimed at sleepy Chandlerville had taken on a life of its own. Atlanta-based CNN had been the first team to arrive at the school the day of the shooting, not long after the first responders. They'd broadcasted nationally from the start. Other networks followed, even though the details had quickly shaken out that Chandler Elementary wasn't going to be the next Sandy Hook. A single eleven-year-old boy's death at the hands of another had become a poignant obsession for a few days. But Chandler hadn't turned out to be enough of a news sensation to rock the country indefinitely, not the way other recent tragedies had.

Bubba's funeral had been a feeding frenzy for the news outlets, of course, with everyone's grief and shock documented for an international audience. The coverage had expanded from there to include school faculty—spotlighting Kristen Hemmings and Roy Griffin, Chandler's principal, and putting the school board and other local leaders on the spot, as reporters asked their questions and focused their editorials on James and Beverly Turner's demands for reform.

How could child-on-child violence have happened in yet another idealistic, safe suburb? commentators had asked.

Everyday Americans had ranted to neighbors and strangers on blogs and social media. *Hadn't we learned our lesson yet about our nation's eroding moral compass?*

What was the world coming to, politicians had pondered to whomever might throw a vote their way, *when parents can't send their youngest offspring to school with the expectation that they'll be safe?*

Everyone wanted to know why no one at Chandler had recognized the degree of bullying Troy had endured, or how clearly unstable he'd become. And when it was revealed that he'd brought his father's pistol to school in his backpack, the gun-rights debate had fired into overdrive, pitting personal liberty against the public's right to feel protected from their neighbor's lapses in judgment.

And just when broadcasts had begun to sound repetitive, someone's research assistant had made the connection between Cade and Sam, neither of whom had said the first word to the press, and Sam's history with 9/11. Followed by more talk about heroism and courage.

Cade, who barely wanted to talk with anyone anymore, *definitely* didn't want to hear about heroes when one of his classmates had been killed in front of him and his best friend had been shot. Sam had continued to decline interviews, too, except with the police. Friends and neighbors and local leaders kept weighing in, though, on gun control and school security and parental responsibility, forming polarizing factions that were ripping at the framework of their small town.

Sam had no interest in adding to that kind of carnage. She'd already watched one city rip itself apart over a trauma no amount of assigning blame would fix. And the fears and the memories and the emotional scars she'd be making public if she were to get involved were already threatening her marriage and her children's happiness. Because she couldn't be home with their father, who was refusing to accept that he and Sam had anything to work through beyond her calming down and settling back into their normal routine.

Hers was the final story the national media had been interested in telling. By late February and early March Chandlerville had been left to flounder mostly on its own, color commentary and marquee talent migrating to juicier events.

The Dickersons were suing the Wilmingtons, but had pretty much kept to themselves otherwise. The Turners still wanted heads to roll at the school and on the school board, as if firing people would guarantee that something like the shooting would never happen again. They'd rallied a lot of Sam's and Brian's friends and neighbors to their cause. Exploratory school board meetings had been held weekly for over a month, during which Roy Griffin kept covering his butt and showing all signs—according to Julia, a member of the school board—of throwing Kristen under the bus, so he could blame her for anything found lacking at Chandler.

Because someone *was* going to be held accountable. Someone always was. As if all of them wouldn't feel responsible, in their own ways, for the rest of their lives.

Sam thought about it every night—going back to the shooting in her mind and searching for some way to stop Troy sooner. She thought about Cade and Joshua, worrying over how all of this was affecting them. She'd thought more and more—more than she had in years, the way her New York therapist had once said Sam would have to, if she ever wanted to really get past what had happened there. And more than anything else, she thought about her husband, who was still staying as positive as ever for the boys. But Brian had grown angry and sullen with Sam, after her repeated refusal to move back home. And when he'd kept insisting, she'd stopped speaking with him altogether about anything but their children's well-being.

She'd initially promised him she'd need only a few days to pull herself together, when she'd asked Julia if she could stay in her and Walter's spare bedroom. But waking day after day to solitude and thinking, really thinking about all that had happened—precious days of not having to face Brian's confusion and determination to talk her into coming back—had turned into weeks, and then months.

She still spent as much time as she could at their house, taking care of the boys, cooking breakfast the same as she always had. Except that she left now when Brian came downstairs. After he headed for work, she'd return to do whatever chores she could at the house while it was empty. In the afternoons she helped Cade and Joshua with their homework, until their father came home from work.

Neither of the boys wanted to talk much about either her move across the cul-de-sac or the shooting, Joshua probably because he was so young, and Cade because he was still in shock about the shooting itself. His silence was to be expected, according to the child psychologist she and Brian had consulted, who'd tried to speak with Cade in a few therapy appointments in March.

After Cade had sulked in silence through each one, Dr. Mueller had recommended waiting another month or so before trying again. Cade clearly wasn't ready to open up. As long as the kids were following a relatively normal schedule, the doctor had reassured Sam and Brian, eating and going to school and not keeping to themselves too much, what Cade and Joshua needed most now was love and time and parents who'd listen when they were finally ready to talk. And Sam and Brian had both assured Dr. Mueller they would be, regardless of their estrangement.

But Sam couldn't *be there* for her husband yet. Her reaction to the mere suggestion of returning home still bordered on panic, and she couldn't explain to him why, not completely. And Brian refused to stop pushing.

How could she stay away and still say she wanted their family? How could she insist she was fighting to save their marriage, while she refused to go back to the way things had been? Why couldn't she keep believing in a relationship that had always appeared calm and under control on the outside, but one she was beginning to realize had increasingly left her feeling terrified and alone under the surface?

It wasn't his fault. They'd become this thing they were together, putting a positive face on the fallout from 9/11 and hoping for the best. And if the shooting at Chandler hadn't happened, maybe they'd have made it. Maybe. But Bubba was dead, and Sam had been there, believing her son was going to die, too. And when she'd woken in the hospital to her husband's empty assurances, something inside her had snapped. Or maybe it had finally started to heal. But that was crazy, right? She'd thought so at first, the same as Brian.

And she might still be thinking she was being as reckless as her husband did, if it weren't for the kindred spirit she'd begun to share her night walks with. Someone who was dealing with a lot of the same hushed, under-the-surface things. Someone she'd promised to be there for every night, even if no one else ever knew about it. Especially because she suspected no one else knew.

Over the last month she'd begun to share her shadows with a soul far too young and tender to feel as lost as Sam felt. But there he'd been one night—a new light shining into her world, waiting for her on the swings in the community park that was her nocturnal destination. And there he was again tonight, as she left Mimosa Lane behind and stepped onto the crunchy cedar chips that the landscapers spread around the playground equipment.

"What can I do to help you, Nate?" she asked as she took the swing beside Cade's best friend.

It's what she always asked, and *would* always ask, as long as he kept coming back.

She pushed away from the ground, lifting her feet until her swing was airborne, flying, floating, with spring shadows whispering all around. Her companion didn't respond. He hardly ever did. He'd ask her a question every now and then. How was Cade? Did she go to Bubba's funeral? Was she mad, because of what Nate's parents were saying in the press and trying to do to the school? Did she ever think about that day, or about what could have happened?

He never offered anything about himself. She wasn't even certain he listened to her answers. But she answered all the same, as honestly as she could. They passed the darkest moments of each dawn just like this, when the night was at its most fragile, collapsing in on itself to be reborn into morning.

"You must be anxious about today," she said. She didn't expect he wanted his "big day" any more than she had hers three months ago. "Just walking in the door of the school for the bake sale that morning was enough to make me sick."

She winced as her mind filled with the sound of adults and children screaming. A sleepy little bird in one of the oak branches above them sounded off to the sun that wasn't quite ready to rise. Nate jumped at the joyous warble. Then he kicked off too, swinging like Sam. He arced back and forth, out of time with her. His beaten-up high-tops dragged the ground with each pass.

"I thought I was ready," she said, when she usually would have waited longer, hoping to draw him out.

But tonight she was too worried to keep silent. Nate was returning to school later today, for the first time since the shooting, his circumstances wickedly similar to what she'd faced three months ago. She couldn't know for certain what he was going through. But it was all she'd been able to think about for hours, while she worried for him: Nate and all the other children at Chandler who'd been so in danger that day, and how the memories of it would affect him now, the way hers had attacked the morning of the bake sale.

Startled by what sounded like a jet plane soaring overhead, she looked up, swallowing her panic. She forced her vision to focus on the crystal-clear winter sky above the treetops, just to be certain nothing was there.

"It sounded simple enough to everyone else," she made herself continue. Nate hadn't stopped swinging. He hadn't rushed home the way he had a few other nights. "The bake sale was just another day for the rest of the world. Fun. Easy. Moms love that sort of thing, because we get to be a part of your lives for a while when you spend so much time away from us. It was special. I wanted it to be so special for me and Cade and Joshua. But I was terrified, too. That was another long night just like this one, waiting for the morning to come. I sat right here swinging by myself, not sure if I could make it back home or to the school. I wanted to run away. A part of me still wishes I had, so I wouldn't have had to be there to see what Troy did to you and Bubba and all the other kids. What he's done to himself and his family and the people who love him."

Nate skidded to a halt. The little bird—a cardinal—in a flash of disappearing red, fluttered off. Wind swirled at the brittle leaves left over from the fall, wrapping morning chill around them.

She'd mentioned 9/11 to Nate once before, and how it made things harder for her even now. She'd wanted him to know that maybe she could understand something about what he was feeling. He hadn't responded in any way before now.

"How . . ." he said. He inhaled in a gulp, like he was fighting not to cry. "How did you finally forget, so you could go to school that morning the way you did?"

It was halting, personal questions like this that had convinced Sam that Nate had known she'd be coming to the park the first night they'd met. And that maybe he'd planned to find her at the playground, so he could ask the few questions he had.

He was searching for answers, which was a healing thing. Sam hoped so at least. As much as she hoped what she'd been doing each of these nights would help, instead of confusing him even more.

Nate pushed off again, swinging higher.

Her feet snagged on the dust and dirt at their feet.

"You don't forget it," she said, knowing it and feeling it and hating it.

He picked up speed, leaning deeper into each swing, pushing harder, probably tuning her out.

Until tonight she hadn't been certain what he needed to hear, or whether he even knew himself. She understood how that was, feeling safer not knowing. Only how did you get better, when not knowing sooner or later began to make *safe* feel an awful lot like giving up? And she didn't want to see this boy make the same mistakes she and Brian had.

Nate wasn't talking to Cade anymore. She'd heard from Julia that Nate never left his house. Yet James and Beverly were sending him back to school—to the place where the unthinkable had happened to his life—thinking that having a normal day with his friends would help their son move on. The same way Brian still thought Sam's returning to her *normal* self at home was the answer.

"You don't want to forget, Nate," she said. "Forgetting is the last thing you should do. You have to find a way to live with what you saw and heard that day, and everything it's making you feel. Even if it keeps things from getting better as fast as you and other people want them to, you have to keep looking back at what you went through. It never gets okay, not completely. And you don't really want it to. Because thinking something that horrible is okay, or not thinking about it at all, will hurt you. Don't forget, Nate. No matter what you do or what anyone else says. Don't try to make yourself forget . . ."

***

Brian stood in the shadows of Mimosa Lane's playground, where his boys had laughed and screamed and played with friends and fought and grown up together, listening to his wife bare her heart to another family's child.

Sam hadn't slept well in more than a decade. And now Brian didn't either. He'd slept less and less every night since the shooting. Since she'd come home from the hospital and moved into their friends' guest bedroom.

The last few weeks, he'd spent the early hours of each morning haunting the garden Sam had let grow wild since January. And then he'd sit and watch the Davis house through the moonlight, waiting for however long it took for Sam to leave and walk far enough down the lane that he could follow her unnoticed.

In January, he'd convinced himself and tried to convince his boys that Sam would be home before they knew it. Things would be better soon. Mom just needed a few days on her own to calm down. He'd smoothed things over with the kids. He'd gone along with the new routine they'd settled into at the house, with Sam coming and going as she pleased but never staying. He'd kept expecting her to come around, to be waiting for him when he got home from work, ready to talk sensibly about what she was going through and how they could deal with it together, the way they had everything else.

Now, three months later, he was an insomniac who didn't know how to explain what was going on to *himself* anymore, let alone to his sons. Oh, and he was stalking his wife. Eavesdropping on the solitude that comforted her in ways she no longer thought he could.

She'd devastated him. She'd left him, without really leaving. She was so close still, it was maddening, but she wouldn't see reason. She was gone from the house the moment Brian came downstairs in the morning and as soon as he got home from work each afternoon. She'd made him the enemy. She was throwing away every loving, concerned, confusing moment of their lives together, and every supportive thing he'd done.

Brian's need to help her and to have her close again so his life would make sense the way it used to had only grown. Even when things weren't perfect before, even when he'd been running himself into the ground trying to make up for the things Sam couldn't do, he'd had her—the brave woman who'd battled back from so much to stay by his side. She'd been the wife and mother to his boys whom he'd trusted to never give up. She'd been his soul mate.

Now she'd abandoned the life they'd built, to *save* their marriage, she'd said. And lately, in their neighborhood park in the middle of the night, she'd found a person she *was* ready to talk to.

He'd watched Sam and Nate for more than a week. He had no way of knowing how long they'd been meeting, hardly talking, hardly visible through the shadows. Sam was clearly still struggling—up at all hours and walking their neighborhood like a phantom. But she was making an effort to face what had happened—with someone else besides Brian.

It was maddening.

It was infuriating.

It was wrong, and he couldn't take it any longer.

Tasting something bitter and hateful and not himself, he pushed through the shroud of bushes and skeletal pines he'd hidden behind. A twig snapped, outing him before he was ready to own the pettiness, the jealousy pulsing through his veins. Sam whirled toward him in her swing, her feet covered by the fluffy pink bedroom slippers he'd given her for her birthday last year.

Nate shot out of his swing. His eyes locked with Brian's for an eternal moment, and then he was racing away, sneakers slapping on asphalt, his swing creaking and jerking back and forth, flying haphazardly without him there to anchor it.

"Do his parents have any idea you two are meeting like this?" Brian demanded.

"You tell me." Sam sounded as calm as every other time they'd talked. But he heard disappointment, too.

It was always there now, in her sweet voice and her eyes and expression, whenever she wanted to talk, but only about what she wanted to talk about: everything she was convinced they'd done wrong since moving to Chandlerville, and why she couldn't come home and do it all over again. Bottom line, she didn't believe in him anymore. She didn't believe in *them*. All because she was scared, and for the first time in her life she was refusing to face her problems head-on. Which meant she couldn't face him.

The gentle, open, understanding love she'd just showered on Nate and kept trying to share with Cade the few times she did get him to talk was no longer there for Brian. Not unless he agreed that everything they'd built their Chandlerville life on was absolute crap.

"I've been a little too busy at home," he bit out, "to be chatting up our neighbors about where my wife spends her nights."

He felt the unwanted explosion rising inside him. But he didn't let it out. He couldn't. She was hurting, he reminded himself. He wanted to help her. He had to find some way to get through to her. Things had gotten completely out of hand.

"I understand," she said, pushing off, swinging back and forth as if she were once more alone, or he was dismissed, or she simply didn't give a damn what he did next.

Fuck her understanding.

"Come home, Samantha." He grabbed the swing's chains and stopped her, moving until he was in her path and looming over her. She wasn't avoiding him again. Not this time. "This has gone on too long. I've tried to be patient, but we have children to raise, and they're confused. We have a marriage to save, and a community falling apart around us. Don't you think you've been selfish long enough, blaming me for our problems, or whatever else this is?"

He heard himself attacking his wife, instead of comforting her, which made him even more furious. Didn't she see what she was doing? She was tearing them apart.

She stood, her body brushing his. She slipped away, because he was suddenly too afraid of his own anger to stop her. For now, she went only as far as the curb. But how long would it take before she'd wandered so far, he'd never get her back?

He had less of her, knew less about her—less about himself and who he'd thought he was—by the day.

"I'm not coming home," she said. "Not until you understand what I've been saying."

"You're not *saying* anything." Nothing that made the least bit of sense to him. "We're hardly ever in the same room together anymore, because that's the way you want it. All you seem to want is to give up on getting any better, and to give up on our marriage getting back to what it was, and to tell me it's all my fault because I want to keep fighting for you. Come home. Then we can talk—about the shooting and Nate and New York and whatever else you need to deal with. That's the only way we're going to work this out."

"I'm trying *not* to give up on us, Brian." She sounded so scared, yet stronger somehow than she'd been in a long time. "But I understand what you're saying about the boys. And I understand how all of this is making you angry. If you think it would be less confusing, I . . . I talked with Teddy last week about what we'd need to do to make the separation official. Maybe if we did that, we could tell the rest of our friends and the school and the boys and it would be easier for everyone."

He grabbed her arms so quickly, he didn't realize he had until he was fighting the urge to shake his wife until she took back the latest bomb she'd exploded in his life. He let her go instead, and watched the same shock he felt at his loss of control bloom across Sam's moonlit face.

Teddy Rutherford. The aging, graying, good-ol'-boy Southern lawyer who'd handled updating their wills when Joshua was born. Brian's wife wanted him to talk to their lawyer about filing for an official separation. He shook his head. He tried to laugh.

The alien sound that came out left him queasy and made his wife look like she might be sick, too.

"For God's sake, Sam, we're *going* to work this out. We don't need Rutherford or anyone else nosing into our family business."

"Anyone else? Like the therapist Mallory recommended we see together?"

Mallory and Pete had been there for both of them through all of this, listening and trying not to take sides the way Julia had. It had taken until last week before the ex–social worker had chewed Sam and Brian out about getting counseling to deal with their issues. But while he and Sam had agreed to counseling for the boys when Cade and Joshua were ready to talk about the shooting, Brian and therapy were a no-go.

Would you consider it? Sam had asked. *For us, would you do it, so some of this can really start to get better?*

Consider being ambushed all over again with everything that's gone wrong with you and me and our family? he'd demanded, while he and Mallory and Sam talked on Julia's front lawn. He hadn't needed a shrink after 9/11, and he didn't need one now. *All I've done is try to help you, the way you said you needed to be helped. We're fine,* he'd insisted. *You're upset, and I totally get that. You should have all the support you need. If you want to see a therapist again, do it. But you're the one who didn't want to keep working with your doctor in New York. After all this time, don't try to rope me into going with you, because what you're doing is somehow about me. I'm not the one who has a problem dealing with things.*

Except that he was stalking her all over the neighborhood, and arguing with her in the middle of the night while their boys slept at home. Because he missed his wife so badly, he was losing his mind. He reached for her again, a man grasping for the crumbs of his happy life. She backed even farther away, gutting him.

"You're going to get through this," he insisted. "You're not alone, Sam. I'll help. We all will. I know you don't think I understand, but that day at Chandler was hard for me, too. It was a terrible reminder of what it was like on 9/11, and we can talk about that. But Cade's okay. We're all safe. Our entire family is right here on the lane, the same as we were before, and we're going to be ok—"

"Stop it!" His wife, the other half of himself, was looking at him as if *he'd* made all this happen. "Stop—"

"Believing in us?" he snapped with a fresh surge of almost hatred. "Wanting us? Fighting for something normal and safe and peaceful for our family, the way you and I have all these years, only now you're giving up? All while you're helping someone else's child in secret, because it means you can feel better about checking out on the rest of us?"

He wasn't being fair. She'd never *not* been there for their sons, all three months she'd been at Julia's. But fuck being fair.

She'd flinched when he'd raised his voice, but she was closer now. And he was shaking, his fists clenched, the control he'd spent a lifetime mastering deserting them both until he found himself fighting back tears. His terribly hurt wife looked as if she wanted to reach out and soothe him, and instead of relief, all he could feel was shame—and even more anger that she'd pushed them to this.

"I need you to stop," she said. "Stop trying to get me to say that I'm okay with nearly being shot, or nearly watching our son be shot, or nearly being blown off the face of the earth on 9/11, or watching babies lose their parents. I stood there in our son's cafeteria, Brian, and watched a boy we know who'd already killed another kid very nearly take away Nate and Cade, too . . ."

She did reach for him now, her hand shaking and cold and clinging. He'd seen this before, in New York, and she was unrecognizable to him in these moments. Someone beyond her own reach and his. The woman holding on to him was a broken reflection of his bride of more than fifteen years. And she was saying that the only way he could keep her was to fall apart with her, instead of holding on to the last of the strength and faith that had gotten them this far.

"I need you to stop," she begged.

"Damn you." It was a whispered curse, but his throat hurt as if he were shouting. He'd had enough. Three months of enough. "How selfish can you be? You're out of control. And you're a coward, Sam. You want me to stop? Why? So you can feel better about quitting everything we've fought so hard for? Because that's what you're doing. You're quitting on me, the boys, our life here. You're throwing it all away, everything we've built. You're throwing *us* away, and you want me to help you."

She shook her head. "I know it makes no sense to you. I know that you think I'm just making excuses. So you think all you have to do is convince me to calm down and go back to the way I was. And then I'll see that everything I'm feeling isn't real. But there's no calming down, Brian, from feeling this alone with who I am and what I've become. And there's no going back to the life we had. You're right. I'm out of control. *We're* out of control. I think we have been for a long time. And those feelings don't belong to the quiet, careful place we've built for ourselves here. So there is no *us* anymore to throw away. There's just me, *this* way. And you, needing me to be something else."

When he didn't respond, when he had no idea what to say, her touch disappeared. The rush of emotion they'd both been riding drained away. In its wake, her expression became smooth as glass. Calm. Deadly serious. They'd been here before, too. This was the Sam he'd prayed he'd never see again. The woman she'd promised they'd seen the last of when they left New York behind.

"You're quitting again," he repeated. "Just like before, when you no longer wanted anything to do with what we'd made for ourselves in Manhattan."

"I'm being honest." She backed up. "And this is nothing like New York. For the first time in a long time, I'm dealing with my fears instead of shoving them aside. I'm thinking about them, the way my therapist couldn't get me to. And I'm doing it so we can have a chance. I'm as responsible as you are for never really dealing with all of this. I asked you to help me become this person who can't handle anything. And I'm still not sure what I'm doing at Julia's or out here with Nate. But I need you to meet me halfway, Brian, if I'm going to figure any of it out. And that's not happening. The Sam you thought I was is gone, and you don't want the one who's here instead."

"That's not true." Panic shredded him at the sound of her losing hope. "I love you."

"Not this way."

She was scattering before him, shutting down again and reminding him that he was the one who was failing. He was the most broken of the two of them. Because nothing, neither 9/11 nor the shooting at Chandler, had happened to him. But he was falling apart, too, though he didn't want her or the boys to see it. More each day without her, he was feeling the same lost, alone, alien things she was describing. And he hated them both for it, because *he* wasn't the one suffering from PTSD and the traumas she'd endured.

I asked you to help me become this person who can't handle anything...

I need you to meet me halfway...

"Sam, please. I'm sorry. Stay and talk with me . . ."

"What's the point?" She shook her head. "I'm never going to be the Sam you want me to be again."

And then she ran, just like Nate had, disappearing down the same dark street.

Chapter Six

Sam let herself through the white picket fence into the Davises' backyard, and then into the house through the door that led off Julia and Walter's immaculate deck.

Sam, please . . . stay and talk with me . . .

Brian was the only man she'd ever loved—would ever love—and she'd broken his heart. They'd been headed for this place for so long. Now she was driving her husband there at warp speed, shoving their marriage over a dangerous cliff with no idea where they'd land.

He was so angry. Her even-tempered Brian, always calm through every storm, steady and focused and dependable, had yelled at her for the first time in their marriage.

Shaken, she'd stopped by their house on the way to Julia's, rushing inside to leave him a note and hoping he wouldn't return until she was gone. Then as she'd slipped out the back door into her overgrown, neglected backyard, the disappointment that he *hadn't* barged in to force her to keep talking had trampled on her faith that her marriage still had a chance.

She'd stared at her skeletal rosebushes as she'd left—not a bloom in sight—and had finally accepted the truth that maybe there was so much distance between her and Brian now, there was no way to heal it. And she'd been his partner in crime, loving her husband all these years for making it so easy for them to find themselves right back in this nowhere place, as soon the next major crisis challenged them.

Whatever it takes, she'd promised herself the morning of the bake sale. She'd been determined to do whatever it took to move forward for her family. And she still was. Why couldn't Brian see that, no matter how angry he was?

Tears still streaming down her face, she closed the Davises' kitchen door behind her. She prayed Julia wasn't waiting for her the way her friend often did in the mornings, when she and Sam would sometimes talk over a cup of tea before Julia left for her day of taking meetings with Chandlerville citizens, answering questions on behalf of the school board. Sam made a beeline for the downstairs guest room, only to skid to a halt halfway across the kitchen.

The rooster-shaped electric clock perched on the wall beyond the oak farm table said it was barely six o'clock. But as if it were the most normal thing in the world, curvy, nurturing Julia and exotically tall, pulled-together Kristen Hemmings sat at the table drinking coffee, dressed for the day, while beneath her coat Sam still had on her nightgown and slippers. And there Mallory was, standing next to them, looking concerned and determined and . . . ready for the kind of straightforward conversation Sam couldn't handle at the moment.

She was already feeling lower than pond scum, after deciding not to make breakfast for her boys for the first time since she'd moved out. She was shaking so hard she could barely stand still. She didn't want Cade and Joshua to see her this way. And whatever Mallory and Julia and Kristen were there for, she wasn't up for that either. Mallory had become increasingly insistent that Sam deal with her husband, rather than retreating further and further away from what they were doing to each other. But this wasn't the morning to get into something so troubling, and certainly not in front of Kristen.

"I'm sorry." She wiped at the corners of her eyes with both hands.

She'd promised herself this wasn't who she was anymore—a woman who ran from her problems or hid away, allowing life to trample all over her. But damn it if she wasn't again moving toward the guest bedroom.

"I'll let you three talk." She was passing the table at what could only be described as a walking sprint when Kristen put a hand on Sam's arm.

Sam jerked away, appalled at her own rudeness. Kristen had befriended her the morning of the bake sale. There was absolutely no reason to be afraid of her now.

"I'm sorry," she apologized again. She was feeling more pissed by the second, actually, as she glanced at Mallory. "It's just that I've—"

"She's still having a hard time," Julia explained over her, "since the shooting."

"I know." Kristen said. "And I'm the one who should apologize for barging in at such a ridiculous hour. I wouldn't be here if it weren't important," added the taller, more beautiful, more composed, more *everything* woman.

"This meeting isn't about you," Mallory added. "Though I for one wish it were. Please, Sam. Hear us out."

This *meeting*?

Sam stared at her friend, who hadn't been in favor of pretty much anything Sam had done since the few moments they'd shared in Mallory's clinic the morning of the shooting. What had Mallory said back then?

Just get through lunch any way you have to, and you've won.

Feeling like more of a loser by the second, Sam melted into one of Julia's cane-backed chairs and grabbed a napkin from her cat-shaped napkin holder.

The cute orange tabby was curled around itself, with flower-printed paper napkins sprouting from its hand-painted tummy. Everything in Julia and Walter's house was either cute or homey, just like the couple themselves—idealistic and Middle America and maybe just a little too perfect for their own good. Especially since the shooting, which had taken an emotional toll on their family the same as it had everyone else in town. Even in the Davis household, "idealistic" was getting harder for everyone to swallow.

Sam dabbed at her eyes and shucked off her jacket, the sleeves flipping over the back of the chair. She ignored her friends and smiled at Kristen with a look Sam hoped was more, *How can I help you?* than, *Please go away; you terrify me.*

Chandler Elementary's AP had called her a hero that day at the school. And for just a moment Sam had felt like one as she absorbed Kristen's admiration and story of how Sam's *Times* interview had inspired her to dedicate her future to changing young lives for the better. But if Kristen was there thinking Sam was up for another go at challenging anyone to be better at anything, she'd wasted her morning.

"This is an awkward situation," Kristen said. "And I'm sorry about that."

She sounded uncertain and anxious and other things that didn't suit her. Julia had been incensed last night, talking about how Kristen was taking the brunt of a lot of the local outrage and panic about the shooting, while Julia and others on the school board patiently tried to explain the AP's heroic efforts that day, as she'd calmly run toward danger with Sam and had gotten as many people out of the cafeteria as she could.

"You and Brian both have made it clear," Kristen continued, "that you want to be left out of the never-ending debate the community's having about the Wilmington shooting. I can understand. Things are getting messy, and your family has been through enough. But I tried to send you a personal message through Cade and then your husband—"

"Brian and I are . . . having some communication issues."

"Yes, I realized that after speaking with Mallory." Kristen touched Sam's shoulder in sympathy, casting a worried glance toward Julia. "I've been so wrapped up in dealing with the press over the shooting, and the counseling that our students and faculty have needed, and getting the school board and super-intendent the answers they've requested . . . I just last night real-ized you were staying here instead of at your home."

"Just last night?" Sam stared up at Mallory. "I see."

Mallory and quite possibly Julia had spoken with Kristen about Sam and Brian and their situation. Yet neither woman had thought to mention this morning's little impromptu party to Sam.

"I know Cade's been upset." Sam's empty stomach twisted. She was transforming her napkin into a pile of lint, pulling it apart instead of screaming, *Why are you doing this to me?* at her friends. "His father and I have tried talking with him about how his grades have been slipping. But he's not wanting to talk about much yet, and we've been advised not to push him unless things get worse. We were hoping the school would continue to understand."

"Of course," Kristen said. "We'll support Cade any way we can. I'm not sure I agree with you about whether or not now's the time to push him for some answers. I'm very worried about Cade, too. But he's not why I'm here. There's another, more pressing matter I needed to discuss with you . . ."

Sam sat straighter.

"Is Joshua okay?" Her youngest had seemed fine, though he was pretty much pretending that nothing had happened at all. Denial was a normal stage of recovery from a trauma like the shooting, Dr. Mueller had said. And for some people, for young children especially, that phase of the grieving process could last longer than for others.

"As far as I know, yes," Kristen reassured her.

"This isn't about your boys or your family." Mallory slid into the remaining chair, close enough for Sam to reach out and take her hand if she wanted to. The four of them were grouped comfortably in Julia's kitchen, as if they met like this all the time.

"Oh." Sam's relief felt petty and selfish, when clearly something was terribly wrong for someone else. "Then how can I possibly help?"

"I asked Mallory's advice on how to approach you," Kristen said, "since we don't really know each other well. And you've had a difficult few months, and I hate to intrude on that, or on Julia's morning, because I know she has a busy day ahead at city hall. But I have a feeling you might be my best shot, and I'm hearing rumors that made me wonder if you're already involved, and . . ."

Kristen clasped the edges of her unbuttoned suit jacket and adjusted its tailored fit, as if tweaking her appearance would keep her focused. She always wore suits, Julia had mentioned, no matter how casual the rest of Chandler's staff dressed or how pastel each of Kristen's suits turned out to be. She seemed to veer toward the ice cream parlor side of the color wheel, whether it was high summer or the dead of winter. But regardless of that concession to femininity, Kristen and her formal work clothes perpetually exuded confidence and professionalism.

Except this morning she looked anything but certain about whatever she'd come there to say.

Sam remembered Kristen's kind words and understanding that day in the school parking lot. Now the other woman seemed to be struggling for answers. Sam's heart melted, along with the last of her resentment for being ganged up on. She reached to smooth away the wrinkles on the assistant principal's bubblegum-pink sleeve, but instead pulled back and laid her palm on the table.

"What can I do?" she asked.

"I told her," Julia said, "that you were talking with Nate a little."

"What?" Sam stared across the table. Her best friend's hands were clenched around her mug of steaming coffee.

"I've followed you a few times at night. I'm sorry . . ." Sweet, optimistic, *take your time getting better, you can stay with Walter and me as long as you need* Julia couldn't have sounded less apologetic. "But I was worried. You kept wandering away at night for hours. I haven't said anything to Beverly or James, because I know Nate isn't talking to them at all, like Cade's avoiding you and Brian. And the Turners are steamed about you and Brian not siding with them in their legal war against the school board.

It looked like Nate was relaxing with you a little, and I didn't want to interfere with that. I trust you, like I'm certain the Turners would if they were . . ."

Julia glanced at Kristen and then Mallory.

"If they were ever in town long enough," Sam finished for her friend, "to do anything more than vent to the school board?"

The Turners' fear for their son and explosive need to vent at all the wrong people was one Chandlerville story the national media hadn't stayed long enough to cover. Because the day-to-day reality of a busy family still struggling months after a crisis didn't sell advertising spots.

Sam and Julia had discussed how Nate's parents were still traveling constantly for work, James especially, despite their concern for Nate. The couple was doing what they thought was best. But too many times their drive to get back to a normal life had left a silent and still-healing Nate in the care of the live-in housekeeper/nanny his parents had hired to homeschool him while he recovered from the shooting.

"Nate seemed to be opening up to you a little," Julia said. "And then Kristen mentioned how worried she was about his coming back to school today, and that she'd visited the Turners about it over the weekend but they wouldn't speak with her. And Mallory thinks it's too soon, too . . ."

Julia, always upbeat, sounded fresh out of bright sides to look at. Kristen, always in control, had her hands clenched in front of her, practically wringing them. Mallory appeared to be as calm as ever, but she was meddling, something she typically loathed doing. And someone else besides Brian had been monitoring Sam's solitary morning wanderings and innocent run-ins with Nate.

Sam slumped deeper in her chair. Did they really expect her to approach the Turners about how to deal with their son's recovery?

Do his parents know . . . ?

"I can't talk with Beverly and James about Nate. He trusts me not to. But you have to believe me. I'd never do anything to cause that boy more pain and confusion."

"Of course you wouldn't," Kristen said.

"I haven't mentioned seeing him out so late," Sam explained, "because he seems to be struggling and . . ."

And she was struggling, too? Hadn't she needed someone to understand how lost she felt, with her own memories and fears swirling through her mind, and her husband refusing to understand? No. There was more to it than that. There really was. There had to be.

How selfish can you be?

"His parents are pushing him too hard," Mallory chimed in. "They want him better, whether he's ready to be or not. And no matter how much they love him, they can't accept that he's not there yet."

Sam inhaled sharply. Hearing someone else say what she'd been trying to get Brian to realize about *her* brought tears to her eyes, for herself and for Nate.

"Yes," she said. "And that can be a very scary place. A lost, lonely place."

Nate needed his parents to accept what he was going through, not rush him through it or help him run from it, not the way Sam had run all these years, relying on her husband to help her. It had become a lifestyle, her wanting to be better without actually doing the work her therapist had insisted was necessary.

You have to grieve the life you've lost, Sam. You can postpone that for as long as you want. Forever, if you want. But until you deal with the scary memories that feel like they're taking everything away, they'll always be there. There's no shortcut, no matter how much support you have or how far away you move. There's only what you're running from, and what being stuck in that place can do to you and the people you love . . .

"What Nate's dealing with is like"—she swallowed against the memories—"knowing you're giving up and knowing you shouldn't, but having absolutely no way to stop how much you want to quit no matter how hard you try not to."

Kristen nodded again. Julia wiped at the corners of her own eyes. Mallory reached for Sam's hand and squeezed. What had Mallory said in her clinic in January?

I know you want today so badly, you're being reckless.

I'm a disaster, Sam had responded. But she'd gone to the bake sale anyway, because she hadn't wanted to disappoint her family or herself.

"Nate shouldn't be going to school today," Sam said. "Not if he's not ready."

"I was thinking the same thing," Kristen said. "But—"

"He shouldn't!" Sam said even louder.

Kristen blinked.

Sam pressed her hand over her mouth.

The AP hadn't asked her opinion, not really. Sam had no idea why Kristen was there. But it certainly wasn't to be shrieked at. Sam had been the recipient of enough well-intentioned if misguided advice about her own life to absolutely refuse to do that to a top-notch educator like Kristen. But someone had to get through to James and Beverly Turner.

It had been building inside her, the determination to speak to someone about Nate. She'd been thinking about it for days now, each night after she'd spent time with him and watched him become more agitated. She'd almost said something about it to Brian at the park, before he'd lost it with her. Not that he'd go to bat for her with the Turners now.

But the powerful women circled around Sam would. She'd felt so alone in her worry for so long, despite living with her best friend, that she hadn't seen the solution to Nate's problem staring back at her from across the breakfast table each morning. Julia—or Kristen or even Mallory—could reason with the Turners, who lived just a few houses down from the cul-de-sac, and explain what a trauma like the Wilmington shooting could do to a heart and a soul and a young life like Nate's. They could make Beverly and James understand how potentially dangerous it would be to push their son to move on from what had happened before he was ready.

"Will you come back to school today?" Mallory asked.

"What?" Sam hadn't heard her friend correctly. *Sam* returning to the school? "No. One of you should—"

"The Turners aren't speaking to anyone from Chandler," Kristen said, "except at the school board hearings."

"Or anyone from the community," Julia added. "I've tried, but to them I'm the enemy because I'm on the school board. When Walter said he didn't want to get involved, I got Brian to stop by their house, but Beverly shut the door in his face."

Brian had tried to talk with the Turners?

"Then they're not going to listen to me," Sam reasoned.

Brian knew James Turner professionally. Her husband had done some design work for James's law firm, for a remodel of their midtown Atlanta office space. There were a lot of old-money families living in the larger homes on Mimosa Lane, and her husband was a pro at making social contacts that might one day evolve into something lucrative for him and the partners at his firm. But Sam had never even met James. And she and Beverly had spoken only a few times over the years, always about the boys. It wasn't as if their families knew each other beyond being friendly acquaintances because Cade and Nate had hung out all the time before the shooting.

"Nate will listen to you," Julia insisted. "He already is, Sam. And you've been through something like this once yourself. He's opening up to you. Think about him and what today's going to be like, before you make up your mind."

How . . . ? Nate had asked her.

How had she survived and started over and gotten back to her life and gone on?

But didn't he see what everyone else did? That she hadn't gotten on with anything or moved on anywhere. Not really. She was still in the same place he was, stuck where the world that everyone else thrived in didn't work for her. She was hiding in Julia's guest bedroom, for heaven's sake, and arguing with her husband in the middle of the neighborhood before the sun came up—after barely talking to him for three months.

Sam dashed at her eyes, furious with her friends for setting her up this way. But she also couldn't bear the thought of Nate facing this morning alone because *she* was too afraid of going back to Chandler to help him. That would actually make her the coward Brian had called her—while she'd been accusing *him* of not wanting to face reality.

Kristen was watching her intently, hopefully.

The younger woman always seemed to sparkle with so much energy, it made Sam wonder whether she ever stopped moving. Kristen ran 5Ks and half marathons and coached two girls' basketball teams at the YMCA. She'd been full of life and love for their community since she'd moved there to take the job as Chandler's assistant principal, after teaching for six years in South Carolina.

But all that energy and enthusiasm had . . . dimmed somehow. Kristen's eyes were ringed with dark circles and haunted by the same horrible day and loss the rest of them were grappling with. And she was looking at Sam in almost the same way Nate did sometimes—as if Sam had all the answers, because she'd been to this dark place before.

"Come back to school," Kristen said. "Help Mallory and me take care of Nate today. Help us decide what Chandler and his parents can do to help him. I'm very afraid we're losing this young man, Sam. Our school. Our community. And we can't let that happen."

***

"You gonna sit with me on the bus today?" Joshua asked Cade for like the fifth time.

He hadn't stopped asking since Cade woke up with his kid brother sitting on the side of his bed already talking away. Joshua asked the same thing every day now, since Cade had gone back to school the week after Troy killed Bubba.

"You gonna eat breakfast?" Cade asked back, sinking deeper into his stool. "Or just annoy me until my head explodes?"

"Your head exploding would be cool."

"You first, egghead." Cade looked over his shoulder from where he and his brainy little brother were sitting at the kitchen island.

Their dad would be downstairs any minute, telling them they were gonna be late for school. Maybe he'd say something about Joshie wasting time and not eating. Maybe he wouldn't care. Without Mom there anymore—once she got Cade and Joshua settled and eating in the mornings and she went back to Mrs. Julia's—their dad hardly seemed to care about anything in the mornings, except for asking Cade how he was doing, and worrying when Cade didn't know what to say.

His dad worried a lot now, even though he kept saying everything was going to be better soon.

"Mom didn't make breakfast this morning," Joshua complained.

Like Cade hadn't noticed.

Only he didn't want to talk about it. He didn't want to talk about anything, but especially not about why Mom wasn't there. He didn't want to talk in the mornings. He didn't want to talk on the bus, or when he got home from school, or any other time. And all Joshua wanted to do was talk to him, like it would make everything better. Like talking wouldn't make everything a lot worse.

"I like cereal." Cade scooped up some of the chocolate corn puffs he'd poured himself, after he'd filled his brother's bowl with the same sugary crap and doused it all with milk.

"Mom doesn't like us eating only cereal for breakfast." Joshua copied him and took a huge mouthful.

Milk dripped down his chin. He wiped at it with the wrinkled sleeve of his favorite rugby shirt. Mom wouldn't have liked that either. She'd have told them to use one of the napkins that matched the place mats she'd made. Only they weren't using any of them that morning.

"Well, Mom's not here, is she?" Cade dropped his spoon into his bowl and chewed. His stomach felt sick, the way it always did when he ate sweet stuff right after he woke up.

Joshua wasn't asking any more questions, and he wasn't looking at Cade anymore, which should have felt good. Except Cade was being mean, just because he didn't want to talk about why Mom hadn't been downstairs baking when their alarms had gone off. He was being mean to his little brother because he was scared.

Even though she wasn't sleeping at home anymore, Mom had promised she'd be there every morning. She'd promised when she'd told them she was moving across the cul-de-sac—*for just a while*, she'd said. *It will be okay*, Dad had said, *because Mom will be back soon, once she's feeling better.* Meantime, she'd still be taking care of Cade and Joshua and the house and breakfast and afternoon snack and homework time.

Only that had been months ago. And Dad wasn't acting like he really believed any of what they'd said anymore, not for the last week or so. It was almost like he was going away, too, just not like Mom had. And then that morning there'd been no amazing smell to get Cade and Joshua out of bed. No hug when they'd come downstairs. No Cade just looking at his mom, when she wasn't looking at him, trying to make himself believe that she really would come back. And then Dad would feel better again. And Cade could stop feeling like—no matter how many times stupid people called him a hero because they thought he'd helped Nate and Mom keep Troy from killing anyone else but Bubba—it was *his* fault their family would never be together again.

His family was like the LEGO pieces Cade's brother kept losing everywhere, popping on and off and being left behind when you weren't looking, more and more things disappearing, until what you were building would never work.

"I like Mom's muffins better." Joshie slouched on his stool.

"I like her breakfast, too." Cade burped up chocolate, not wanting to talk about it. But he wanted to stop being so mean to his little brother, too. "Mom makes good muffins."

His voice sounded like his baby brother's when Joshie was trying not to cry, and Cade hated it. He hated how he felt like that all the time now, wondering whether Nate did, too, only his best friend wouldn't talk to him at all. And he hated how he wanted to hug Joshua now, because of how much they were both missing their mom and how weird Dad was being.

He nudged Joshua's shoulder. Joshie nearly fell off his stool, which made Cade smile. His kid brother shoved back. He wasn't strong enough to push Cade very hard, but Cade grabbed the counter anyway, like he'd lost his balance. Joshie ate another bite of cereal and laughed through chewing it, happy again, because nothing ever really got to him too much.

Cade wished he could be that way. He never had been, just like Mom. He thought about things a lot more than Joshua or Dad. And he hated that most of all, because now . . . their parents and their family were so messed up. More than they'd been before. And that was all Cade could think about until he got to school. And then at school, the things he couldn't stop thinking about only got worse.

He wished . . . everything could go back to the kind of messed-up it had been before he'd gone and made things so much worse.

He shoved his little brother again. The milk from his brother's spoon spilled all over the countertop. Joshua jumped on Cade, tackling him and nearly knocking both their stools over. Their bowls of milk and soggy chocolate puffs slid across the counter, Joshie's crashing to the floor.

"Enough horsing around, you two," their dad said as he came down the stairs and picked up the bowl.

He grabbed a kitchen towel and mopped up the cereal off the hardwood and then the mess they'd made on the counter. Cade and Joshua straightened and stared at him, waiting for him to explode.

He didn't. And he'd come into the kitchen so quietly, they hadn't heard him. He tossed the towel into the sink, and that was when he saw it. Cade looked at Joshua, and then they both looked at Dad to see what he'd do.

Mom used to always leave Dad notes. And Dad had kept every one. Cade found them once, in a shoe box in the big bottom drawer of his dad's office in the basement. Pieces of paper, all different colors, covered with Mom's swirly handwriting saying the kinds of things his parents used to say to each other all the time, and Cade and Joshua used to act like they were going to barf when they heard them.

Miss you already, a note would say. Or, *Think of me today and smile . . . Call me and I'll tell you a dirty joke . . . Love you bunches . . .*

Only there hadn't been a note in three months, not since the last morning they were all together in the kitchen. Not until today. And when Cade had seen it, he'd hoped it meant something good, even if Mom hadn't made breakfast.

Instead, his dad's head dropped as he read this one, like he was trying not to let it upset him in front of Cade and Joshua. Cade knew what it said. He'd read it while he'd made the cereal.

I'm so sorry.

Dad pulled the Post-it from the counter. Instead of putting it in his suit pocket to save for later—for the box of memories he kept of Mom—he wadded it up and threw it into the sink along with the cereal.

"Is your homework done?" he asked, not that he sounded like he cared.

Cade shrugged. That way he wouldn't be lying. He *wanted* to have his work done. He used to like doing schoolwork. Especially things like the essay project that he should have finished last week. But he just . . . couldn't. Not last night's assignments. Not any of his homework since Troy went nuts and ruined everything because Cade hadn't stopped him.

His dad was staring at him. Cade could feel it even though he was looking at the glob of chocolate cereal and milk still on the counter. Did Dad know? Were they really going to talk now? Would it finally be over, and someone would make Cade say what he was so afraid he'd say if he wrote his essay, or finally got Nate to talk to him, or really told his parents what was going on?

That he'd let them all down, not telling Mom or Ms. Hemmings what Troy had said that morning in the bathroom. And that he couldn't stop letting them down even now.

"Grab your things," his dad said instead, heading for the garage through the door from the kitchen. He'd wait for Cade and Joshua to make it to the bus stop before he drove into Atlanta for his job. "You'll be late."

Late for school.

Late for another day like all the other days Cade had hated since January. Only this day would be worse. He wished he could ditch class today. He really did. He'd skipped, like, six or seven times already, twice last week, and never gotten caught. But he knew he wouldn't today. He couldn't.

Cade looked at his little brother, hoping for a sloppy grin to cheer him up. But Joshie was looking at the counter, too, like Cade had been, pushing around a lose corn puff with his finger. Cade got off his stool and walked to the sink. He pulled out Mom's note, uncrumpled it, and wiped it on his jeans to get off the milk that had soaked into it a little. He shoved it into his pocket, then walked back to his brother, who was watching him now.

"We'd better get to the bus stop early," he said, "if we're going to sit together."

Joshua grinned at him. And even if it wasn't one of Mom's half hugs or Dad's thumbs-ups, it made Cade smile. He could always count on his bratty little brother to cheer him up, no matter how much they fought. At least one thing about their screwed-up family was still the same.

So he'd sit with his brother. It wasn't like Cade talked to any of his friends anymore, anyway. The only person he wanted to say anything to was Nate, who was supposed to be coming back today. So today Cade would stay at school, too, even when he knew just how to slip away as soon as everyone got off the bus, and no one would miss him. Even when he knew Nate still wasn't going to talk to him.

He grabbed his backpack and handed over Joshua's.

"LEGOs for brains," Cade said, wrapping his little brother in a headlock and dragging him toward the door to the garage.

"Dork," Joshie squeaked into Cade's armpit, trying to wrench free as they walked out of the house.

Cade let him go and shut the kitchen door behind them. Their dad already had the automatic garage door open and the car engine on. He'd pull to the end of the driveway to wait while Cade and Joshua walked to the corner. They'd all look at the Davis house and wonder whether Mom was watching from inside, but no one would say a word about it, not to one another or the neighbors.

"Let's go," Cade said, leading the way, grateful to have his brother walking beside him while everyone at the bus stop turned to watch them.

"Thanks," Joshua said as they headed for the crowd at the corner.

"For what?"

"Sitting with me. I hate the way people stare like they know something's wrong and they can't not look away, like our family's a train wreck or something."

"Yeah," Cade said. He hated it, too. All of it. "Just ignore them."

He caught sight of Nate standing at the curb with his mom. Cade stumbled, fighting not to run to his friend, or away from him, or do anything but walk closer, slowly, as if it were just a normal, stupid school day like all the rest. It was the first time Cade had actually seen his friend since talking to him just after the shooting, and Nate didn't even look up. Cade felt his eyes getting wet and his nose start to run, because he'd been right. Nate wasn't going to say a word to him, not the whole ride in to school. Not when they got to class, either, which made Cade's wanting to be there for his friend's first day back kinda stupid. But Cade would stay.

"Who needs them anyway," he said, refusing to cry.

Joshie nodded and shrugged. He looked at Nate, too, and then at Cade again. But for once, the kid kept his questions to himself.

"Yeah," Joshua said. "Who needs these buttheads anyway."

***

"I can't believe you did that," Sam said to Julia, while Sam and her friend stood at Julia's front windows, watching Cade and Joshua catch their bus. "You invited Kristen and Mallory over here to ambush me?"

Brian was in his car at the end of their drive, the same as he'd been every morning. He waved at the bus driver when she honked and headed down Mimosa Lane with the kids. Like every other day, Brian then stared across the cul-de-sac at Julia's house, as if he could see them standing behind her sheers, watching back. He'd be leaving soon, regardless of the fight they'd just had or the note she'd left him or how any of this was affecting him.

That was just the way her husband was. He was responsible. Stable. He was always where he was supposed to be, doing exactly what he was supposed to be doing. While Sam was the wild card, throwing everything out of sync. Never more so than now.

"When Mallory called this morning," Julia said, "Walter and I were . . . arguing. I didn't think before I invited her over, and then she was saying Kristen would be here, too, before I could make much sense out of what they wanted to talk about."

"You and Walter?" Sam asked, worried for her friend, even if she still felt a little betrayed. Things had become increasingly strained in the Davis house, as Walter took Bubba's death and Troy's unbelievable rampage harder than either Sam or Julia could have anticipated.

"I would have done anything to get my husband out of my hair at that point," Julia said, "and expecting company before his first cup of coffee did the trick. He was gone in fifteen minutes, mumbling about stopping at Thanks a Latte on his way into the city. I'm sorry. I know that sounds terribly selfish."

"That you and Mallory set me up, or that you and Walter aren't getting along? Julia, every married couple fights."

"Not like this." Her friend headed back toward the kitchen. "Not about . . ."

"Not about him drinking so much every night he can't think straight in the mornings?" Sam followed her, watching Julia grab the sponge from its holder behind the sink to wipe around the coffeemaker that she'd cleaned twice already, while Sam and Kristen and Mallory had discussed plans for the morning that Sam had no idea if she could follow through with. "About you thinking the problem's going to go away on its own?"

Julia threw the sponge down and faced Sam. She was dressed for the day in a navy blue ensemble she'd no doubt bought at Talbots or some other überconservative store where she found her *uniforms*, as she called them—the sweater twinsets and coordinating tailored pants and skirts that filled her closet and kept her stylish and comfortable.

The Davis family wasn't wealthy, but Walter's job as a CPA for a downtown firm made them comfortable enough that Julia had never had to work. She could spend her free time on anything she'd wanted to. As long as Sam had known her, caring for her family had consumed Julia, followed closely by volunteering in their community, including being appointed to the Chandlerville school board—the salary from which Julia donated to the local Boys and Girls Club.

"It's not getting better," Julia admitted.

"I know." When Sam had moved into the guest bedroom, neither one of them could have known that Julia would end up needing a sympathetic ear living down the hall almost as much as Sam did. "He's drinking every night."

"He's getting *drunk* every night," Julia corrected. "Sloppy drunk. In front of the boys, and they're tired of it. I tried to talk him into going back to bed this morning, he's so hungover. I could have called him in sick to work, but I think he'd rather be there than here. And the boys know it. There's no glossing over it with them. Between their jobs and school and friends and dates . . . They're finding a reason to be out of the house these days more than they're here, just like their father."

Justin, the oldest Davis boy, was a freshman at the local community college, studying photography, while Austin was a senior at Chandler High School. Both were the apples of their parents' eyes. The Davises had always been close even though they'd faced the same day-to-day challenges as other Chandlerville families. Three months ago, anyone in the community would have agreed that the Davis family had a bond nothing could penetrate. Julia had devoted her life to ensuring it.

Then the shooting had happened.

"Walter coached Troy and Bubba and Nate," Sam said. "He was in a bowling league with all three dads. What's happened and the community still fighting over it is hitting him hard."

"Yes," her friend agreed. "Except he's not doing a thing about dealing with it." Julia pinned Sam with a knowing gaze. "Just like some other people I know."

Sam held up her hands, her awful confrontation with Brian earlier replaying in her mind. "I've asked my husband to talk about things realistically. I've asked him to meet with a counselor, so we can get help dealing with this. I'm letting you drive me back to school today to be there for Nate if he needs someone, when I doubt we'll make it halfway there without having to pull over at least once so I can hurl on the side of the road. I'm trying my best to deal with everything I can, Julia. I really am."

Her neighbor pulled her into a hug. "I know you are. You're doing what you think is right for your boys and for Nate, too. You're not giving up on Brian. And I'm right here for you, if you need me. Always."

"You, too." She and Brian were lucky to have such wonderful friends, even if Julia and Walter's relationship seemed these days to be almost as dysfunctional as theirs was. "We'll never be alone, you and I. Never. Right?"

Sam sounded desperate. She *felt* desperate. It wasn't even eight o'clock yet, and she wanted to crawl back into bed and sleep until tomorrow. As frustrated as she still was with her friend, she'd never get through the rest of what she had to do today without her neighbor's help.

Julia nodded fiercely. "You bet your Yankee butt," she promised.

Chapter Seven

"Do you have the Kelsey proposal prepped and ready?" Jonathan Whilleby asked the moment Brian walked through the door of Whilleby & Marshal Associates.

"What?" Brian had sat in the parking garage for almost an hour, and he still couldn't think about anything but this morning and Sam. He barely remembered saying good-bye to their boys.

His mind wouldn't settle. He was a total mess these days. He couldn't think, or work, or sleep, or . . . tell his wife he loved her unconditionally, just the way she was now. And that was clearly what she needed to hear. What he should have said this morning.

But how did you love someone who was ripping apart the security that had kept you going for so long?

For God's sake, Sam, we're going *to work this out . . .*

He'd yelled at her. Berated her. He was terrified of never getting her back. He'd said unforgivable things he'd promised himself he never would. Because who would he be, how would he go on without her?

"The Kelseys?" Whilleby prompted. He was the firm's founding partner and senior architect. He wasn't prone to panic, but his manner at the moment registered just shy of frantic. "I know it's been a difficult time, and we've tried to be patient while you and your family work through this. But you've postponed the Kelsey presentation twice. They've been waiting in the conference room this morning for half an hour. Tell me you're ready."

The Kelsey proposal.

Right.

Brian wiped his face with his hand. He needed at least one cup of coffee before he could charm the socks off his workday. He opened the overflowing briefcase he wished he could toss across the firm's entryway. He rifled through the mess of folders and papers inside that he'd tried and failed to work on last night, all weekend, and all last week. His fist clenched on the spine of the portfolio he wasn't ready to present, even though this account had been his baby from the start.

The Kelseys' massive renovation was the largest project he'd bid on and developed entirely on his own. It had practically dropped into his lap, because he'd known Ginger and Jefferson for close to six years through their kids' school.

The Kelseys owned the most expensive and secluded spread on Mimosa Lane. The *estate*, everyone called it. Their home was set back in the woods beyond Brian and Sam's cul-de-sac, at the crest of a hill, like a manor house overlooking the rest of the kingdom. It was three stories, with terraced lawns front and back, a separate mother-in-law suite and two gated entrances— one for family and guests and the other for deliveries and groundskeepers. It was a study in conspicuous consumption. And it was a drop in the bucket of the assets Jefferson had acquired by being a fearless, talented and more often right than he was wrong entrepreneur.

Jefferson and Ginger bought and sold and rented property like they were dabbling in the latest fashion trends. They owned a condo in Atlanta and other properties in various cities across the country and beyond. They didn't care that they'd priced themselves out of the real estate market with what they'd already done to their Mimosa Lane house. They wanted what they wanted the way they wanted it, and they'd decided Brian was the architect du jour who could satisfy their latest whim.

The Kelseys were having their third child—a girl, finally—and what had first been Ginger's interest in turning a spare bedroom into a nursery was fast becoming a revamp of the entire top floor, from the studs out. No expense was to be spared for the arrival of their princess.

"I have their plans right here." Brian held up the portfolio for Whilleby to see.

He was still wearing his overcoat, making it stifling hot inside. He unwound the scarf Sam had bought him as a stocking stuffer at Christmas—ordered from Barneys in New York, where she'd snagged him something, no matter how small, for the holidays every year since they'd married. It was too warm outside now to be wearing it or his wool coat, but they reminded him of his wife. So he kept putting them on each morning, the same as he had since January.

He stuffed the scarf in the top of his briefcase.

"I'll be with you in five minutes," he said. Ignoring the skepticism in his senior partner's gaze, he took the hallway toward his office.

"Fine." Whilleby's glacial tone was his way of announcing just how *not* fine Brian's performance had been lately.

Brian had no way of knowing how many passes the partners intended to give him, even though they'd been patient since the shooting. And at the moment, he didn't give a good damn. He'd put everything on the line for the firm for years, rather than busting his ass building a career in the type of architecture he would be able to do only if he struck out on his own. The partners owed him a little more time to set the rest of his life to rights. He ducked into his office's quiet dimness. Without flipping on the lights, he flopped into his plush desk chair.

"You look like a man with the entire world on his shoulders," a concerned voice said from the doorway behind him.

"Hell . . ." Brian pivoted from staring at the window that was covered floor-to-ceiling by blinds. "You would know, Pete. It wasn't four months ago that you had everyone in the neighborhood wanting to stage an intervention to yank your head out of your ass so we'd get you and Polly back after Emma's death."

His friend leaned against the doorjamb, crossing his arms over his chest, one ankle propped in front of the other. "Mallory took care of that faster than the rest of you could have."

Mallory had moved to Mimosa Lane with no clue how to become a part of their community, but desperately wanting a place in their world. The Lombards had been grieving for Pete's wife, who had died the January before. Somehow, all the need and emotional hurt Mallory and Pete and little Polly were dealing with had created a bond among the three that was unshakable.

And Mallory's remarkable survivor's story of growing up living on the streets with her homeless, mentally ill mother had created an instant connection between her and Sam, once Sam shared a bit of her 9/11 memories and how hard they were to handle. Mallory seemed to have that effect on everyone she met.

"You're a lucky bastard," Brian said to his friend of almost ten years. "Your fiancée is an inspiring woman."

"So is your wife," Pete said.

Yes, Sam was. Despite what he'd said that morning, Brian had always known she was. He'd always told her how proud he was of her, especially that day at the hospital. But she was so certain now that she couldn't count on him or anything he said.

So why had she stopped by the house on her way back to Julia's, not to make breakfast for the boys but to leave Brian the first note she'd written him since she'd moved out?

I'm so sorry . . .

She was driving him insane. Every damn bit of this situation was, because he couldn't get a handle on any of it. He'd barely been able to look at the tiny yellow square she'd left on the counter. He'd wanted to rip it to shreds.

Somehow, he'd made his wife feel unwanted and misunderstood, which was categorically untrue. But in other ways, she was right. He clearly *couldn't* handle hearing her say the things she had that morning, no matter how much she thought she needed to say them.

His wife was giving up, and that he'd never accept.

"You two haven't worked anything out yet, have you?" his friend asked.

"Look," Brian answered. "I have a meeting I'm already late for. And my wife's made it clear she doesn't want to talk to me—not about working things out. I evidently don't understand her, or anything we've tried to build together since we left New York. She's determined to make me agree that we've been doing it all wrong. And my reassuring her that I'm trying to understand, and that I just want to help her get over all of this before it drives us even further apart, is making things worse instead of better." *I'm never going to be the Sam you want me to be again . . .* "Working things out with me is clearly the last thing she needs right now."

"Yeah." Pete rubbed a hand across the back of his neck, beneath the hairstyle his position with the fire department required him to keep shorter than any of their other friends. "But what do *you* need, Brian? What do your boys need? I get that Sam's spinning right now, even more than the rest of us. She's a loose cannon. And trust me, Mallory's not happy that she's still at Julia's, instead of home with you and whatever the two of you need to go through together. But that doesn't change the fact that she's your wife, and . . ."

A faraway look dimmed Pete's gaze.

Brian grimaced.

They'd had this conversation a long time ago. How, good or bad—and Pete and Emma had had their own share of bad times, just like every married couple did outside of romance novels and TV sitcoms—Pete would give anything for the chance to see her again, and to talk with her about what had happened and the mistakes he'd made when it was clear she wasn't going to survive the cancer, but he hadn't been able to let her go. He still blamed himself for how hard a time Polly had after her mother's death, and his complete withdrawal from everyone for a while, even his own child.

"It's not the same situation, man," Brian said.

"I know. You two still have a chance to work this out."

"Not if my wife has anything to say about it."

The Sam you thought I was is gone . . .

"Yeah, well . . ." Pete sighed. "Mallory just called and woke me up on my one day off this week, telling me to get over here

and talk to you in person. Sam's on her way in to school to help
with Nate on his first day back."

"What?"

"Kristen Hemmings stopped by Julia's this morning and
asked Sam to help out."

Brian stood and braced his hands on his desk.

"Sam's hardly left the neighborhood since the shooting," he
said. Each and every time she'd run an errand, someone in town
had found a way to let him know—as if an APB had been de-
clared on his wife. He could count on one hand the number of
people besides their neighbors who'd seen her since she'd come
home from the hospital and the media frenzy over the shooting
had kicked into overdrive. "But now she's on her way back to the
school?"

"Julia's driving her in, so Sam can wait in Mallory's office."

"For what?"

"For Nate to need her. Because he's still messed up, but his
parents think he needs to be back at Chandler with his friends."

"James and Beverly need to get back to focusing on work
full-time, you mean, without worrying about whether things are
okay at home."

"That's got to be a lot of pressure on a kid. And Sam might be
able to help Nate feel his way through that, if what Mallory's
hearing from Julia is even part of the pressure your wife's feeling
to pull herself together for you and your boys."

Brian stared his friend down.

"I've been there every day for her since 9/11. I've *never* pushed
her to do or feel anything she wasn't ready for. I've given her all
the time in the world she's needed to get better, and I haven't be-
grudged her a single bit of the solitude and privacy she's said

she's needed. I haven't taken a day for myself in more than a decade without first checking to make sure she's okay."

"Hell, I know that. I'm the last person who'd judge you for doing what you have to do for your family. I know how much you love Sam, how demanding this job is, and how much you're juggling so she can heal. But maybe Sam hasn't known what she's needed, is all I'm saying. Like Nate and his parents can't really know. And she wants to be there to help him figure some of this out, even though going back to Chandler must be scaring the ever-loving shit out of her. And whatever's going on between you two," Pete pressed, "you don't want to regret not being there for *her*. If it turns out to be a bad scene, even if she resists your help, at least you'll know you tried."

Like Brian had tried just that morning, and had completely screwed things up?

He was no good for Sam or his boys this way.

"I found her with Nate," he said. "They've been meeting at the park, early enough that no one's suspected. I yelled at her for interfering in the Turners' problems, then for not being there for our family. I let it get ugly . . ." He shook his head, reliving it all. "I should have been more patient. But she was refusing to talk sensibly, and then she seemed almost . . . relieved."

"That you knew about Nate?"

"That our marriage might not make it, because I can't accept the stuff that's been coming out of her mouth since she woke up at the hospital. Not when she sounds like she wants me to fall apart with her, and if I don't that means *I'm* the one who doesn't want to make this better."

Meanwhile she was pushing her already fragile well-being to the breaking point, to help Nate Turner through his own confusion over the shooting?

Brian dropped his head. "How did things get so screwed up?"

Pete stepped to his side.

"Screwed up is the way life likes to be sometimes," he said. "But things don't stay that way, not if you refuse to give up. Mallory taught me that. And for the record, she thinks it's good that Sam's still fighting, even if Mallory's not sure it's really against you at all."

"Well, if it's not against me"—Brian swallowed the compulsion to lose it all over again—"what is my wife fighting against?"

Pete pounded his shoulder with an open palm, which was as close to hugging it out as they'd ever gotten.

"Cancel that client meeting," his friend insisted. "Let's get you over to the school so you can find out."

***

Sam looked even more exhausted at nine o'clock in the morning than when Kristen had seen her just before dawn at the Davises' house. But Sam was there when Kristen hustled into the school's clinic, right where she'd said she'd stay in case the Turner boy needed her.

Kristen eyed the deceptively fragile-looking woman sitting on Mallory's cot, dressed in pink-and-grey sweats. Sam was breathing too shallow and too fast, as if she needed to put her head between her legs and inhale into a paper bag.

"Come with me," Kristen said. "I'm afraid it's an emergency."

She didn't wait to see whether or not she was followed as she headed to the second floor. She'd already been gone too long from the Baxter classroom. The tread of Sam's tennis shoes, out of rhythm with the familiar squeak of Mallory's rubber-soled work shoes, rewarded Kristen's faith in human nature and heroes. Both of the women could be counted on in a crisis, regardless of the cost to them personally.

"Is he okay?" Sam asked.

Kristen stopped outside Mrs. Baxter's classroom, cursing the Turner parents all over again for creating this situation. They should have taken Kristen's advice and homeschooled Nate for what was left of the spring semester. That would have given him time to recover more fully over the summer. But Beverly and James no longer trusted Kristen. She should have known, they insisted, what had been going on between Troy and Bubba.

"No," she said to Mallory and Sam. "Nate's not okay."

"His parents are on the way?" Mallory asked.

"We've left messages at both of their places of work. The father is out of touch until this afternoon. Mom will be here as soon as she's free from a conference call."

"Then . . ." Sam said. "Then maybe we should wait."

"We can't." Kristen gestured for the other two women to precede her into the classroom.

Sam walked into the room slowly, Mallory still at her side.

Lord, please don't let this be a mistake, Kristen prayed.

"Everyone else is at art class." Kristen kept her voice low, leading the pair to the supply closet in the back of the room. "Mrs. Baxter didn't realize the boys were missing at first. By the time she did, they were already holed up in here."

"Boys?" Sam asked.

"Cade is with Nate."

***

"Cade's in there, too?" Sam asked, shock leaving its bitter aftertaste on her tongue.

Sam stepped to the darkened closet's open doorway with Kristen and Mallory. Mrs. Baxter had joined them.

"Neither one of them will talk to me." The poor woman sounded beside herself.

Kristen steered the boys' teacher away gently but firmly.

"Ready?" Mallory asked, once they were gone.

Sam swallowed. "The walls aren't closing in around us, right?"

Mallory hugged Sam to her side. "Sure they are. That's pretty much what every day of the last three months has felt like to me."

"And the floor?" Sam could have sworn it was shaking.

"It's rolling beneath us, trying to knock us on our asses."

Sam snorted. "You're not a very good liar."

"But I'm an excellent friend. And I'm right here. Do whatever you need to do."

"And what would that be? What on earth am I supposed to do?"

"Start with talking to your son."

Cade was in there. And no matter how many times she'd tried, Sam couldn't get through to him. And she didn't want to make the divide between them even wider by saying or doing the wrong thing now.

"He blames me," she whispered. She turned away from the closet.

"Are you sure about that?"

"I've walked out on my family. Of course he blames me." The fear that he and Joshua and Brian would never forgive her was a constant companion.

"Don't you think it's time you found out for sure?" Mallory turned Sam back toward the closet. "Maybe today is the day the two of you can figure out what's really going on. Together."

Together.

How long had it been since Sam had truly done anything *with* someone else? Brian, the boys, even her friends. She'd tried, the day of the bake sale, and so many times before. But for so long her world had felt almost as if it were wrapped in cotton. The numbness that had sustained her since leaving New York had kept everyone and everything at a safe, muffled distance.

That was what had made Brian's accusations that morning sting so badly. He'd been right. She *didn't* want to hurt anymore. She'd give anything to give up and be home with him, just like before, and to be able to hide from realities like lost boys and angry spouses and even Julia and Walter's marital problems. Except Sam refused to allow herself to do that anymore, to her friends or her sons or her husband or Nate. Or herself. That wasn't the life she wanted to live, no matter how hard and terrifying the alternative might be.

"Ready?" Mallory asked again.

Sam shook her head. "But since when has that mattered?"

She stepped to the closet. As grateful as she was to have Mallory there, her friend's nearness also made Sam crazy. She'd already been in the school and the classroom for too long. Her nerves were shot. Flashes of memory wouldn't leave her—of the kids the day of the shooting, and of her own students from so long ago, children scared and crying and needing Sam to make it all go away.

Will my mom be there? she could still remember Krista Watson asking, while the little girl's hand clung to Sam's.

Krista had been the very last child Sam had coaxed out of their school, so they could walk through the maze of dirt and mess that had once been the Twin Towers, on their way out of

Manhattan. They'd had a long walk ahead of them, and each step had been a battle for Sam to keep from vomiting up everything in her system, and then running as fast as she could until she'd found Brian and they escaped forever the city that they'd loved.

I don't know, Sam had lied. *Someone will be there, though. The mayor's told your families where to find you guys. People are making sure someone will be there.*

Meanwhile, Sam had known that Krista's single mom had been a day trader on a floor that had taken a direct hit from one of the planes.

Please? The little girl had stared up at Sam, as if Sam were the only thing that could make her world okay again. Her tiny hand had squeezed around Sam's even harder. *Will my mommy be there?*

Yes, Sam had promised.

She'd told Krista the unforgivable lie they both had needed her to hear, while Sam imagined what was to come, almost as if it were playing out in her mind like a movie clip: Krista watching other kids whose mommies hadn't worked in the towers getting the hugs and kisses she never would; Krista looking at Sam when whichever family member could be located finally arrived, still begging Sam to not make this the worst day of her life; Krista walking away or being carried away, broken and knowing that Sam had lied to her, and that her world would never again be the way it was before . . .

Sam didn't flip on the light as she entered Mrs. Baxter's closet. Instead she knelt, and in the shadows just beyond the doorway she saw Cade sitting with his back against the wall and his legs stretched out: her own son, needing something she wasn't certain she could give him, because all she wanted to do was race away from this terrifying moment, too.

"Hey, buddy," she said, the way she'd greeted both her boys most every morning of their lives.

Hey, Mom, they'd always say back.

So simple. Moments like that were so easy to take for granted. Only now Cade was looking at her with his big, blue eyes, silent and wary and hurting, the way he'd looked at her every day since the shooting. Beyond him, all the way in the back of the narrow, cluttered closet, Nate was staring, too.

Sam glanced over her shoulder at Mallory, then back at the boys. "What are you guys doing in here?"

Cade looked down at his feet, then at his friend, who, Sam realized, was quietly crying. In all the times they'd met at the park, she'd never seen Nate cry. Relief flooded her. Finally, he was letting some of what he was feeling out. But her heart hurt, too, because the release had been triggered by his not being able to handle today.

"He's scared," Cade said, his gaze still on the ground.

Sam nodded, then realized her son wouldn't see it. She cleared the freaked-out mother from her voice. "He has a lot of reasons to be."

"He doesn't want to be here."

"He ain't the only one." Sam sat on the ground just a few feet away. They were talking. Her son was finally talking to her. She swallowed her smile of relief. She was terrified of breaking the spell. "Do you think he'd mind if I stayed for a while?"

Cade shrugged. "I don't think he cares what anyone does. He just sat on the bus this morning and ignored me. In class, too. He won't talk to me here or at home. Not that I blame him. It's just . . ."

"Hard," Sam said, hanging on each word her son said.

She'd wondered some nights as she walked up and down Mimosa Lane whether Cade would ever trust her enough to talk with her like this again. They'd been so close before the shooting, and now he felt like too much of a stranger to be the same sweet kid who'd waited for her to come back from her walk the morning of the bake sale, because he hadn't wanted her to be alone.

"It's not your fault," she insisted. "Either of you. This stuff, what Troy did . . . It's impossible for the adults around here to figure out. You and Nate, you're doing the best you can. You have to stop being so hard on yourselves. Be angry and upset, but not at yourself. And take whatever breaks you need to, like hanging in here for a while. That's okay for now. Anything's better than pretending that stuff's okay when it's not . . ."

"Like you did?" Cade looked at her, angry. Accusing. "All along, especially that morning, you acted like you were okay. And then after . . . You moved out, because you said things were so bad."

"Yeah. I've really messed that up, buddy, not dealing with what I was feeling. Wishing it away for too long, instead of facing what happened to me. I'm sorry. You have to know how sorry I am for what's happening between your dad and me. I should have been more honest with you and Joshie, and your father. Not facing my problems when I needed to . . . it hurt a lot more people than just me. That's why I'm saying it's fine for you and Nate to not deal with too much *for now*. It's too soon for you guys. But eventually, you're going to need to."

Silence spread between them. Her son pulled his legs up. He tucked his knees under his chin, his arms crossing around them, the way he did when he had thinking to do. It gave her a little more space to slip deeper inside the closet.

"What are you doing in here?" she asked again.

"I didn't want Nate to be alone. I know he doesn't care, but I'm not disappearing when he needs me. I'm not leaving him alone."

"The way I've left you and Joshua?"

"And Dad." Her son spit the words at her like poison he'd swallowed for too long.

Sam reached for him. He shied away from her touch, and something inside her ripped open, grabbing at her next breath.

"I know how alone your dad's feeling, honey. I feel the same way. I miss him and you guys every minute we're not together. And I'd do anything to fix this for all of us, to get better and stop feeling the way I do. But . . ." She didn't want to make excuses. This wasn't about her. But what if Cade never gave her another chance to explain? "Sometimes you need to work things out on your own, for everyone's sake. So what you're feeling stops making it impossible for you and other people to be happy."

Her son picked at the torn spot in his left sneaker just above his pinky toe. He glanced at his friend again. "You mean like hiding in a closet is okay, even when you're not supposed to, because going to art class or the lunchroom or anywhere else is making you feel like you're going to puke or something?"

"Yeah, kinda like that."

Julia's house had been Sam's "closet" all this time, so Sam could get stronger. Which she had, she realized, or she never would have lasted this long back at Chandler, or been ready for this moment when her son and his friend needed her.

She wiggled just a little closer to Cade, who didn't move away this time. In fact, he stretched his legs out again. The way they were sitting, their feet were so close they were almost touching. Almost.

"Why are you here?" he asked.

"Because I might be able to help Nate, maybe more than other people can right now. And with your help maybe he'll let me, even if he's not talking to you the way you haven't been talking with me or Dad. Will you help him with me?"

***

Your mom's a hero, everyone kept saying to Cade.

Everyone who knew anything about her and Dad's life before Chandlerville had always said so. Since the shooting, even more people were saying it. The same people who didn't know anything, because they were talking about him being a hero, too.

If Mom was a hero, why was she still at Mrs. Julia's? If she could really help Nate, why did she look so scared now? As scared as Cade had felt since Troy had gotten crazy and Bubba had gotten dead and Nate had turned into a kid Cade didn't know anymore, just like Cade didn't really know his mom.

"Will you help me talk with your friend?" she asked again.

She was acting like Cade couldn't tell how bad off she was. And *now* she wanted to talk, when he really, really didn't. Not ever, not about Troy and Bubba, and especially not like this, with Nate listening. Only she was talking about their family, too, and that felt really good.

Talking with her again felt really, really good.

And really messed up.

As messed up as him following Nate into the closet, when Cade knew it would make both him and Nate feel worse. They hadn't said a word, but Cade hadn't left, not even when Mrs. Baxter kept calling them. He'd just sat in the dark with his friend, like he'd sat at his desk all morning, staring down at the ground and not answering Mrs. Baxter's questions when she called on him, because he knew he'd sound scared if he tried. Like his mom sounded now. He'd been afraid he might start to cry, like he almost had that morning with Joshua.

Because Nate wouldn't talk to him. Not on the bus. Not in class. Not in the closet. His friend was never going to talk to him again.

"It's my fault," Cade blurted out.

There, he'd said it.

Was that what his mom wanted to hear to make it all better?

"What's your fault?" she asked.

"You wouldn't be here, and Nate wouldn't be here, if I'd told."

And he wouldn't be pretending like he cared about anything anymore while he waited for someone to find out the truth.

It was all his fault.

Cade looked at his friend. They'd promised after the shooting, before Cade had been moved with the other kids who hadn't been hurt and Nate had been taken to the ambulance, not to tell what they'd known before lunch. That Bubba was pushing Troy around too much. And Troy was acting weird and sounding scary. That Mr. Perry was hitting him with his belt and making Troy stand up to Bubba or else. And Cade and Nate had had a chance to tell Cade's mom and Ms. Hemmings or Mrs. Baxter that morning—only they'd kept their traps shut instead, because Cade had said to.

No one had asked Cade anything about Troy, not really, not any more than they'd asked the other kids. Not the police or the school or even his parents, who were supposed to know when he wasn't telling the truth. Every day, Cade had been waiting for Troy to finally tell someone about that morning in the bathroom.

Then someone would want to know why Cade and Nate hadn't stopped Troy before lunch. Or maybe Nate's parents would ask why he and Cade never talked anymore, and Nate would tell them. And then everyone would finally stop calling Cade a hero and start hating him the same way they did Troy.

"How is it your fault?" His mom glanced at Nate, sounding even more afraid now.

"We knew," Nate said from the dark.

It was the first thing Cade had heard him say since that day at the school. Nate hadn't spoken when Cade and his parents visited his hospital room. Or any of the times when Cade had sneaked over to his friend's house, even though Mr. and Mrs. Turner were mad at his parents and he wasn't supposed to go. Ten times, he'd tried to get Nate to open his window by tapping on it the way they used to do when they sneaked out at night sometimes. Ten freaking times. After that, Cade had hidden in Nate's backyard some days, hoping his friend would come outside, only Nate never had.

But Cade would never stop trying, even if it took forever. Even if it took admitting what he'd done. He wanted his friend back.

"You knew what?" His mom looked out the door to the classroom, at whoever was out there listening.

"What Troy's dad was doing." Cade wiped at the stuff running out of his nose, not caring who heard. He hated this. All of it. Everything had gotten so bad. He'd lost Nate and Mom and Dad and even Joshua, really. Everyone felt so far away, he hadn't been able to say anything to them. Everyone thought he'd done something good that day, because they didn't know.

"How . . . What did you know?" his mom asked.

"Troy told us his dad was whaling on him." Nate stared up at the ceiling. His head thumped against the shelf behind him that was full of the math books they didn't use in class, because Mrs. Baxter made her own handouts and things that were easier to practice with and learn from. "And that Mr. Wilmington told Troy to stop Bubba or else. Bubba was being a jerk, and Mr. Wilmington was being a jerk, and everyone was pushing Troy around and laughing at him and . . . he was going to make it stop, he said. He said he was going to make it all stop. And we . . ."

Mom's foot was next to Cade's, resting against his the way she used to when he was little and they'd sit on the floor together to read, and it had seemed like just being with him made her a little happier. And then he was resting his leg against hers, wondering whether this was how she'd always felt when she'd gotten so quiet and wanted to be alone. Like she hadn't slept in months, the way he hadn't since Troy shot Bubba. Each night, it got harder to think about anything else when it was dark and there was nothing else to do.

He couldn't make it stop.

He kept seeing Bubba smiling mean down at Troy, and Troy shaking and holding Mr. Wilmington's gun, and Bubba bleeding, Nate bleeding, everyone but Cade bleeding . . .

He yanked his leg away.

"Nate wanted to tell," he said. "Just like he stood up to Troy in the lunchroom. He wanted to tell, and we should have, and if we had, none of this would have happened."

Bubba was dead. Troy was locked up somewhere. And Cade and Nate and Sally and everyone else from lunch that day could have died, too. And now Cade's friend hated him.

His mom squeezed his knee. "And you guys have been keeping this to yourselves, what you found out about Mr. Wilmington that day, because you think you should have stopped Troy?"

Cade didn't say anything.

Nate didn't either.

Cade's mom looked out into the classroom again. Someone else must be out there now, besides whoever had come with her. For a minute she looked like she wanted to run away almost as much as Cade did.

Then she looked back at him and Nate, all sad-like, trying to smile.

"Feeling guilty like that has to have sucked big-time," she said. "I'm so sorry."

She was crying, just a little, the way she did when she didn't want anyone to know. But Cade could always tell when his mom was crying, even when she hid it.

And she was saying the same thing she'd written to Dad that morning. *I'm so sorry* . . . Like it was all her fault, not Cade's.

"But you saved us," he said. She *was* a hero. He'd always known that, somehow. Only it had made him mad since the shooting, because *he* hadn't been a hero when he could have helped Troy and Bubba and everybody. "You and Nate kept Troy from killing the rest of us." While Cade had stayed on the floor with Sally and tried not to hurl. "Why are you sorry about anything?"

"That's how sorry works," Mom said, sounding less scared, her voice stronger. "You feel bad. You feel sorry. Even if it's not your fault, you want the bad things to stop, and you feel awful that you can't make them stop. You have to be careful with feeling sorry, honey. It can take people and time away from you, no matter how hard you try to make the world right again. Especially when you can't fix what's wrong, because you didn't make the bad things happen in the first place. That's the worst kind of sorry."

"Why can't my parents get that?" Nate pounded his head against the shelves again. "They hate what's happened. They think they can make it better and make me feel better by pretending everything's normal again. And by making someone else sorry, like the school board or Mr. Griffin or Ms. Hemmings. My parents just don't get it."

"Probably because you're not telling them what you need to tell them," Mom said, "the way you never told me what you wanted to tell me at the playground each night."

Cade stared her.

What was she talking about?

"I tried," Nate mumbled. "I thought I could say it to you."

What was *Nate* talking about?

"Say it to me now, so I can help you. Say it to Cade, so he can help, too."

Cade felt himself nodding. He didn't understand, but he wanted to help. He wanted to stop feeling sorry, and he wanted Nate to get better, and he wanted his friend back, and he wanted to sleep again without seeing Bubba die and Troy crying after he'd shot him.

Maybe that was why he'd come to school today, too.

Maybe that was why he'd followed Nate in here, needing to talk to him when he couldn't talk to anybody else.

"We'll do whatever we can," Mom said. "But you have to tell us what you need first."

Cade didn't remember doing it, but he and his mom were closer to Nate now, almost right next to him, where the closet was darkest.

"I . . ." Nate sobbed, like Troy had in the bathroom that day. He was losing it, the way Cade had been trying not to for so long.

"I'd rather die than be here . . ." He wiped at his eyes with both hands, while Cade wiped at his. "I'd rather have died that day, if it means I don't have to be here now. I can't. I can't do this. I don't care what my parents think will make me better. I just can't!"

Chapter Eight

"Oh my god," Brian whispered, listening to what was happening in Mrs. Baxter's supply closet, with Mallory and Pete standing next to him, listening too. The AP and Mrs. Baxter were waiting in the hallway, and Kristen had just answered a call on her cell.

He'd had no idea.

None of them had.

No one in Chandlerville had guessed the awful secret his son and Nate had been keeping, silently torturing themselves with guilt on top of everything else they were going through. No one had been able to get through to either boy.

Strike that.

Say it to me now, so I can help you . . .

Sam had been there for Nate for weeks, listening even when it sounded as if Nate hadn't said anything at all. And now she was here for both boys, hurting herself by being back at the school, but staying right where Cade and Nate needed her, for as long as they needed her.

That's how sorry works . . .

"Do you think . . ." he started to ask his friends, but he couldn't finish.

Did Nate really want to die? Was Cade really feeling the same way his mother always had about 9/11—as if *she* could have done something to spare her students the loss of their parents, or Cade could have stopped anything that Bubba or Troy had done?

"How did all of this happen?" he asked. "What the hell are we supposed to do?"

He'd never been able to get through to Sam, not to the point of getting her completely well. And his son had been feeling the same kind of desperation she had. It had been months, and Brian hadn't even known what Cade was going through.

"We'll make sure they get the help they need," Mallory promised.

"And what if there isn't enough help in the world to make this better?" Brian turned to find Pete's arm around his fiancée.

We'll make sure . . .

Neighbors and friends had rallied around Pete not long ago, worried that he and Polly were trying too hard to deal with their grief and pain alone, and that they were failing. All of Mimosa Lane had pitched in to help, and Mallory had turned out to be a godsend. Miracles did happen in some communities. For some people. But not for Sam and Brian. Not in New York and not in Chandlerville.

They'd tried so hard to be okay here—the kind of okay Sam refused to believe in anymore. Word was getting out about their split. Julia and Walter were caught in the middle. Pete and Mallory were involving themselves even further, for whatever good that would do. While Brian's estranged wife and trauma-tized son were sitting on the floor of an elementary school closet, talking with someone else's child about not wanting to be any-where ever again.

"Then for now tell your parents you can't be at school," he heard Sam say to Nate. "That you can't be inside in the middle of the night, and that's why walking around the neighborhood and meeting me maybe makes things a little better. You don't have to be anything you can't be, Nate. But you need to tell your parents why you're feeling this way. You've been keeping a horrible secret, and you have to start talking about it with some-one. Both of you do, or you're going to feel worse and worse until that day in the cafeteria with Bubba and Troy becomes all that you can feel."

Would you consider it? Sam had asked Brian about their see-ing a therapist together. *For us, would you do it, so some of this can really start to get better?*

We're fine . . . he'd answered, just as he had every time since 9/11 that she'd suggested he seek counseling on his own. Just as he had that morning, when she'd tried to explain again what was happening to her. What she believed was happening to them.

He'd always had enough faith for both of them, he'd insisted. He'd always believed that they were fine, or at least that they soon would be. One day. He'd never wanted to be anything *but* fine for her or their boys. He'd wanted to give them the very best he could, so their life in Chandlerville could become what he and Sam had dreamed it would be. Meanwhile, his wife had been suffering much more than she'd let anyone know, reliving the same awful day over and over again, no matter how much of a positive spin she'd helped him put on things at home.

Until it had become all *she* could feel?

Well, if it's not against me, Brian had asked his friend earlier, *what is my wife fighting against?*

All along, Sam had still been fighting herself. And he'd enabled that instinct, making it as easy as possible for her not to face the hard things she had to.

. . . you have to start talking about it with someone . . .

"Oh my God," he said again.

"You couldn't have known," Mallory responded, as if she knew he was talking about more than not being there for Cade.

"I didn't want to know."

That morning, he'd screamed at his wife and called her selfish and blamed her for all their problems. Because she'd stopped putting on a show for herself and him and everyone else. Except he'd wanted to keep holding himself together, like he had ever since New York, rationalizing that it was all for her. So *she'd* get better again. Because maybe *he* didn't know how to live any other way.

He'd been so determined for her to be better, he'd all but driven her from their home with the way he'd bungled her waking up in the hospital. And never once since then had he really listened to his wife without judgment, the way he was now.

I'm never going to be the Sam you want me to be again.

Pete's hand squeezed Brian's shoulder, steadying him.

"I don't want to go home." Nate sounded like a little boy, instead of the strong young man he was growing into. "I can't go home, and I can't be here, and that means . . . what? Where? There's nowhere. I'm nowhere!"

"You're right here with us," Sam assured him. "Cade and I are right here with you, just like I've been there every night in case you wanted to talk. Especially last night, because I knew how hard this morning would be. And I'm here now, even though school scares the mess out of me just like it did the day of the bake sale, even before the shooting. Cade's here for you, too, even if you guys have stuff to work out. He's right here where you need him. And I'm here for both of you. So are Ms. Hemmings and Mrs. Baxter. That's not *nowhere*, Nate. You're never going to be nowhere. We won't let you be."

"His mother's outside in the hallway," Ms. Hemmings said softly, stepping to Brian's side.

"Keep her there for a little longer," Mallory suggested.

"She wants to speak with her son."

"Don't you think it's a little late for that?" Brian bit out, pitching his voice lower but feeling violent at the thought that a parent could have left her child to suffer in silence the way Nate had been.

The way Brian had pretty much left Cade without the support he needed. The way his denial had left Sam to fend for herself for so long.

"I don't have the authority to keep her away from Nate," Kristen said.

"Let me talk with her." Mallory headed out of the classroom.

Brian could hear her and Beverly speaking in the hallway, but his mind would process only what was being said in the closet.

"I can help you talk with your parents," Sam insisted.

"Me too," Cade chimed in. "I'm sorry, Nate. I'm sorry I said not to tell that day. I . . ."

"Shut up, okay?" Nate said, sounding more like himself. "It's not your fault. Bubba was a bully. Troy was a stupid shit. And I didn't tell, either."

"But you tried to stop him," Cade said. "And I . . ."

"You kept Sally safe."

"And you kept us all safe." Cade sounded miserable, and there was something else Brian had never heard before in his son's voice: shame. His boy was ashamed, the same as Sam had felt all these years, wanting to not be as messed up as she was by what had happened to her.

"We're all safe *now*," Sam reminded them. "And you both were very, very brave that day. Everyone did what they thought was right. Everyone wishes they'd done more. How do you think I feel, Nate, not stopping Troy before you were shot, or before Bubba was? Ms. Hemmings and the teachers and the rest of the adults in the school—we all wish we could have kept everyone from being hurt, or stopped Troy from doing something so awful. You all could have been killed right in front of us. And I just had to stand there, watching it happen . . ."

Sam's words hiccupped to a halt. The closet grew silent. Everyone in the classroom beyond seemed to be holding their breath. Brian sure as hell was.

They'd all heard it.

The panic and anxiety and fear that Sam had never shaken. He'd known to expect it when she'd woken up in the hospital. He'd known she'd be remembering another school and another group of children and another community grieving over a senseless act of violence that never should have happened. He'd tried to reassure her before she could fall apart. He'd tried as hard as he could to hold them both together.

Only she hadn't crumbled to pieces this time.

She'd walked away from him and the optimism that used to make her feel safe, saying she couldn't take it anymore.

"Is my mom out there?" Nate asked.

"I hope so, honey," Sam said. "She was on her way from work."

"She'll be pissed that I messed up her day."

"No, she won't. She'll be glad to be here for you. I'm sure she came as quick as she could."

"My parents were so happy I was back at school. It's all they could talk about this morning, especially my mom. All weekend, too."

"They were happy you were feeling well enough to try." Sam sounded as if she were trying to convince herself as much as Nate. "Sometimes we want so much for the people we love to be better, we can't see that they're not ready yet. And then people like you and me want to make everyone happy again after we haven't for a long time. We think it's our fault everyone's sad and worried about us. And we don't speak up when we should, or say how we're really doing, or make ourselves work through stuff we know we should, because other people are expecting us to be over things already. Trust me, that makes everything harder in the long run and everyone even more upset. Then big days like today that should be good, end up being the worst days of all, when we can't do what we thought we could, and we know we're disappointing the people we love."

Big days.

"Jesus." Brian had to get to his wife. He moved to step into the closet.

"Don't." Pete gripped his arm. "Let her talk."

"You don't understand." Brian struggled to be free. "I—"

"We understand," Mallory said, once more at her fiancé's side. "We've been through this with Polly, dealing with how angry she was at her mother for going away forever. It's not your fault, Brian. And you can't fix it right now. Sam wouldn't want you to try. She wants to do this for Cade and Nate."

"If this is stuff she hasn't been able to say to you in person," Pete said, "let her talk it out here."

Brian stopped trying to pull away. Pete was right. If he interrupted his wife now, it would be because *he* needed to. He needed

Sam to understand that he'd never meant to leave her feeling like she was letting him down because of how badly she still hurt.

Brian stared into the closet. What was it doing to her overtaxed system to be there for Cade and Nate like this?

You're such a coward . . .

"Do you want me to help you say the things you really need to say to your mom?" she asked Nate.

There was a long pause.

"I'll go with you," Cade said. "We'll tell your mom everything. I'll tell her it was me, not you, who got everyone shot, because I didn't let us do anything about Troy when I should have. It's not your fault." Cade's voice broke, tearing at Brian's heart.

"Neither of you are to blame," Sam insisted. "And everyone's here to help both of you. Never forget that."

"You'll . . . you'll talk to my mom with me?" Nate asked, just as Beverly and Kristen joined Brian and Pete and Mallory at the closet door.

***

"How did it go?" Brian asked Sam.

She knew he'd stay the rest of the morning, the moment she'd caught sight of him outside the closet, standing with Mallory and Pete. He'd silently followed her and Cade downstairs, where she'd known he'd stay while she and their son finished talking with Nate and Beverly Turner. And there Brian was, calmly waiting outside the conference room Kristen had shown everyone but Brian and Mallory and Pete into.

Cade had headed back to class after sitting beside Nate while his friend talked with his mother, and Sam tried to help Beverly understand what Nate was saying. Cade hadn't really looked at

Sam again or talked to either her or Brian directly once they left the closet. And as soon as things had started to wrap up in the conference room, he'd split, yelling for her to leave him alone when she'd tried to hug him, and saying he wanted to go back to his class instead of home to Mimosa Lane with Sam or Brian.

Sam closed the conference room door to give Beverly and a much calmer Nate a chance to speak privately, hoping the pair were in a place now where Nate could say whatever he needed to. She stopped next to her husband, wanting to collapse into him, fighting the tears that welled up at the hopeful smile spreading across his face.

He'd been outside the closet almost the whole time, Kristen had said. He'd heard what Sam said to the boys—things he'd never let her say to him without trying to talk her out of her feelings. He thought he understood her now, and maybe he did, a little more, anyway. He'd stayed. He wanted to talk. Maybe this was their breakthrough.

But Sam couldn't do it. Not here. Not after the last two hours of being terrified for two damaged sixth graders. Not after staying where she hated being, because that was where her son and his friend were, and she wasn't leaving them alone with their fears. Now she couldn't stop hearing little Krista's voice, mixed with Nate's voice, and Cade's voice, and the sound of countless other children needing her.

She'd called Julia on her cell about half an hour ago, and her friend had just texted that she was waiting in the parking lot for Sam to finish up.

"How do you think it went?" she asked her husband. "It was awful."

That took care of Brian's smile, and she wanted to kick herself for it.

When they first met, she'd loved his fearlessness. He'd been a man built to weather any storm with style and confidence and humor. Her perfect match. Then everything had changed after 9/11. At least, *she'd* changed, as she'd leaned more and more on his strength and his conviction that they could still conquer anything together.

He'd been entitled to his anger that morning. It was lousy of her to be asking him, after all this time, to stop being the supportive, capable, fearless cheerleader she'd adored. But stopping was what she needed—what she thought *they* needed—and she wasn't up to going another round at trying to explain why.

"Ms. Hemmings sounded encouraged when she came out a few minutes ago." He looked confused.

Sam didn't blame him.

"That Nate's finally asking for help," she said, "and his mother might be finally listening? Yes. But he's been dealing with too much on his own for months. And his parents have been so proud of him for pulling it together enough to come back to school. Now he thinks he's let them down, on top of everything else. He's had a good couple of hours, but that doesn't fix the rest."

"Beverly's not acting like he's letting her down, is she? She and James may be myopic about their careers and their vendetta against the administration and the school board. But they wouldn't keep pressuring Nate to feel better when he's not. Not after today."

"No. But in his mind, he's disappointing them, just like he and Cade think they let Troy and Bubba down."

The same way she couldn't stop feeling as if she'd failed her husband and sons, letting herself get to this place and bringing them all to the brink with her. No matter how she looked at it, she couldn't get around the fact that if she'd faced her fears sooner—really faced them, instead of blinding herself to the effect they were still having on her and everyone else in her life— her family would have weathered the Chandler shooting and a lot of other things better.

She hated the way she'd made Brian feel that morning, even if she didn't regret having stood her ground. She hated the sight of the muscle ticking along his jaw now, because she once again wasn't making any sense to him at all. But she'd promised herself to be honest from now on about how she was feeling and what she needed.

"I should go," she said. The last thing she wanted to do was irritate her husband to distraction for the second time that day. And Cade would be okay without her, at least for the rest of the school day. She *had* to get out of there. "This is really a bad time to do this."

"Don't," Brian grabbed her by the shoulders before she could get past him. "We need to talk about—"

"No. *You* need to talk about it. And maybe we're both finally wanting to talk about the same things, and I appreciate your being here, and I think you and Cade and I should definitely sit down when he's ready, and try to understand some of what he's going through, too, maybe even with his therapist. But I can't do this anymore today. I can't be here for another minute, even if it would make you feel better."

Sam wanted to slap her hand over her own mouth.

It had taken her so long to admit the awful truths she'd needed to say to her husband, she couldn't seem to stop herself now. This was why she stayed out of his way at the house in the mornings and the evenings. She didn't want to keep hurting Brian like this. Cade and Joshua didn't need to see them fighting, because the frustration wouldn't stop pouring out of her, no matter how much she still loved them all.

"I want to talk about us." His grip tightened. "I want to talk about what you said to Cade in the classroom. I wanted to say how sorry I am." His voice cracked, his eyes closing as he bent his head to hers. "I haven't given you a chance to say those things to me when you needed to. Maybe I didn't want to hear them. Or I didn't . . ."

"You didn't want to feel them with me?"

The words tasted like hate when she said them. As if the betrayal was so deep, so personal, maybe she did hate her husband a little, almost as much as she hated what she'd become.

She prayed every night that they'd salvage the best parts of their marriage and return to a place where love was the strongest emotion they felt for each other. Not fear and resentment and disappointment and blame. But that wasn't where they were today. And as much responsibility as she was willing to take for the mistakes they'd made, she hadn't stumbled into this place alone.

"We were so close once, Brian. Then after everything that happened in New York, we both changed so much, only with you it was in a hundred invisible ways. You stopped being with me, and started taking care of me and then the boys and everything else, deciding what we both needed to be so we could stay together. You needed to keep going strong, and I needed to get better. Only you couldn't unless I did. So we started being so careful. And I told myself I *could* get better, just by following your lead. And then we stopped talking about the really important things. And no matter what we said and did with each other and the boys to make it seem like we could wait forever for me to come back, you didn't get it any more than I did. I was *never* coming back from 9/11, not to the way I used to be. Neither of us wanted to accept it. You still don't. I've tried my best to be what I thought I needed to be, so I could stay close to you and have at least something of the life we wanted. But I can't do that anymore."

In his mind, she'd failed these last few months.

And in her own mind, too.

That was the terrifying truth, in all its unvarnished glory. She hadn't been focusing on making herself stronger all these years that she'd hidden away from the world. She hadn't gone to the bake sale that day in January to help herself heal. She'd simply been trying not to be a burden any longer, to her family and her husband.

It's my fault, Cade had said about what he thought he'd caused. Sam's heart had broken for them both in that closet, because for the last three months she'd been feeling the exact same self-loathing as her son.

But Troy would have self-destructed eventually, given the pressure he was under and the lack of support he had at home. Just as this shadowy place her marriage had arrived at had likely been foretold from the moment those planes flew into the Twin Towers—just as so many other relationships had fallen apart over the years, in the community of survivors that remained. The same way the strain of the shooting was already taking its toll on so many families in Chandlerville, including Julia and Walter's.

Not accepting that reality was an emotional sinkhole she tried daily to drag herself back from. And she kept telling herself not to blame Brian for being who and what he was. For being the strong one who'd done so much for her that she hadn't been able to stay, if she ever wanted to learn how to once again do for herself.

"I don't know how . . ." Brian let her go, giving her the out she'd wanted.

Her husband sounded as close to giving up as she'd ever heard him. She couldn't run, she realized. Her legs wouldn't move. Not because they were numb this time, but because she couldn't stand the thought of not being there beside Brian as the next words tumbled from his mouth.

"I don't know," he said, "how to feel what you want me to, and not fall . . ."

"Fall apart like me?" she asked.

He'd supported her and been patient with her and waited for her, while she'd had the luxury of coming undone and never finding her way back together again. She owed him so much for giving her the time she'd needed to find this place of healing she was starting to understand. It must seem as if she were throwing how selfless he'd been back in his face. That was what she felt guilty about most of all.

"I know," she said. "I took up all that space in our marriage and our family, and you never had the chance to really deal with anything else but me. But the thing is . . ."

His bright blue gaze was brittle. But he was listening, instead of rushing to console her, or arguing as if he thought she was attacking him.

"The thing is what?" he asked.

"If you don't know how to break," she said, backing away a step, heading toward the door as the panic and fear and doubt grabbed for her again. "And I can't go back to being the way I was when we thought everything was fine . . . then what are we doing, Brian, except staying in the same place we were when we left New York? How are we ever going to get through the worst parts of this, and move on to whatever's on the other side?"

***

Kristen watched Cade's father while Mr. Perry watched Sam flee.

There was no other way to describe the other woman's frantic exit through the school's front entrance. And Brian looked poised to race after her as she rushed through the outer school office, then into the hallway, on her way to Julia Davis's car.

Something stopped him—something deeply personal that Kristen had no right to impose herself on. Except, like she'd said that morning at the Davis house, she'd been very worried about Cade, even before the boy's revelations while he'd talked with his mother and Nate. There were some things Kristen needed to discuss with one of his parents, and she'd already asked too much of Sam today.

This family deserved a break. And she was about to make their already difficult day even worse.

"Can I speak with you for a moment, Mr. Perry?" she asked.

He cast a fleeting glance toward his wife. Then he held out his hand to Kristen.

"Brian, please. Thank you for being so responsive this morning, and for giving Cade and Nate and my wife the time they needed to talk."

"It's my pleasure, Brian." Kristen shook his hand as she smiled. "Your wife is a remarkable woman. If I didn't know that already, I would certainly have discovered it today."

Brian nodded. "Sam's always had a way with people. She . . . feels things and picks up on things that hardly anyone else would. She finds a way to understand what people are going through. All the kinds of things that I'm no good at."

Kristen tilted her head, thinking that Brian and Sam had always seemed like the perfect team whenever she'd seen them together.

"I hope today wasn't too difficult for your wife," she said. "I talked her into doing it, and I can't imagine what would have happened if she hadn't been here to speak with Nate and Mrs. Turner."

Kristen cleared her throat as Brian checked his watch and glanced down the hallway to where Pete Lombard was waiting, talking quietly with Mallory. Pete and Brian had arrived outside the Baxter classroom together. Both men would need to get back to their days, the same as Kristen and her clinic nurse did. She'd stalled long enough.

"I realize your wife must be exhausted," she said. "But I'm afraid there's more for her to do today, for you both to do—with regard to Cade."

Brian's attention snapped back to Kristen.

"Cade's upset," he said. "He's been keeping a lot to himself since the shooting."

"Yes. And up until recently, we've thought we were able to deal with Cade's school issues here. We wanted to give you and Sam as much time as you needed, to take care of other things at home. But I'm afraid we've let a few things go a little too long, because of the other issues my staff and I have had to address. And it's come to my attention that late last week we reached the point where you and your wife will need to become involved."

"Involved with what?"

Brian's demeanor changed from that of the competent, cool parent and businessman she'd always admired. Instead, Kristen found herself staring at a man who seemed to be clinging to a razor's edge of control.

"Sixth-grade midterms were held the latter part of last week," she said. "And I'm afraid that after Cade's performance, combined with his other missing assignments this semester, your son is on a precarious path toward failing sixth grade if we don't take some immediate action."

"Excuse me?"

Brian's astonishment was understandable. Cade was a straight-A student. He had been. He would be again, if Kristen had anything to say about it.

"Your son's been struggling for a while," she said, "which is perfectly understandable. Mrs. Baxter and the rest of his teachers tell me they've been in touch with you about the situation."

"About the missing assignments, yes, and his lack of participation in class and with his friends. But no one's said anything about failing."

"His midterm grades were posted to our database over the weekend. The exams he took—science and history and art—he failed outright. Social studies and math and language arts were entered as zeros because he was out sick those days. Those averages should improve once we get his make-up grades in, but—"

"Out sick?" Brian braced his hands on his hips. "When?"

"Wednesday and Friday of last week." Kristen mentally reviewed the attendance record she'd checked. "We have an excuse on file from you for each absence."

"How?" Cade's father asked.

"How?"

"What kind of excuse?"

"A written letter, I would imagine. We can check with Mrs. Baxter. I assume it would be the same method you've used every other time your son's stayed home since January. That's another matter I'd planned to schedule a phone conference about. There's a maximum number of days we can allow a student to be absent from school before it begins to jeopardize his eligibility to graduate. It's understandable that Cade would need some additional downtime, after what he's been through. But we'll have to formally modify Cade's education plan if we're going to—"

Brian held up his hand, silencing the information she'd typically have communicated in a much less rambling way.

"As far as I know," he said, "my son's been in school every day since the week after the shooting. My wife and I haven't been keeping him home ourselves, and we haven't been writing excuses for his absences. He certainly wasn't sick last week. I don't know where he's been going during the day the last three months when he hasn't been here, but Cade hasn't been home with one of us."

Kristen blinked at him.

"Oh, dear," she said.

She'd already worked out extra-credit opportunities with each of Cade's teachers, chances for a bright, dedicated student to make up work and the midterm tests he'd either missed or failed. But none of that was going to be very effective if they couldn't keep the boy in class.

"It seems we have a much bigger problem than I'd initially thought," she said.

"Of course we do." Brian motioned for Pete Lombard to join them. He took his cell phone from his pocket and began menuing to a contact. "Let me make a call to my office. Then I'd appreciate any more time you can give me this morning. My son's not going to fail sixth grade because his mother and I have been as oblivious to what Cade's going through as James and Beverly Turner have been with Nate."

Chapter Nine

"Wow," Julia said, sitting at the foot of the guest room bed Sam had collapsed onto. "You've had a busy morning of saving lost boys."

"I didn't save anyone," Sam said through the migraine that was building from too many panic attacks today, too much adrenaline, and two dysfunctional run-ins with her husband.

"I heard from Mallory. Nate's home with his mother, and Beverly's taking the rest of the week off to work with him herself, instead of using the nanny or a tutor."

Julia always, *always* meant well. And she'd been Sam's closest friend since she and Brian arrived on Mimosa Lane—two Yankee wildflowers digging their raggedy roots into the rich Georgia soil that was better suited to nurture Sam's heirloom roses. But despite Julia's best intentions, her idea of helping sometimes felt like having a frontal lobotomy without anesthesia.

She seemed to always know exactly what Sam didn't want to discuss, just when Sam wanted to discuss it the least. Julia's secret weapon was her personality, the sweetest of temperaments that almost made you believe it didn't hurt so badly that she wasn't satisfied until she helped you, however she thought you needed helping. And right now, Julia seemed to think that what Sam needed was to talk about what had happened at Chandler that morning.

"Yes." Sam ground her thumbs against her closed eyelids, wondering how much pressure she'd have to apply to push straight through to the back of her skull. "Nate seems to have hit whatever rock bottom he needed to, to finally deal with his parents and capture their undivided attention."

"Mallory said something about Cade helping you when you talked with Nate . . ." Julia sat on the bed beside Sam. "How did that go?"

"Fine, as long as it was about Nate. As soon as it wasn't, Cade went back to his class like nothing's changed. Does he really think we're going to let this drop, now that we know what's been bothering him?"

"Mallory says he's been blaming himself all this time, while no one's known that it's been more than the same shock the rest of us are dealing with."

Sam's eyes were stinging, but she was too tired to cry.

"I should have known . . ." she said. It had been one of the many things eating at her while she talked with Brian outside the conference room. "I should have been there more at home, listening to him, so he didn't feel so alone."

She should have known something was wrong, the way he was avoiding talking to her. She should have known it was more than just her moving out. They'd been so close, and he'd pulled away so completely. But she hadn't wanted to push herself on

Cade, or demand that he forgive her for the changes she'd forced on their family.

"Don't do that to yourself." Julia shoved off the bed. "You've needed to be here, taking care of yourself—and you still managed to be home every morning and afternoon for your boys. Don't value yourself and your well-being less than you do everyone else's, even your family's. You need to take care of yourself, or there won't be anything left for the rest of the people in your life."

She stared down at Sam, still in her workday uniform. Her eyes were alive with something darker than their normal hazel-green. She was a different woman than most people in Chandlerville knew. Most of their friends and neighbors saw only a former PTA president, a coach's wife, a homemaker and hostess, and a selfless representative on the school board.

Sam wasn't most people.

"You first," she said, sitting up, thinking it was high time for Julia to talk about some things *she'd* rather not talk about. "Why don't you and your boys stand up to Walter and figure out what the hell's going on with him, before he gets worse? Why don't you focus on your own family as much as you're killing yourself to save Chandlerville's soul? Don't you have another school board hearing tonight about the shooting, like there's been a hearing every other Monday night for a month and a half? Why don't you *not* go to that for a change? You say no one's listening to anyone at those things anyway. Sitting through them is making you crazy. Why don't you stay here instead and deal with the husband who's making you crazy? Do that for yourself, and maybe then you can tell me to stop feeling like a failure as a wife and mother for leaving my husband and sons, while I have a slow nervous breakdown."

Sam was as shocked as her friend by her tirade, but it was too late to take the words back. Her nerves were shot. She was strung out from being at school, even if she'd managed to help Nate and maybe even Cade a little. She hated herself for every harsh truth she'd spewed at Brian, when he'd rushed back from Atlanta and stayed half the morning to support her and their son. But none of that was an excuse for deflecting her own problems by pointing her finger at someone who'd opened her home and her heart to Sam so unconditionally.

Julia started to say something. Her jaw clamped closed again, so hard her teeth clunked. Then she sank back onto the bed, her shoulders drooping.

"Walter doesn't realize what he's doing when he's drunk," she said. "He's never been like this before. I don't think he even realizes how much he's drinking."

"And that makes it okay?" Sam was sick of seeing the Davis family suffering, while Julia hoped this would all just go away. "He was so drunk he hit you a few nights ago."

"He never hit me! It was just a little shove, when he was trying to get by me."

"You almost took a header downstairs to your basement."

"I caught myself. And I'm still not sure I didn't slip on the tread at the top."

"I'm sure." Sam felt like a weasel. But she was glad they were discussing this finally. She was afraid for her friends—Julia and Walter both—if things didn't change. "You two might still seem like the perfect couple to everyone else. But I've lived here for three months. Your husband is a wonderful man, but he needs help. He's never been like this before. Something is wrong, Julia, and you can't keep letting him hold whatever it is inside. If he won't let you or the boys help him, then there are other ways. You could—"

"What? Get him to go to treatment? Therapy? How's that kind of thing working for you and Brian?" Her friend shook her head. "Walter won't go. He's as resistant to something like that as Brian has always been. Both of them think the world is black-and-white, and there's no sense talking about the stuff in between. They can handle it all on their own, because they always have. But boys terrorizing each other until one of them is dead, one in the hospital, and another in jail . . . Three sweet boys, Sam. It's tearing Walter up. I don't know why it's hitting him so much harder than the rest of us. He won't talk about the shooting at all, except to say that he can't believe it happened, and what good is helping kids the way we always have, if we can't protect them from things that mess them up so badly that they turn on each other?"

"None of us can believe it."

Sam thought of Cade and her son's confusion and insistence that he was to blame.

"When I moved in here," Sam said to her friend, "who'd have thought we'd both end up in the same place?"

"Lonely?" Julia asked, nudging Sam's shoulder with her own.

Sam nodded, nudging back. "But never alone."

She thought of how charmed the lives on Mimosa Lane had seemed to her when she and Brian had first moved here. And how quaintly the national media had painted Chandlerville, as if it were a modern-day Mayberry. In reality, most of the families they knew had two parents who worked, many of them all the way downtown like Brian and Walter and the Turners. Or mom and dad were divorced or struggling with the same complex family problems as people anywhere else in the country.

Ideal lives and ideal places like Mimosa Lane had their own cracks and dents and rusted-out chips that took away from the good stuff. Especially when no one wanted to confront the bad things in their midst, until it was too late to deal with them.

***

"I need to speak with you, Brian," Whilleby said before Brian could make it to his office after returning to Whilleby & Marshal around one o'clock.

He thought about continuing to walk, as if he hadn't heard the voice of doom beckoning him to the pit of despair. He felt a careless smile consume his expression. He let his thoughts wander to Cade's favorite movie, where "the pit of despair" was one of his favorite scenes.

Since the boys were old enough to care, Saturday nights had been movie nights. The whole family would pile into the media room in the basement that had, over the years, morphed into a playroom that often resembled bedlam. Kids' stuff stayed strewn everywhere, no matter how much Sam sorted and organized. On any given weekend day, there used to be five to ten of the boys' friends over to play foosball and air hockey and video games and LEGOs, blaring music through the surround sound speakers and watching ridiculous kid TV shows and movies that seemed selected to drive adults from the basement. Until someone, usually Brian, ventured down again to clear everyone out because it was dinnertime.

But like the boys playing all afternoon with friends, Saturday movie nights were gone now. So was his family being silly and easy with one another, no matter what else was going on in their lives. Since the shooting, he and Sam had lost twelve Saturdays, all while Brian had been stewing over how unfairly she'd been treating him, stalking her at night but not confronting her until this morning, waiting around for her to come to her senses.

"Brian?" Whilleby asked. Brian had started walking again—toward his office and not his senior partner. "I have a pressing business matter I need to discuss with you."

Brian already knew what the pressing matter was—he was off the Kelsey project.

Jefferson had left a voice mail on Brian's cell, saying how disappointed he and Ginger were to hear about the change. They understood his personal situation and sympathized with his decision to step away from their redesign so another associate could finish the plans Brian had poured his creative heart and soul into before the shooting. But they were disappointed.

And Brian had been . . . relieved when he'd heard the news.

Standing outside the school listening to his phone messages after talking with Kristen about Cade, his disappointing clients had paled in comparison to his worry for Cade and Sam and his marriage. The design work that had annoyed him more than it had inspired him lately didn't rate a second thought now. Maybe it never had.

He'd made being indispensable at W&M a primary focus since he'd uprooted his family and moved them to the Deep South. He'd been lucky to have landed this opportunity. And yet he'd secretly seen working here as something he'd had to settle for, when he still dreamed of striking out on his own to do the more environmentally conscious projects he'd been pursuing in New York.

Sam and the boys had needed so much of his time, he'd reasoned with himself, there was no way he could put enough into a start-up venture. So he'd given up on running his own shop, and he'd patted himself on the back for the sacrifice. Only now his family was falling apart, regardless.

From the start, Whilleby & Marshal's brand of conservative, upscale, mostly corporate design hadn't satisfied him. But he made good money. And over the years he'd used his crazy schedule at the office as an excuse not to look too closely at what was happening to the people he'd done all of this for.

"Mr. Perry!" his senior partner bellowed.

The shocking sound of the understated man's anger, his use of Brian's last name, caused several associates to poke their heads out of their offices to see who was about to get his ass fired. Their attention swiveled from the senior partner to Brian. One by one, they ducked back into their own spaces.

Brian gazed into Whilleby's furious features—at least as furious as Brian had ever witnessed. The man's complexion was blotched with red, and he was scrutinizing Brian as if he'd never seen him before. Whilleby's mouth was so firmly closed, a white line had formed around the man's lips.

"I need to speak with you *now*." Whilleby was the partner who'd hired Brian away from the small New York firm that had given him his start right out of school. Back then, the man had seen a bright future in Brian's cutting-edge designs and commitment to environmentally friendly solutions. "We need to discuss your recent performance."

"No," Brian said, a piece of who he'd once been clicking back into place—the recklessly driven young man who'd married an equally committed schoolteacher named Samantha, both of them fresh out of graduate school. Together they were going to take on the world and make it a better place for the children they'd dreamed of having. "You really don't, sir. I understand completely whom I've been letting down all this time."

He walked into his own office, closing and locking the door to ensure his privacy. Heading around his desk, he looked down at the schematics for the Kelsey project he'd left spread out the night before. The family's high-end choices were in line with the firm's upscale rep. Hardly any of it reflected Brian's instincts for giving the Kelseys what they wanted in a unique, modern way no one else could have designed for them.

Because Jefferson was such a high-profile catch for the firm, Whilleby had micromanaged the proposal from the moment Brian pitched it to the partners. His touch was everywhere, drowning out Brian's aesthetics. Brian had lost control of his vision, telling himself it was the price he had to pay to support his family. He'd been making similar concessions, practically from the moment he'd first joined the firm and realized that cutting-edge and environmentally friendly were things Whilleby liked a lot better in the firm's press release about Brian's background, than the partner did in Brian's day-to-day work.

Control.

When was the last time Brian had really felt it, reached for it with confidence and fought for it, knowing he had a shot in hell of coming out on top?

An image of Sam running from him at the park that morning flashed through his mind. He relived the soft sound of her and Cade talking on the patio back in January, when Brian had felt excluded from their special moment, but had shrugged it off. And then there was today at school, hearing his son crying in a closet along with a friend about the guilt and shame they'd been silently enduring for months, while Brian had thought everything would eventually right itself, as long as he kept himself and everyone else under control—meanwhile Cade was cutting class and flunking his courses, and Brian had had no clue.

And it felt as if he couldn't stop any of it now.

Flashes of memories and personal failures rushed through him with a roar that sounded like the explosion of buildings, of families, of a marriage. He braced his palms on top of the desk and the Kelsey papers, fighting to keep it together the way he had for so long, so he could give his family what they needed. What *he* needed—a safe and happy life that no one could steal away again.

Except he hadn't helped a single one of the people he loved, or even given his best to the career he'd once thrived in. He'd been going through the motions for years and tuning out the warning signs that he was failing, while snapshots of the life he'd been meant to live lingered in the back of his mind.

We're fine . . . he'd said over and over to himself and his wife.

Suddenly he was the one roaring, the sound deafening and coming from somewhere inside Brian he hadn't touched since that day in New York when he'd raced to reach Sam, after she'd finally made it out of Manhattan to Queens with her shocked, horrified students. That was the last day, the last time he could remember feeling totally alive and wanting anything except for that horrible day to never have happened to them at all.

What's the point, Brian? I'm never going to be the Sam you want me to be again . . .

I don't know how to feel what you want me to . . .

If you don't know how to break, and I can't go back to being the way I was . . . then what are we doing . . .

"Goddamn it!"

He swept his arms wide.

The Kelsey papers flew, along with his conservative desk set, the blotter, family photos Sam had lovingly framed for him, and the cold dregs of the coffee he hadn't finished drinking last night.

She was right.

Sam was right.

The world he'd so carefully navigated all this time, the unfulfilled choices he'd congratulated himself for making the best of, had been more about protecting himself than he'd wanted to admit. He and his family had been living a half-life of *his* making. They didn't talk about important things. They didn't face problems together, not even what had happened in January. Despite his hopeful words and positive attitude about the life they'd made in Chandlerville, he'd given up somewhere along the way—on himself and Sam.

A part of him *had* resented that she never really seemed to get better, no matter what he did. He'd been exhausted the morning of the bake sale, and hoping desperately for a break. So instead of listening to his wife and getting her to tell him how she was truly feeling, he'd been secretly glad for the silence that had grown between them over the years. He'd turned away from that window and the sound of her opening her heart to their son. He'd wanted to put that "big day" behind them and finally move on. He hadn't wanted to deal with all the reasons behind her continued nerves and fears.

The long-ago New York day he thought they'd turned their backs on was still testing him and Sam. The Chandler shooting was still testing them. And just when they'd needed to be at their best as a couple and as parents, everything had fallen apart.

He'd yelled at his wife for giving up. But Sam had had the courage to start over and demand more from their lives. *She'd* found the strength to reach their son again today and get Cade to open up a little.

Don't try to talk right now, honey, he remembered himself saying in the ER after the shooting. *You're not making any sense . . .*

"Goddamn it to hell!" he whispered.

How did he make this right?

He had to make this right.

It couldn't be too late for his marriage. His family. Fear and shock flooded him, powerful emotions he'd never let himself feel as bravely as his wife had, each and every day she'd found a way to keep going.

Thinking only of her and the sacrifice she'd made that morning—hurting herself by going back to school and staying for as long as she had, because Nate and Cade had needed her—Brian sat and pulled out the keyboard tray for his computer. With a click of his mouse and a few keystrokes, he logged into the firm's e-mail system and then his account.

He directed the message to Whilleby, copying the other partners. His fingers began typing the message before the thoughts could fully form in his mind. He could feel the perspiration coating his upper body, soaking into his crisply starched shirt.

This wasn't smart.

It wasn't responsible.

He was damaging the professional relationships that had been the backbone, the secure core of his and Sam's move to Atlanta. But this was exactly what he needed to do for his family. He'd known it since speaking with Kristen, and since trying outside that conference room, and failing for the second time that morning, to speak calmly with his wife about their future.

It had taken him long enough, but Brian could feel himself accepting the truth that *he* hadn't been okay for a long time.

Now all he had to figure out was how to win back his wife, so he and the woman he loved could finally begin healing together.

Chapter Ten

"I'd like to see my wife," Sam heard Brian say. "Could you get her for me?"

Julia had left Sam to rest, while she prepared whatever she needed to for one of the fabulous dinners she cooked each night for her family, whether Walter or the boys turned up for the meal these days or not. Sam hadn't been able to nap, her mind refusing to settle.

She'd needed to regain enough energy somehow to be there when her boys got off the bus. She'd promised herself she'd find a way to approach Brian when he got home from work. She wanted to apologize for not giving him a chance at the school. She wanted to listen to what he had to say. She wanted this to work, the hesitant step toward reconciling he seemed to sincerely want to take.

Now there Brian was, pursuing her still when he should be back at work, while Sam hovered in the hallway to the left of Julia's front door, out of sight but close enough to hang on every word.

"She's resting, Brian," their friend said, instead of welcoming him in and handing him a glass of sweet tea, the way she once would have. "She's exhausted from this morning. I helped Kristen talk her into going, and I don't think—"

"Get Samantha for me," Brian interrupted, "or I'll come in there and find her myself. Sam?" he called, loud enough to be heard throughout the house.

As if in a trance, she found herself standing in Julia's immaculately decorated foyer. Her headache suddenly gone, she stepped farther away from the hallway and stared at her husband as if she'd never seen him before. It had been forever since she'd heard him sound anything but accommodating to anyone. He looked younger, too. Rougher. More . . . vital than he had since their move from New York.

He looked like the man she'd fallen in love with.

"I'm going to have to ask you to leave." Julia was closing the door as she spoke. "Like I said, Sam's resting, and everyone needs to stop pushing her to—"

"I'm never going to stop pushing." He placed his palm on the door, his gaze locking with Sam's. "I'm sorry, but this isn't just about our marriage. It's about Cade, too. Sam, please . . ." His voice caught, tugging at Sam's heart. "Please talk with me."

"Is . . ." She stepped closer, stopping beside Julia. "Is he okay? You're home early from work. Has something else happened?"

Brian checked his watch. "The boys' bus won't be here for another hour. I wanted to speak with you first, so we can deal with our son together."

We . . .

Together . . .

Instead of relentlessly optimistic, Brian sounded frazzled. Maybe even a little scared.

"He had such a hard time this morning." Sam couldn't stop thinking about it. "He did such a great job with Nate, but there's so much he's not letting us know."

You're really something, Mallory had said the morning of the shooting.

You've been a hero for me for twelve years, Kristen Hemmings had gushed.

Except Sam's son was hiding his darkest fears from her, as if he didn't trust her with them. She'd thought she was doing the right thing, staying with Julia and putting some distance between her and Brian and the mistakes they were making. She'd wanted to protect her boys. And look at what had happened instead.

"I spoke with Kristen after you left," Brian said. "There are some things we need to tackle together, if we're going to help Cade through this. Things I . . . can't handle on my own. Our son needs you, Sam. I need you."

She blinked at the sound of her husband asking for her help, instead of shielding her from whatever problem needed to be dealt with. She glanced behind her, realizing that Julia had found somewhere else to be.

"Come walk with me." Brian held out his hand. His fingers were shaking. "We have to do something about Cade before we lose even more of him."

Slipping her hand into her husband's, Sam let herself be drawn from her friend's house into the warm spring sunlight. She was momentarily blinded by the dazzling day.

Brian's car was in the Davises' driveway instead of their own. He'd driven straight there after doing whatever he'd done to arrange the rest of the day off from the firm that frowned on downtime and family time or any time that wasn't contributing to their bottom line.

He tugged her closer as they walked down the lane, heading toward the larger lots and houses where there was less through traffic to deal with. Not that there was much traffic at all this time of day. Mimosa Lane's adults were often at work well after kids sprinted off their buses at the end of the school day.

Sam's mind wouldn't stop racing, distracted by thoughts about their neighbors and other people's lives and families. Anything but pushing Brian to talk. She was suddenly certain she didn't want to hear what he was so determined to say—after months of her desperately wanting his undivided attention.

"Are you okay?" he asked.

No. She was feeling codependent and weak. She'd begged since January for his honesty. And now that she seemed to have it, a part of her wanted to bury herself in his strong arms so he could make reality go away again. When she tried to pull back, he wouldn't let her go. He sighed. The thumb of his left hand smoothed over hers as they walked through the flickering shadows cast by the tall pines ringing the yards on either side of the street.

"I know I said all the wrong things at school," he said. "And this morning, and at the hospital, and every time we've talked since the shooting. Even before then. I know you're hurting and I want to help, but I don't know how, or maybe I don't want to know what you really need, because every time I try to make things okay, I only seem to make them worse . . ."

Sam caught herself from responding right away. She squeezed his fingers, trying to think of a way to explain what she wasn't sure he'd ever understand. She let go of his hands and crossed her arms, shivering amidst the warmth surrounding them.

"I need you to do me a favor," she said. "Or we're not going to get very far with this talk, either."

It wasn't an ultimatum. Not really. It was her line in the sand. One she'd marked off months ago at the hospital, and she wouldn't back down.

"Anything," Brian said, so eager and sincere she was dying to believe him.

"Stop using that word. *Okay.* Stop saying it, please. When we're alone, when we're not in front of the boys or our friends or anyone else, stop asking me to be *okay* for you."

He pulled her to a stop beside him.

"I wasn't." He blocked her, when she would have walked past him. "I'm concerned about you. I have been all day. I was simply—"

"Asking if I was *okay*, as if being okay is the goal. And once I get there, we'll finally be making progress."

"No. In fact I came here to . . ." He raked a hand through his hair. "So let me get this straight. You don't want me to care about you now? Is that it? Because I came here for Cade, but also to ask what you needed from me, Sam. I'm willing to do whatever it takes, but I don't know how to stop caring about you getting better."

"I love that you care about me." Except now she was desperate to be back in Julia's guest room bed, hiding from the love of her life and this moment and how their relationship seemed to be hanging in the balance. "I love you, Brian. But trying to be *okay* all these years has destroyed too much. And whether it makes sense or not, whether you mean it or not, I need you to stop saying that word. Maybe being messed up is better than being okay. Have you stopped to think about that? Look at what Cade has been hiding from us. Being okay and careful and not falling apart is what our family does, but look at what avoiding the hard things has done. Forget about me. Look at how we've taught our son to deal with his problems!"

She was shouting, loud enough that anyone outside for blocks—or inside with their windows open, enjoying the beautiful spring day—could hear. But was it loud enough to finally get through to the man she'd built her life around?

Brian looked ready to yell himself. Then his features became a battle for control, as if he didn't know what to feel or say or be. The stranger staring down at her was nothing like the confident, carefree man she'd fallen for the first night they'd met.

After a childhood spent loving and trying to live up to the expectations of perfect parents who'd valued above everything else their perfect home and perfect social connections in an upscale, moneyed Connecticut suburb, Sam had escaped to NYU with a full-ride scholarship for her undergraduate and master's degrees. She'd been living a life that felt on the cusp of being what she'd always imagined the *real* world would feel like. Brian had stumbled into that reality as the buddy of one of her male friends, at a dinner party Sam was hosting—if offering cheap wine, boiling pasta, and heating Ragú counted as dinner.

The eclectic mix of guests had been perfect, the conversation had been lively. Brian had been the last one to leave her apartment that night . . . because, he'd said right then and there, he'd wanted to get to know Sam better, more than any other woman he'd met.

They'd walked to a nearby diner and talked all night: about their equally disconnected families, their degrees, their dreams, and their determination to make a difference in the world. He hadn't laughed, as her parents had, at her insistence that even though teachers were underpaid and overworked, it had to be the greatest job of all, feeling every day as if you were making a difference, changing the world one eager mind at a time. He was aiming for the same things with his architecture—wanting to specialize in designing and constructing green homes and communities and even corporate spaces. Making a difference by making where people worked and lived and played both beautiful and environmentally responsible.

He'd pursued his passion after they'd graduated, gotten married, and begun their careers. They both had. And they'd still stay up all night as often as their busy schedules allowed, talking and loving each other and drinking wine that wasn't so cheap anymore, and believing that they had the secrets to this life licked. They'd been a team once. A perfect fit. Then their rarefied world had exploded around them, literally, and the differences between them had begun to stack up, higher and higher until ignoring them had been the only way to stay together.

Starting with their move to Chandlerville, when rough-around-the-edges Brian had flawlessly adapted to Mimosa Lane's upscale, suburban culture—for her. And Sam had morphed, she was very much afraid, into a neurotic replica of the nervous, needy woman who'd raised him. And now she was making him second-guess himself and everything they'd ever had.

"I wish I could tell you I was okay," she said, "and really mean it." He was staring down at her with a blank expression on his face, as if her honesty were crushing him. "I wish we were still like we were when we first met, when we were kids, before we had kids of our own. Free and confident and invincible, instead of so very careful. But we have to accept that big parts of those people are gone, Brian. We need to figure out how to handle who we are now, what we've become, even if this isn't where we thought moving to Atlanta would get us."

It was everything she'd meant to say that day in the hospital. It hadn't been a conscious choice, asking him for a separation. It had been a reflex, a panicked attempt to get him to see her, really see her for the first time in years. For days afterward, she'd waited for him to get angry, to talk her out of it, to shake her and fight for her, and listen to her, mess and all, never dreaming that it would take them three months to get here.

Brian reached for her now, tugging her closer. Their foreheads touched in the sweet way they'd once greeted each other—and said good-bye—every day.

"I don't know what I can handle anymore, Samantha." Her full name sounded like heaven tumbling from his mouth. It had shortened over the years to Sam, the name everyone else but her parents had always called her. But with Brian, at first, it had always been Samantha. And he'd always made it, and her, sound so special, so beautiful, every time he said it.

"You don't have to know," she insisted, desperate for him to believe her. "I get it. I'm driving you and the boys crazy. I know I haven't been there for Cade, not the way he's needed me. I don't blame him for not talking to me."

"Stop it." Brian shook her. Staring down at her now was that young crusader she'd first met. "None of this is your fault. We both did this. And Cade *is* talking to you. You got him to open up today. I never could have done that. He blames himself for what happened to Bubba and to Troy—and to Nate. I've been living with him for three months, and I didn't see it. I was too absorbed with our problems, and I wanted to believe he was doing fine. Or maybe I couldn't think straight about anything anymore, not with you gone. You're . . . everything for us, Sam. It's all wrapped up in you. Can't you see that? Without you, none of the rest of this makes any damn sense."

They were locked in a bone-crushing embrace before she could think what to say, kissing each other like their first kiss outside that all-night diner in Manhattan.

She'd never remember who reached for whom first. But she'd also never forget the perfect feel of this moment that a part of her had worried they'd never find. They were together again. One. Connected on so many levels that each brush of their lips and tongues and hands as they roamed the other's body was a physical representation of the love coursing through them, between them, from one of them to the other and back.

This. This was what it had always been like, as if long before they'd ever met, they'd been destined to fit perfectly with each other. As if they'd searched their whole lives until that moment at her shabby dinner party, when something had clicked and everything they should have been had suddenly seemed possible. Because they were no longer alone, and the someone they'd been put on this earth to share their lives with was finally there.

And that someone was holding her again as if he'd never let her go. The same man who'd let her drift away for years was molding her pliant body into his harder one. He was wanting her with a fierce, desperate need. As if he couldn't help but curve his hand down her spine and then her bottom, lifting and pulling her against him until they both gasped at the electricity that was building, arcing.

"God . . ." Brian whispered against her ear, sending goose bumps everywhere. "Samantha . . ."

"I love you," she whispered back, while she slowly, determinedly began to create space between them. Air. She needed air and enough distance for her to think.

Breathing hard just like she was, her husband was staring at her lips. His gaze rose to meet hers.

"You love me," he said, "but you're still not coming home, are you?"

She shook her head, resolved.

She thought of Julia, who was still hoping that Walter would come around on his own without her having to take a stand. Walter, who loved his wife more than life itself. Only he'd let drinking to escape the horror of what had happened at Chandler become a threat to them both. They needed to talk about some difficult things, but they were both too afraid to. Maybe Julia and Walter were too close to the pain they were feeling to be able to find their way through this together. Maybe Sam and Brian had been, too, until she'd stepped away from the wandering path they'd been locked into.

All she knew was that she couldn't move back home. Not until she was certain they'd found enough of themselves again, individually, to make being together really work.

"Because I use the wrong word when I try to tell you how worried I am about you, and how much I care?" Brian was flash-fire furious. His hands balled into fists at his sides. "Damn it, Sam. I'm doing the best I can, and I know it's not good enough. But I don't have anything left. I've been fighting this for so long, trying to figure out what to do to make everything o—" He stopped himself from saying that hated word. He took a deep breath before continuing. "I can't remember when I wasn't trying to figure out how to make things better for all of us. And I know I've done too much of that on my own. I know we need to communicate better, and I need to listen more. So, talk. Tell me what you need, and I'll do it."

She took one of his fists and rubbed her thumb over his knuckles. She smiled up at him, hope filling her heart.

"This," she said, tears shimmering across her vision until Brian became a kaleidoscope image, sunlit, of everything she'd always known he could be. "Honesty. Acceptance. And, yes, anger and failure. We're both failing at this, honey. I need you to accept that, too, or we're going to keep making the same mistakes and one day . . ."

"One day you're going to turn this *time* you said you needed into a permanent separation."

He pulled away.

She didn't tell him she'd never meant to say those words, or that being away from him was the last thing she wanted, ever, when he and the boys would always be her home.

"I can't go back to the way things were," she insisted.

"And I'm not asking you to. But our family needs you now, Sam. I need you."

"I was disappearing, Brian. Most days I feel like I still am." She didn't know who she was anymore. Who *they* were. "And I'm no good for you or the boys like this. When I woke up in the hospital, the first instinct that came to me when I saw my husband standing beside my bed, trying to console me, was to get away from you. I have to figure that out. *We* have to figure that out, or I'll just keep hurting everyone."

Instead of growing angrier, he took her hand in his. Seconds passed. Minutes. Until every emotion dragging at Sam faded, except the need to keep feeling her husband like this, peaceful and accepting beside her.

"You said we needed to talk about Cade?" she asked. "Is it about what he said to me this morning, when we were talking with Nate?"

Brian shook his head. He tugged her to his side and started walking again. They were almost at the park now, where things had gotten so ugly between them so early that morning. A breeze kicked up, rosy and fresh and new, like spring itself.

"He's been skipping school," Brian said softly.

"What?" Dread filled Sam. Neither of their kids had ever needed the kind of supervision that was required with children who didn't want to learn. Both Cade and Joshua had loved school from their very first day of kindergarten.

"He's been forging notes from home, complete with my signature, saying that he's not doing well and needs time away from class."

"Brian . . ." Sam stumbled.

Her husband wrapped her in a hug, resting his cheek against the top of her head, continuing to walk beside her. "He's in trouble, Sam. I have no idea where he's been when he's not at school. He's missed so much class, and now he's failed or skipped every one of his midterm exams. He might not graduate sixth grade without summer school if we don't get him back on track. We have to talk with him. But I . . ." Brian was holding on to her as desperately as when they'd been kissing. And it felt just as good, just as right, regardless of the circumstances. "I don't know what to say to him. I haven't for months. I've messed this all up. I told myself I could handle it, and that you'd be back soon and everything would go back to normal, and now it's out of control. Please, Sam. Come home with me, at least for this afternoon. We need to talk with Cade together, before things get any worse."

Chapter Eleven

Cade walked into his house with Joshua bouncing along beside him, the same way his little brother always did. Because for Joshie, nothing was wrong that Mom's cooking and one of Dad's *okay* thumbs-up and a new box of LEGOs couldn't fix. His little brother had chattered all the way home on the bus, while Cade had been too scared to say a word.

He'd been scared of coming home. He'd been scared the whole time he'd stayed at school. He was still mad at himself and Nate and his parents and now his brother.

All day at school he'd thought Nate might come back to class, but he hadn't. Then Cade had felt sick about what his parents had heard him say in the closet, only they hadn't heard everything yet. All day, he'd thought they'd come get him. Or that his mom would be waiting when he and Joshua got home, to pester him with more questions he didn't want to answer.

Only he and his brother had had to let themselves inside using the keypad on the garage door. All the other doors had been locked still, the way Dad left them every morning. No one else was home. There were no snacks laid out when they got to the kitchen.

Mom had always been there in the afternoon, the same as before the shooting. She'd always ask about school and home-work, even though Cade was a pain these days and mostly ignored her. Today he'd thought she'd be there for sure, after she'd said she wanted to help him, and not just Nate.

"This is just weird." His little brother dropped his backpack in the middle of the kitchen and pulled himself up on an island stool. "Weirder than no breakfast. What's going on?"

Cade dumped his stuff in the same spot as his brother and trudged to the pantry. He pulled out the first two boxes he found and held them up.

"Cheez Doodles or Fruit Roll-Ups?" he asked.

"I want a grilled cheese. Mom's grilled cheese and tomato soup."

"Cheez Doodles it is." Cade slapped the box on the counter in front of Joshua. He headed to the cabinet for glasses, and then the refrigerator for milk.

He could still feel his mom next to him in the closet, and her leg resting against his. He could still picture her looking worried for Nate in the conference room with Mrs. Turner, and looking worried for Cade when she'd glanced over at him and he hadn't let her know he was watching her.

Joshua ripped open his box of snacks. The kid drank the milk Cade put in front of him, too, without saying anything else. And his chatterbox little brother always had something to say.

Cade dove into the chewy fruit things, leaning against the counter by the sink instead of sitting with Joshua. He didn't want anything to eat, but that would make his brother ask even more questions. Cade wanted to hide in his room, but Joshua would just bang on his door, wanting to know what was wrong. And then their dad would get home, and *that* was when the real questions would start.

Or maybe not. And that would be even worse. Because after today Cade didn't want to hide what had happened with Troy anymore, but maybe no one really cared. Maybe no one would come and find him, the way he'd followed Nate into the closet so Nate wouldn't feel alone when he was feeling so bad. And the way Mom had followed them both in there, and then Dad had followed her to school. Maybe no one wanted to follow Cade after hearing what he'd done, no matter what Mom had said about it not being his fault. Was that why he'd gotten away with everything so far, even the things his parents didn't know about yet?

"Did something happen at school today?" Joshua asked through a mouthful of fake cheese.

"No."

"Then why are you acting so weird?"

"I'm not."

"You're being nice to me, and you're never nice to me after school. Are you in trouble or something?"

"No."

"Are too. What did you do? Because you know I'm going to find out. Everyone can hear everything in this house. Why do you think Mom and Dad never fight when we're here? Did you do something bad? Is that why Mom hasn't been here all day today?"

"God! No, you little brat."

Cade snatched the Cheez Doodles away from his brother and pulled a fistful out of the box. He shoved them into his mouth.

"Then why do you sound like you're going to cry?" Joshua licked orange dust off his fingers.

Which almost did make Cade cry, because he really wished his mom were there to tell Joshie to use a napkin. Or to tell Cade he'd messed up big-time with Troy, and that he should have ratted on the kid when he'd had the chance. And, no matter what she'd said at school, that it was all his fault Bubba was dead and that Nate had been shot and that everything was so messed up now, because he should have told them everything sooner, while someone still cared. Only he hadn't, and now everything was ruined. Even his family.

A Cheez Doodle caught in his throat, along with all the things he couldn't say to his brother and wished he'd said to his mom and dad that morning. His stomach burned, twisted, pushed to his throat. He tossed the box into the sink and raced for the downstairs bathroom, barely making it before he hurled.

His snack, his lunch, his breakfast, every awful feeling he'd been feeling about himself and his friends and his mom and dad . . . It all came up, until he was hanging over the toilet, his hands on his knees, trying to breathe and to make it stop. When it finally did, he flushed and washed his hands. He rinsed out his mouth and told himself he couldn't hide there in the stinky bathroom for the rest of the day.

Joshua at least would come find him eventually. In fact, why hadn't he already? Cade walked back to the kitchen to see what was up, telling himself he wasn't going to let whatever came out of his brother's mouth next mess with him. But when he got there, Joshua was already talking—to Nate.

Cade's friend was sitting at the island with Cade's kid brother, as if it were no big deal that Nate hadn't been over since he'd gotten shot.

"What are you doing here?" Cade asked from the hallway.

Joshua stopped talking.

He and Nate looked at Cade.

"My mom said I could come over for a few minutes if I wanted to," Nate said. "I told her your mom would be here."

"Well, she's not." Cade was angry again, even though he was glad to see his friend. He was still feeling sick. He should have stayed in the bathroom. "So I guess you should go back home, before you get into trouble."

Nate got off his stool.

Joshua stared at both of them.

"I know I've been pretty lame." Nate dug his hands into his jeans pockets, making Cade realize he'd done the same thing. "I've been pretty pissed about everything. But I . . ."

Nate's voice was getting that way again—like in the closet. Like he felt the way Cade felt when he cried at night and no one else could hear.

"I haven't been pissed at you," Nate said. "I don't blame you for what Troy did."

"Yeah, right." Then why had he ignored Cade ever since the shooting, when Cade hadn't been able to talk to anyone else about anything, and he'd needed his friend? Even when he'd cut class and camped outside Nate's house half the day, only to walk back to school to catch the bus home with Joshua . . . He'd known there was no getting Nate's friendship back, but he'd needed to be close to his friend anyway. "Whatever. It's not like I care."

Nate stopped looking like he was going to cry and started looking like he wanted to beat on someone.

"You said you cared this morning," he said. "But you're just weaseling out now, is that it? 'Cause that's what you're best at."

"Like you're best at forgetting who your friends are?" Cade glared at his little brother, who'd gotten off his stool, too, and was headed Cade's way.

The kid stopped between him and Nate.

"What's wrong?" Joshie asked.

"Everything." Cade was tired of answering questions that weren't important, when no one was asking the right ones.

"I didn't forget you or anyone else," Nate said. "I just couldn't talk about it."

"Who can?"

Cade's mom and dad never talked about what was really bothering them. And Cade hadn't talked to them before today about the shooting. But Nate was different. Cade had really thought he and Nate would be different.

"I've tried," his friend said in his crying voice again.

"You mean like you tried to open your window every night I came over the first week you were home from the hospital, and your parents weren't letting you see anyone? What about all the other nights, when I was stupid enough to keep trying? When I was thinking you blamed me for everything and never wanted to talk to me again, because you never called or texted or said anything to me? Not even on the bus this morning. Not even in class. Like we didn't know each other anymore. Like we'd never been friends at all."

Joshua was tugging on Cade's arm. Cade realized he was walking toward Nate, his fists not in his pockets anymore. His baby brother was trying to keep him from taking a swing at his best friend.

"But you've been talking to my *mom* about everything?" he said. "You didn't even talk to me today in the closet. You sat there, staring like a dork until my mom showed up. You didn't want me, your best friend. You wanted *her*. She's the reason you're here now, right? She's the one you finally showed up here to talk to."

"Stop yelling at me, man." Nate had stepped closer, too. They were nose to nose.

"Then stop being such a girl and just say it. You blame me. It's all my fault you got shot."

"I didn't say that. Stop saying that. I just—"

"Chicken shit," Cade spit at him. "You're too chicken to say it. You still blame me. You'll always blame me."

"You're the chicken shit!"

Nate's fist came up fast. Pain exploded on the side of Cade's face, and then he was swinging, too, making contact on his friend's body somewhere hard enough to make his hand hurt worse than his face.

Both of them went down, still throwing punches, rolling around on the wood floor. And the whole time, Joshua was dragging at Cade's arm and then Nate's and then Cade's again, yelling, "Stop it!" over and over, while Cade couldn't stop yelling himself.

"Say it!" he kept saying. "Say it was all my fault, and *you're* the hero. Say I got you and Bubba shot. Say I should have stopped Troy after we left the bathroom. Say it. Say it, you chicken shit!"

Cade was crying now. And so were Nate and Joshua. And none of it was making the hurt inside better. Nothing was making it go away—the sound in Cade's head of Troy firing his dad's stupid gun, and the squeaking sound Bubba had made when he'd looked down at the blood all over his T-shirt, just before he'd fallen to the lunchroom floor.

"Say it!" Cade screamed. "Say it and make it stop . . ."

Stronger hands than his little brother's clamped onto Cade's arm and pulled him to his feet, away from Nate.

"What the hell is going on?" his dad demanded.

Cade's mom stood behind him, her hand over her mouth.

***

Sam and Brian had let themselves into the kitchen from the backyard, expecting to find their boys doing their homework at the island like they did every day after school. Or at worst, they'd be lounging on the sofa in the family room watching cartoons because Sam was late.

Instead, she and her husband had walked in on bedlam, with Cade shouting things at Nate that broke her heart all over again for the ways she and Brian hadn't been able to reach him since the shooting.

"Enough!" Brian shouted, while he tried to keep the still-struggling boys away from each other.

"Mom!" Joshua raced to her and wrapped his arms around her in a hug she never wanted to let go of.

"What happened?" she asked. And what was Nate doing there, when he should be home with Beverly?

"Nothing," the older boys said in unison.

She looked down at her youngest, who glanced at Cade, who was glowering at Nate.

"Nothing." Joshie hugged her tighter.

Brian sighed and turned Nate loose. "I think you should be getting home. Does your mother even know you're here?"

Nate nodded his head. There was a swelling bruise on his cheek, and he looked for all the world as if he wanted Cade to keep pounding on him.

Sam's son looked just as bad. Beaten up. Guilty. Sick. Cade looked sick, his complexion ashen the way it sometimes got when he had the stomach flu. He watched his friend turn to go.

"Nate," he said in a watery voice, as Nate reached for the back door.

Nate didn't answer, but he stopped and waited.

Everyone in the kitchen waited, Sam and Brian and Joshua, hoping that these two could find their way back to being friends again.

"I really am sorry," her son said, fingering his own cheek and then his fat lip.

His friend nodded. Then Nate left, slamming the door and leaving a shell-shocked kitchen in his wake.

"Mom?" Joshua asked. "Why's everyone acting so weird?"

Sam looked down and forced herself not to mutter the first reassuring excuse that came to mind. She knelt and took Joshua's face between her hands. Brian held on to Cade's arm to keep him from bolting.

"Because we're having a tough time right now," she said to Joshua. "Aren't we? It's been hard ever since the shooting. And no one's been dealing with things well around here. That has to stop, so things like this won't happen anymore."

Joshua nodded. There were a thousand questions swirling in his eyes, but he hugged her again instead of asking them, making her so grateful to Brian for getting her back here, when she'd been half planning to wait until morning to face Cade, once this crazy day was a memory and maybe she wouldn't feel so out of control.

"I'm sorry it's been so hard," she said to everyone, checking to see whether Cade was listening. He wasn't looking at her, but his shoulders rose and fell on a sigh that spoke volumes. "We need to start dealing with a lot of things, don't we? About what's going on with me. And you boys. All of us. We need to talk until we figure things out as a family. No one is in this alone—no matter what we're feeling. We need to trust that. We need to trust each other."

Trust could be the hardest thing in the world to get back, once you'd let it go. Even with family. *Especially* with family.

Joshua nodded again. When Brian let go of Cade's arm, their son stayed where he was instead of making a break for his room or outside.

"Could you head upstairs?" she asked Joshua. "Start on your homework. One of us will be there in a bit to check on you. But we need some time with Cade first."

Joshua looked at his brother until Cade looked back. Something strong and unspoken passed between them, these two guys who often fought more than they played. But they always made up, and they were always there for each other, making Sam so proud in the midst of so many regrets.

Cade nodded.

Joshie grabbed his backpack and trudged up the kitchen stairs toward his room, casting a lingering look over his shoulder.

"I want to do my homework, too," Cade said.

"You mean you actually went to class today, after your mom and I left the school?" Brian sounded frustrated, and very, very worried.

Of course, frustrated was all their son picked up on.

"What do you care!" Cade shouted at his father. He sneered at Sam, but there wasn't much meanness behind it. He sounded more lost than angry. "What do either of you care?"

He made a dash for the door Nate had escaped through.

"Not so fast." Sam blocked his path. "I let you get away from me at school, because I didn't want to embarrass you in front of everyone and you needed a break. But we're home now, and we're going to talk."

"Home?" He slouched against the kitchen cabinet. "Like you're staying? That kind of home? You weren't here for breakfast.

You weren't here to help us with homework when we got off of the bus. You weren't here after saying how much you wanted to help me at school. Since when is this *your* home anymore?"

"Don't talk to your mother that way." Brian pointed a finger at the stool closest to them. "Sit down and have a little respect while we try to figure some of this out."

Sulking, Cade trudged around the kitchen's island and sat. Sam took the stool beside him. Brian stood on the other side of the island and leaned both hands against the counter.

"Your mother wasn't here this afternoon because she and I have been talking," he hedged. His quick glance acknowledged that she might very well still be at Julia's, hiding from the world, if he hadn't all but dragged her away. "And her being here every time you turn around, to make breakfast and after-school snacks and to check up on the homework you've been lying to us about doing, *is not* all that makes her a part of this family. You know that, Cade. You know how much she means to all of us, and how hard it's been around here with her gone . . ." Brian cleared his throat, looking down and spreading his hands on the counter before reclaiming his son's attention. "I think you owe her an apology before we go any further."

Sam inhaled to say that no apology was necessary. But her husband's next glare was for her. She narrowed her eyes at him, but she kept her silence. Cade was too absorbed in his own misery to catch the exchange.

"I'm sorry," he said to his lap. "I know it's my fault you got so upset and had to move out. I know you don't want to come back. I don't . . . I don't want to be here anymore, either."

"None of this is your fault, honey." Sam wiped at her eyes. She looked to Brian for help. What did she say? Now that Cade was finally talking, what did they say to help him get past this idea that keeping quiet about Troy's family situation meant he was to blame for what his friend did? "And I've been working hard every day to be able to come back. There's nothing I want more than to be living here with you and Joshua and your dad again, I swear."

She glanced at her husband, willing him to believe her, despite how confused and angry he must still be. Crossing his arms, he nodded, and his acceptance of the promise she'd just made their child felt even better than the hugs and the kiss they'd shared on their walk.

"Where have you been the days you've ditched school?" Brian asked, his voice rough with his own fight for control.

"Nowhere . . ." Cade said. "Nate's mostly, just hanging behind the trees in his backyard in case he came outside to play. But he never did. It's not like I wanted to be there, while he keeps ignoring me like we were never friends. It's just . . . I couldn't stay away . . ."

"Where do you want to be?" Sam asked, sighing when her son shook his head, staring down at the island without blinking, while tears pooled in his eyes. "Do you want to be back at the school that morning, with Troy," she pressed, "so you and Nate can find some way to stop him?"

Her son looked up, surprised.

He nodded, swiping at his tears with the sleeve of his shirt.

"That's what all the adults want, too," Brian said. "The ones like Nate's parents, who are yelling at the school board and the teachers about how something should have been done to stop Troy. People are blaming Roy Griffin and Ms. Hemmings and Mrs. Baxter and anyone else they can think of for what one mixed-up kid did, because they think that will fix what happened. But nothing will go back and take that gun out of Troy's hand. Not the school board firing someone, or the Dickersons suing Troy's parents, or you saying it was all your fault. Did you know? Did you know Troy had a gun in his backpack? Did anyone at the school know what he'd decided to do?"

Cade's eyes were bottomless with guilt.

"I didn't," he said. "I swear I didn't. But I should have. Or I should have told someone how upset he was, so someone else could have stopped him. Nate wanted me to, but I . . ." He looked at Sam, then at his lap again. "I didn't want to mess up Mom's day at the bake sale. I thought we could handle Troy, Nate and me. But when Troy started shooting, I just ducked while Nate and Mom stood up to him. I . . ."

"You protected Sally," Sam reminded him. "You stayed on the floor with her, and put your body between her and Troy's gun. I saw you, and it scared me to death, how brave you were being." Sam gripped the edge of the counter, reliving those moments when she'd been certain her child would be gunned down in front of her. "You did what your instincts told you to do. How does that make any of this your fault?"

"You and Nate were hurt."

"Because of Troy, not because of you."

"But you moved across the street, and Nate wouldn't talk to me, no matter how hard I tried to get him to. Not until his parents made him come to school today."

"Because we're all hurting." Sam covered her son's hand with her own. "You and me and Dad and Nate and his parents and everyone else in town who knows you guys, we're all hurting and not handling it very well." She glanced at Brian again. The love and understanding and respect she saw in his expression—for her—was everything. He'd looked at her that way at the school, too, when she and the boys had first stepped out of the closet—as if her husband were really seeing her again, for the first time in what felt like forever. "That's the way it is a lot of times, when scary things happen. Folks don't know what to do. They're upset. They can't make things better. So they go looking for someone to blame—and sometimes they blame themselves, like you are."

"I'm sorry we've let you down, buddy," Brian said. "We thought we were giving you space. Just like I've been giving your mom space since January. And I've been wrong, about both of you. I should have found a way to reach you." He looked at Sam. "Ever since the shooting, I should have listened more to what your mother's been trying to tell me. I think . . . I think maybe I was afraid, too. But we can't let that stop us anymore. We have to do whatever it takes to get better, all of us. We have to face this together, as a family, from now on."

Cade wiped at his eyes again.

So did Sam.

Brian, too.

No one said anything for a long time, the gentle moment a tiny flicker of healing all its own.

"Why have you been skipping school?" she finally asked her son. "You blew off three of your midterms, honey. And you couldn't have studied for the other ones, with the scores you made on them. You had to know what that would do to your grades, and that the school would talk to your dad and me about it."

Cade shrugged again.

"Maybe you wanted them to talk to us?" Brian asked.

Another shrug.

"Because you couldn't?" Sam added. "You didn't know how to talk about what you were going through, so you were hoping someone else would realize there was a problem and make you?"

Like Sam had been waiting all these years, hiding how lost she still felt, even from herself. Had she been expecting Brian to read her mind or force her to come clean or just understand and somehow magically make everything better, without her having to face the things *she* had to?

"Like Troy didn't know how to tell anyone about how he was hurting?" Brian asked. "So he kept hurting until it made him do those horrible things he thought would make it stop."

Cade stared at his dad, shaking his head. "I'm not like Troy. I'd never—"

"Of course you wouldn't." Sam pulled her son into a sideways hug she expected him to resist. He didn't, even though his shoulders were too stiff for her to cuddle him close the way she longed to. "Of course you'd never hurt anyone that way. But you've been hurting yourself, honey, rather than getting the help you need. And even if you don't know what you need, you have to trust your dad and me to be here for you. Whatever you say, whatever you do, it's okay with us." Sam cringed as she said the word that she'd banned her husband from using. When she glanced at Brian over their son's head, a world of understanding passed between them. "We'll be here for you, whatever you're going through, and we'll help any way we can. But you have to give us a chance."

"The way you did when you moved out?" Cade jerked away. "You're not even here anymore. You're not giving us a chance. So why should we give *you* one?"

"Your mother gave me years of chances," Brian said in her defense. "She's staying with Mrs. Julia because she couldn't get better here. Because together, neither one of us wanted to admit how bad things had gotten."

"But I'm always here for you, Cade," Sam said, falling in love with her husband all over again, even though there was still so much for them to sort out. "And if you need some time, too, away from school, then you don't have to go back for a while. Just like Nate doesn't. In fact . . ." A flicker of an idea began to form in her mind, a crazy thought that she shoved away for the moment. "Never mind. Just know that whatever you need, we're here for you. There's nothing we can't fix together, as a family, as long as you talk to us about it."

Cade glared at his father. "So now you're glad Mom doesn't live with us?"

"No." Brian stepped around the island and put his hand on his son's shoulder. "I'd give anything to have her back with us tonight. But being at Mrs. Julia's is good for your mother right now, until we help each other fix a few more things. Things that I have to work out as much as she does. But we *are* working on it, and I'm listening to her like I wasn't before. I'm listening to both of you from here on out. We love you, whatever else is going on. Can you understand that, Cade? Will you let us help you through this?"

Cade looked back and forth between them, still scowling.

Then he propped his elbows on the counter and rested his head in his hand, exhaustion seeming to swamp him from one heartbeat to the next.

He cut Sam a scared look, like he didn't really want to know, as he asked, "So how much trouble am I in at school?"

Chapter Twelve

"Sam?" Kristen said, after answering Sam's knock on her front door. There was a touch of surprise and something else in her voice.

She towered over Sam, tall and strikingly beautiful in that athletic way Sam longed for. Standing beside Chandler's AP, Sam always felt like an elf.

"I'm sorry to bust in on you like this," Sam said in a rush. Staying put was much harder than she'd thought it would be when she'd pulled into Kristen's driveway. Racing back to her car and returning to Mimosa Lane sounded far more appealing. "Is this a bad time?"

"Yes," Kristen said. "I mean, no . . ." She waved Sam inside. "I was on my way to tonight's school board meeting, but I have a few minutes before I have to leave."

The school board meeting. How could Sam have forgotten, after harassing Julia about it earlier? She followed Kristen into her modern, split-level condo, laying her purse on the table in the small foyer.

"You were on your way out." Sam felt terrible. "I can come back."

Of course Kristen would be at tonight's meeting. Depending on what the board decided, once they got around to doing more than holding hearings and listening to irate citizens the way they had been for more than a month, she might be out of a job come fall. "I can come back."

"No, really," Kristen said. "Can I get you something cool to drink? I don't have to be the first person at the weenie roast where they're angling to fry my bacon. I'm thirsty. How 'bout you?"

She led Sam into a bright, friendly kitchen. The indirect lighting was natural, Sam realized—from skylights overhead and the picture window above the sink that Kristen was using as a terrarium of sorts. Tiny succulents and bonsai trees were thriving there. They looked so perky and content. Sam couldn't think of a better botanical fit for Kristen's typically lively personality.

"Beer?" Chandlerville's G-rated assistant principal asked. She pulled a bottle of German ale from her stainless-steel refrigerator and popped the cap with a vintage-looking opener attached to the cabinet at her hip.

"Sure." Sam's stomach felt like a swamp, but why not? Something to soothe the day's never-ending emotional roller coaster sounded like heaven.

She'd spent the afternoon trying to talk with Cade about his problems at school and accomplishing very little. He was still too upset to focus. She'd helped Joshua with his latest LEGO masterpiece. Then she'd left Brian to get dinner ready, while she'd said she was returning to Julia's to lie down. Instead, she'd gotten in her car and headed over here, dubious about what she'd come to speak with the AP about. But she wouldn't be able to get it off her mind if she didn't at least try.

Kristen pulled out another beer, opened it with a flick of her wrist, handed it over, and then saluted with her own bottle.

"Here's to a world where kids don't try to kill each other," she toasted.

"Amen," Sam agreed, drinking as deeply as her host.

They stood in silence for a few minutes. The NCAA Women's Championship clock over the hallway door said it was almost six. Birds were chirping outside. Somewhere nearby, kids were playing, screaming, and calling to one another, the same as they did on the lane. Sam could hear it all through Kristen's open windows and the screens that kept out the South's thriving insect population. She heard no air-conditioning running, though the temperature outside had hit the mid-eighties today. Kristen's brand of peace and quiet was enchanting.

"What a beautiful home," Sam said. "You have a lovely place here."

"Thank you." Kristen took a long drink. "I've fallen in love with this town. I don't think there's anywhere in Chandlerville that I don't feel connected to, even though I've only lived here for three years."

And if the Turners and others had their way—if their witch hunt wasn't stopped—Kristen might have to leave when her contract ran out at the end of the school year.

"You're a phenomenal educator," Sam said. "It will be the school's loss if you lose your job over all of this."

Even this morning, knowing the stress that was looming at the end of her day, Kristen had been so plugged into what was happening with her students, she'd made certain Sam was there to help care for Nate. She'd made time to speak with Brian about Cade.

"They're right, you know." The resignation in Kristen's voice made Sam sick. "I should have known more about the bullying, that it had gone too far. I saw the boys that morning. I thought there might be a fight brewing, but it didn't seem like anything out of the ordinary. There had to have been signs that Troy was so unstable. And I missed them."

"You're telling me it's an assistant principal's job to follow each student home, to see how much pressure he's under from his peers and parents? You're supposed to be there every minute of every day in school, breaking up every fight, weighing every altercation, and labeling bullying at every turn—in case some other child has the unfortunate body chemistry and home situation to turn a grudge into a homicidal temper tantrum?"

All teachers in New York City, public or private, were trained to look for latent violence in students. High-risk candidates were discussed at weekly meetings and followed up on rigorously. The police were involved when needed, as well as social and family protective services if abuse or neglect was suspected. And regardless, some kids still slipped through the cracks. Even with metal detectors in most New York junior high and high schools, weapons turning up in the schools, knives and guns, was a ridiculously common occurrence.

But that kind of world had seemed so far removed from a charming, seductively safe place like Chandlerville, where no one could have anticipated what had happened between Troy and Bubba.

"I've never heard," Sam said, "of an administrator more diligent about training her staff or staying state-of-the-art in crisis preparedness."

"That's true." Kristen tipped her bottle toward Sam again. "Most of my staff calls me 'the Terminator' when they think I'm not listening. Maybe it's the competitive athlete in me, but I wanted us to have the best, and to give the best to our students, even if we live in the suburbs. Especially when we do. I want people from all over Atlanta wanting to move to Chandlerville because we have the best damn elementary school in the state."

"As far as I'm concerned, we do. I've seen private schools that couldn't compete with the services and caliber of educators you've pulled together for our children—or your security measures."

It had all been covered by the media, every detail. During school hours, outside doors were locked so no one could enter, except through the front, where you had to be buzzed through and cleared at the school office. Video feeds at all entrances revealed who was coming and going. And Kristen and her teachers practiced countless emergency protocols—which had been carried out to the letter the day of the shooting. The entire school had been immediately locked down, the danger had been isolated to the cafeteria, and Kristen and the rest of her staff had evacuated everyone they could outside and out of harm's way as quickly as humanly possible.

"Our kids couldn't be in better hands," Sam said.

"I help run a suburban elementary school that's been nationally labeled a hotbed of juvenile-against-juvenile violence." Kristen drained her beer, opened one of the drawers beneath the sink to reveal a recycle basket, and chucked the bottle inside. She slammed the drawer shut. "The local news vans have staked out prime broadcasting spots at city hall this afternoon. I heard just an hour ago that they'll be feeding nationally. Even if we run late again, we'll make the evening news on the West Coast. Eleven o'clock up and down our coast. Sounds like they think a particularly juicy story is about to break. Who knows? We might even make tomorrow's morning shows."

Sam finished her beer and rounded the counter to stand next to a woman who shouldn't feel so alone in all of this. No one should. Not Cade or Nate, or her and Brian, or Julia and Walter, or Kristen. She opened the recycle drawer and tossed her own bottle in, hearing glass rattle but not shatter. No one had to shatter under the weight of what had happened. Not if they all found a way to help one another, instead of tearing one another apart.

She shoved the drawer closed as firmly as Kristen had. "Then I guess we'd better make sure we give those media vultures the right kind of *juicy* to report about."

"We?" Kristen's right eyebrow rose until it was hiding behind her perky bangs.

"We."

"Do I have to remind you how many people will be at tonight's meeting?" Kristen was nice enough not to point out that Sam had been a no-show at the other board meetings, no matter who, including Julia, had thought she and Brian should be there. "You're going to be surrounded by angry people who gave up debating their issues civilly over a month ago."

"Kind of like the bloodbath that a college basketball game can turn into?"

Kristen's other eyebrow rose. "Kind of."

Sam remembered thinking she wouldn't make it through that morning's conversation with Kristen and Mallory and Julia, or her return to Chandler and helping Nate, or even that afternoon with her family. But with the help of her friends and family, she had made it through each moment. Surely she could be there for Kristen tonight, when it sounded as if there might be no one else in the other woman's corner at the meeting.

"Lucky for me," Sam said, "my date's going to be an all-conference MVP center. You can be my blocker, and I'll be yours."

It was the best Sam could do. She was clueless at sports metaphors, having risen to the rank of cheerleading captain in high school without figuring out the first thing about any of the sports she'd screamed her voice raw supporting—except for which of the boys were the cutest.

Kristen laughed, a soft, choppy thing that slowly turned into a tinkling melody. "Do you even know how to dribble a basketball?" she asked. "Let alone how to pick-and-roll and drive the lane for a layup?"

"Nope." Sam laughed, too, enjoying the freedom of making a new friend, and feeling as if there were something, no matter how minor, she could do to help. "But I've got your back. Seriously. You stuck by my side at the bake sale. I'm there for you tonight."

"You don't have to do this." Kristen was suddenly serious. "I appreciate the gesture. And I know how strong you are when you have to be. I'll never forget the way you shoved me to the ground that morning in the cafeteria, when Troy shot at us. But coming tonight would be hell for you. And for what? I can't allow you to do this, just to stand next to me while my career finishes imploding."

"*Allow* me?"

Sam walked to the fridge, pulled out another beer, opened it and handed it over. She was either going to become a part of this community or she wasn't. And suddenly, she couldn't stomach the thought of hiding away for another night from what her town was going through. As a Chandlerville citizen and a Chandler Elementary parent, Sam could either help keep this remarkable woman as their assistant principal, or she'd lose touch with every speck of the educator she herself had once been.

"Just try to stop me," she said. "I'm your designated driver tonight, Ms. Hemmings. You said I'd inspired you to become a teacher. I can't think of a nicer compliment. Now, go make me proud. I'm behind you all the way."

Kristen drank as if Sam had challenged her to chug it. She slammed the empty bottle onto the countertop.

"Let's do it then," she said.

Sam grabbed her purse on the way to the front of the condo and fished out her keys.

"Wait," Kristen said. "When you got here, you said you needed my help with something."

God.

Sam had completely forgotten.

"A teaching job," she said, "and it's going to take someone on the inside to help me make it work this late in the school year."

"A job? For someone you know?"

"For me."

"For you." Both of Kristen's eyebrows rose again.

"It's complicated." It was probably a mistake, because what if Sam couldn't follow through with it once she got started? Only it felt like the right solution for all of them—her family and the Turners. "We'll talk about it on the drive over."

***

Kristen could remember attending a three-ring circus as a child. She'd loved the circus. What wasn't fun about the music and the mayhem and the clowns and the majestic animals showing off as their trainers put them through their paces?

The one thing about the experience she'd never taken to, though, was the tightrope act. And as she and Sam walked into the city hall auditorium where the school board meetings were held, she suddenly remembered why. Even though there might be a net stretched way below the performers to catch them in case they missed a step, the fall still looked deadly. It had to. That was part of the show. But even as a child, Kristen had known she'd hate the sensation of falling. And she had, her entire life since.

Even though she owned her condo outright, and she had money in savings, and she had her stellar reputation up to this point to fall back on if her contract at Chandler wasn't renewed, the thought of not being able to remain an assistant principal in this special community was making her head swim as if she were free-falling. It had taken forever to move through the chaos outside—news trucks and reporters were everywhere, most of them recognizing her and asking for a sound bite that she'd refused to give them.

Sam, true to her word, had done her best to shield Kristen from the worst of it, putting herself between the cameras and Kristen like a seasoned blocker, and refusing to do on-camera interviews as well.

Still, Kristen's legs were shaking by the time they'd pushed their way inside the building and then had navigated the lobby to reach the largest of the auditoriums. She couldn't catch her breath. She'd broken out in a flop sweat, and it was quite possible she needed to switch the silk blouse she wore beneath her suit for something that wasn't soaked and sticking to her skin in several places.

"Remind me to tell you later," she whispered to Sam, "just how bad an idea that second beer was."

"You're doing fine," her cheering section of one replied.

"The meeting hasn't started yet, and it already feels like a disaster. *I'm* a disaster."

"But you look great," said the woman who was so wound up by the crowds, she looked like she might barf at any moment. "Calm. In charge. Ready to discuss things intelligently and rationally. Not the least bit concerned that tonight's decision won't be made in your favor."

They found two seats together in the very front row, and made themselves comfortable a few feet away from the raised dais and tables where the board would sit. Well, Kristen made herself comfortable. Sam more melted into her chair, almost as if she'd feel better if she could simply puddle beneath it, where she wouldn't have to deal with anyone else but Kristen.

"So this would be a bad time to mention that I have a minor problem with stage fright?" Kristen asked, trying to keep things light. She was grateful to the other woman for making such a huge effort on her behalf, but she was worried about Sam as well.

"I'm sure you'll do great." Sam gestured at the quickly filling room around them. "You'll have them eating out of your hands. Everything's great."

"*I'm* sure you're full of crap."

She hadn't been expected to speak at the other meetings. Roy Griffin, Chandler's principal, had been up to bat then. Of course, he hadn't wasted any time before labeling Kristen as the broken link in his chain of command—the reason he'd never been informed about any instances of bullying involving Bubba and Troy, or Bubba and any other child in the school. Kristen, he'd explained, the AP responsible for student discipline and staff training, should have had her finger on the problem and notified her boss of any impending issue that needed to be dealt with. The net had also been cast over the boy's teachers. Roy officially held them all responsible for not being able to read the minds of their students, in order to isolate and prevent every potential problem before it occurred.

Nate's parents were looking for a scapegoat, and thanks to Roy, tonight everyone was looking Kristen's way. When she was called to respond to his testimony, Kristen knew only one thing for certain: she wasn't going to do to her staff what Roy had done to her. She'd take the fall completely on her own, just like the acrobat walking solo on the circus tightrope, before she'd take anyone else down with her.

"You can handle the pressure," Sam insisted. She pulled a box of Tic Tacs from her bag, shook out a colorful handful, and passed half of them over. Her hands were trembling. The tiny woman's entire body was, despite her fierce expression. "You scored thirty points in the conference championship your freshman year at Duke. I know. My husband wouldn't stop singing your praises, once he Googled your college stats. Don't tell me a pipsqueak like Roy Griffin has you shaking in your designer shoes."

Kristen looked down at her Prada loafers and smirked.

Leave it to Sam Perry—a woman who should be lining up, too, to blame Kristen for what happened to her and her child—to have noticed the upscale brand Kristen was wearing, but not to have mentioned it before now.

"I can't wear heels to work. I'd scare the staff and students even more than I already do. So if I have to wear flats, I'm going to treat myself to the nicest, most comfortable and stylish ones I can find."

In a perfect world, maybe she and her new friend would have gone shoe shopping together one day. But Kristen was about to become prime-time news roadkill. And Sam was the local poster child for PTSD. Nothing about their world was perfect.

"That might be the most impressive rationalization for a fashion addiction that I've ever heard," said her pint-size bodyguard.

"My turnaround jump shot from the top of the key is impressive," Kristen said, relaxing and even enjoying herself a little. "Do you think that or my overpriced shoes will win over the board enough for them not to knock me around for failing to protect Chandler's children?"

"Remind them that none of us are guaranteed complete protection in this world," a familiar, deep voice said from behind them. Brian Perry finished walking down the aisle until he'd reached their row. "That's something my wife and I learned the hard way in New York. We'd hoped to God never to find ourselves in another unthinkable situation like that. But here we are."

"What . . ." Sam looked ready to launch herself into her husband's arms, or hide from him. It was hard for Kristen to tell which. "What are you doing here? Where are the boys?"

"Mallory's," Brian said. "She's watching them and Polly at her place. Pete wanted to come, and he's been hounding me for weeks to make one of these things."

"But, Cade . . ." Sam glanced around at the crowd. She lowered her voice. "He was so upset."

"He's fine. When I told him about tonight, he said he wanted me to be here. He's worried about Ms. Hemmings. The kids have all heard what's going down with the school board. I'm guessing he's thinking this is his doing, too."

"What?" If Kristen could have put her hands around Roy Griffin's neck at that moment, she'd have gladly squeezed until the little man squeaked like the rat he was. "This is about workplace politics, and my boss covering his ass at the expense of the school and the community. I don't understand what good either of you think you can do for me, not that I don't appreciate the thought. You should be home with your son."

"I understand." Cade's father knelt in front of them, close enough to his wife to lay a comforting hand on Sam's knee. "I'm not sure what good I'll be able to do, either. But I was talking with my wife and son earlier this afternoon, about listening and being there for people when they need you most, however they need you most, whether or not they think they want your help. Staying disconnected from what's happening in our community all this time has been tantamount to siding with the Turners' out-of-control anger. And I couldn't let that slide for another one of these meetings."

"That must have been one hell of a talk," Kristen said.

After her conversation with Sam at her condo, and then the mind-bending proposition the other woman had made on the ride over, and now Brian's sudden appearance at city hall, Kristen was dying to know what had gone down at the Perry house that afternoon.

"Most talks with my wife are," Brian said. "Once I smarten up and start listening. Keep an eye on her. She can flip your world on its ear and show you things you've never seen before. I haven't decided yet if that's a bonus or a curse, and we've been married for fifteen years. But as long as she's around, you'll never be bored."

He winked at his wife, the lines of tension around his eyes and mouth melting into a smile. Sam looked away, but not before

Kristen caught the blush warming her cheeks. These two had been quietly separated since the shooting. But maybe, just maybe, the most remarkable parents Kristen had had the privilege of knowing were slowly finding their way back to each other.

Brian rose and shook Kristen's hand. "It's standing room only in here, but I'll be cheering you on from the back. I assure you I won't be the only one. Knock 'em dead."

He bent and gave his wife's mouth a soft kiss. Sam's lips followed his as he drew away. His hand brushed the side of her face before he left, the sweet gesture making Kristen smile.

It was the little triumphs that got her through most days now. And the sight of Sam staring after her husband was maybe enough to get Kristen through the rest of the night.

The door at the front of the auditorium opened and the school board members filed in. They took their seats, and the audience settled, too. Ambient chatter softened to whispers and then silence, until there was nothing left to be heard except the swishing of bodies in uncomfortable seats. The district superintendent pounded his gavel.

"I'm calling this meeting to order," Mike Johnson said. "For the record, let me say that holding this additional fact-finding session was voted on at last Monday's ad hoc board meeting, to address matters that arose from Chandler Elementary principal Roy Griffin's report on the shooting incident that occurred in January. It was decided at that time that no press would be allowed inside the auditorium during tonight's proceedings, to protect the privacy of the families and witnesses we expected to be present, and to hopefully speed up the process. Everyone's had their chance to speak their minds. But playing for the cameras and the press, going on and on about the same grievances, isn't getting us anywhere. It's time to settle some of the issues at hand, so our community and representatives can move on to implementing whatever plan is agreed upon. Now, before we begin with the agenda of interviews and discussion, I'm going to ask our secretary to read last week's meeting minutes back for the room."

Control of the microphone transferred to the secretary, and while the woman whom Kristen had never met droned on, she leaned over to whisper into Sam's ear, "Let the circus begin . . ."

Chapter Thirteen

"They're crucifying her," Pete said from where he stood next to Brian, both of them leaning against the packed auditorium's back wall.

"She's holding her own," Brian insisted, even though Kristen's interrogation by every member of the board, with the exception of Julia Davis, who hadn't yet chimed in, had dragged on for over half an hour.

"She'll be lucky if she gets out of this with her job."

"There wasn't a damn thing she could have done to prevent what happened. My son is one of the kids who was almost killed. If I don't blame the woman, what are most of the rest of these people doing here?"

Pete kept eying the restless crowd, the same as Brian, his expression growing grimmer and grimmer as people sat closer to the edges of their seats, mesmerized by the farce the school board was putting on. "Fact-finding session, my ass."

"What the hell is Sam doing down there, right in the middle of all of this?"

Brian had been shocked to see her sitting beside Kristen, changed out of the baggy sweats she'd worn to school and into jeans and the soft pink sweater he'd picked out for her a few years back. He'd been shocked. And he'd been proud. He'd wanted to call for the room's attention and tell them what a remarkable effort it had taken for Sam to make an appearance somewhere this loud and crowded and rife with conflict.

"She's doing the same thing you are, I guess," Pete answered. "What she thinks is right."

"Yeah."

Sam always did what she thought was right, no matter how hard it might be for her or everyone else. Supporting Kristen, talking Nate out of his dark place, walking with Brian down the block and then back to their house to confront their son after walking out on Brian at the school, saying they were never going to be the parents they should have been until he woke up and began to deal with their problems. All of it had exhausted Sam and rattled her even more, but she'd done the right thing, each and every time.

She was his hero.

He'd come tonight without telling her about it—not entirely certain whether he'd stay. But as soon as he'd seen Sam, he'd known this was exactly where he needed to be, for as long as she was there.

"You gonna just let her sit down there all by herself?" Pete nodded toward the seat the AP had vacated when she'd walked to the small podium that had been positioned in front of the board, complete with its own microphone so the rest of auditorium could hear what guest speakers said. "The school board's grilling Kristen like she's tonight's supper. Are you gonna let

Sam sit there in the middle of it, with no one to lean on if she needs someone?"

"No." Brian was already moving. "I'm not."

There were so many people standing around the edges of the auditorium, the only easy way to reach Sam's side was down the center aisle. Walking toward her, feeling every eye in the place shifting from Kristen to him, he forced himself to focus on whatever Mike Johnson was saying next.

"Ms. Hemmings," the superintendent said. "I don't see how you can stand there with a straight face and deny any knowledge that a volatile child like Troy Wilmington was an emotional time bomb, ticking away in your school, just waiting to explode."

"Volatile?" Brian said, realizing too late that he'd spoken the word out loud.

He'd reached the front of the aisle, where he was now standing beside Chandler's assistant principal instead of quietly joining his wife. The day's frustrations and anger and fear rushed through him, the aggression he'd tamped down zeroing in on the latest ridiculous comment coming out of Mike's ignorant mouth.

"Mr. Perry, you're out of order." The superintendent pointed his finger at Brian.

"And you're out of your minds." Brian scanned the honorable school board representatives for the town of Chandlerville.

Six of his neighbors were sitting solemnly at the long table at the front of the room. Each of them was mute now as Mike interrogated Chandler Elementary's assistant principal. As if keeping quiet could distance them from their culpability in allowing this farce to continue.

Brian's gaze finally landed on Julia Davis, who occupied the chair at the end of the table closest to Sam.

"All of you are out of your minds," he said to her and the rest of them, "if you think anyone could have seen this coming. Troy Wilmington is a mixed-up kid who was being bullied by another mixed-up kid, the way mixed-up kids have been going at each other from the dawn of time. No, we don't want that sort of thing going on in our school." The audience began murmuring, countless conversations starting. "Yes, the administration should do everything they can to stop it, as I've been assured they already are. But no one, not even coaches like me and Walter Davis, had any idea what was going on inside Troy's mind or his home or his relationships with other kids. He was the least *volatile* boy I know, which is more than I could have said for Bubba Dickerson. How could Ms. Hemmings or her staff have known that it was the shy, quiet student who'd become a threat?"

"How can you say that?" Charlotte Dickerson stood. She'd been sitting in the front row on the other side of the aisle from Kristen and Sam. She pointed at Brian. The conference room grew silent once more. "My son's dead, and you're saying it's *his* fault? That that Wilmington boy and the father who beat him aren't responsible for getting my Bubba shot? You think just because Bubba teased other kids and was bigger than they were, he deserved to die?"

"Of course not." The fear of that day clogged Brian's throat until he had to force his next words out. "I'm so sorry for what's happened to your family. To all of our families. Cade's still alive, but he's mostly lost to his mother and me still. We're not sure how much of who he was we'll be able to get back, and neither are Nate Turner's parents. But at least we have our children with us still. I can't imagine . . ." He cleared his throat and wiped a finger down his nose to brush away the moisture seeping from his eyes. "I can't let my mind go to a place where it was my son or my wife who'd died that day. It's a terrible place that I've been to before, when I thought I'd lost Sam in New York. I think a part of me will always be there, to the point where I've been letting the fear of it damn near destroy my family. The way this town is using fear to hurt one another now."

Charlotte was openly weeping, sobbing, her husband standing up to curl her body into his while he glowered at Brian, and then the board.

"He's right," Chuck Dickerson bellowed loud enough for the people in the very back of the auditorium to hear. "Charlotte and me will have our day in court to deal with what happened to our boy. But what you folks are doing here, wanting to assign blame to people at the school, so you can wash your hands of this town's responsibility for taking a long, hard look at each of our lives . . . Well, that's just bullshit. And it don't do no one any good in the end. Going after Ms. Hemmings or Mrs. Baxter won't bring Bubba back or fix any of the other kids who were hurt. It won't change the fact that the Wilmington family's lost their boy, too, probably forever."

"Well, I for one think Chandler Elementary has a lot to answer for." James Turner stood up from the row behind the Dickersons, where he and Beverly were sitting. "Where was Ms. Hemmings or Roy Griffin or Mrs. Baxter when that Wilmington bastard gunned down my son? We entrusted teachers and our school staff with our children's safety, and this is what we get? Nate couldn't make it through a morning at school today. Rumor has it your boy's flunking out, Brian. Lord knows what Sally Beaumont and the other kids in Mrs. Baxter's class are going through, not that Beverly and I would know. We've got our hands full dealing with Nate and trying to pick up the pieces of our own lives. And you, Ms. Hemmings, you think you've got nothing to do with any of this?" James drilled Kristen with a killing glare. "Except for how every school policy and procedure was followed to the letter? Well, that's just great. I hope it helps us and Nate sleep at night, as nicely as it does you."

"I've hardly slept a full hour a night since the shooting, Mr. and Mrs. Turner," Kristen said. She looked to Chuck and Charlotte. "Mrs. and Mrs. Dickerson. My heart's breaking for all of the families and children who've been hurt by this tragedy. I've tried to speak with all of you individually, including the Wilmingtons and the Beaumonts. The only parents who've welcomed my attempts to discuss the situation have been Mr. and Mrs. Perry. And I'll tell you the same thing I've shared with them. Our school should have been a safe place for your boys and girls, and I hold myself personally responsible that it wasn't in this instance. But my staff and I did what we thought possible to protect our students, including tracking potentially volatile behavior in instances where we thought there might be a threat to the student body. Nothing, absolutely nothing Troy ever did suggested that he was a cause for concern, or that he'd bring a weapon to school. So now we know that we need to do better, and we will. None of which will make up for what's happened. But I hope you and the board will give us a chance to work harder for you and this community. We're already implementing new bullying intervention procedures and programs, as well as a peer counseling initiative that would make it easier for a student to talk about interpersonal problems before they escalate to such a dangerous level."

"You should start by expelling all the bullies from school," Dan Beaumont said, standing up from one of the back rows near Pete. "Bubba Dickerson should have been out of Chandler Elementary a long time ago."

"My son wasn't a bully," Charlotte insisted, her sadness hardening into the kind of bitter anger that Brian had been swallowing for months. "You shut your mouth."

"Who are you kidding, lady?" Dan stomped down the center aisle. "My Sally told me what happened in the bus lane that day. How Cade and Nate had to pull Bubba off of Troy. Your son had been tormenting that poor kid all year." He rounded on Kristen. "And where were you when all this was going on?"

"Supervising the hundred kids or so who take the bus to school every morning, Mr. Beaumont," Kristen replied. "I'm sorry to say that I don't have enough staff to supervise each and every one of them personally. When I became aware of something going on between the boys on Troy's bus, I intervened and was told nothing was wrong. Until I saw differently with my own eyes, or one of the students changed his story, there was wasn't anything more I could do."

"So my son's dead because you're understaffed?" Chuck Dickerson ranted. "If that's the best you got, lady, then maybe you *don't* need to be working at our school any longer."

"Your boy's dead because he was an asshole," Sally's father said. "He finally picked on the wrong skinny, defenseless kid, and Troy decided to fight back."

"You son of a bitch." Chuck was climbing over people to get to Dan.

"Enough!" Brian stepped between the two men, his hands planted on Chuck's overmuscled chest. The man had been known to bench-press 550 on a light day. He could plow right through Brian if he wanted to. "This isn't going to solve anything or bring Bubba back, Chuck. Don't do this to your wife."

Pete had arrived at Dan's side. He had a firm grip on the other man's arm, keeping him from taking on Bubba's father.

"Kristen and Roy and the rest of the staff at the school aren't the problem here," Dan spit out, struggling against Pete's hold. "You are, Chuck, and your wife, and Troy's lousy excuse for a father. You raised these boys to be monsters. Then you cut 'em loose amongst the rest of our kids and our community, and you didn't give a damn what they'd do, did you?"

"I'm going to kill you." Chuck tried to shove his way to Dan again. He reared back and swung his fist, connecting just below Brian's right eye.

"Brian!" Sam yelled as he went down and the meeting disintegrated into chaos.

"Order!" Mike hammered his gavel as Chuck tackled both Dan and Pete. "Order, this is completely unacceptable."

Kristen helped Brian to his feet. Then, to her credit, she waded into the battle, pulling Chuck away while Pete tried to neutralize Dan.

"Please!" a distraught female voice said, both soft and shrill, and hysterical in a soulless way that somehow captured everyone's attention.

All four men were standing now, bloody and bruised and trying to breathe in enough air to stop wheezing. As one, Brian and Chuck and Dan and Pete turned to stare at the woman who'd slipped unnoticed into the auditorium at some point during the proceedings, to stand in the shadows by the EXIT sign.

"Please," Edna Wilmington begged. Troy's mother's gaze roamed from one corner of the room to another, finally landing on the men standing at its center, then shifting to the board itself. "Please stop this. We're all hurting. My son . . ." She pressed her hand to her mouth. "I can't tell you how badly he's hurting for what he's done. For hurting other children that way . . ." She dropped her hand, clenching it with her other one. "The way I've let my husband hurt him and me for so long. It's my fault." She sobbed the words, her pain so honest and awful, none of them could look away. "Please, the only way this stops is if we stop hurting each other. For our children's sake. We have to stop."

Edna broke down then, her legs visibly giving out. She'd have sunk to the floor, but Sam had reached her side. Brian hadn't seen his wife move, but there she was catching Edna close and helping her to a nearby seat. After kneeling in front of the other woman and exchanging a few soft words, Sam walked slowly back toward the center aisle. But instead of collapsing into her own seat, she continued to Brian's side and took his hand, staring evenly at Dan and Chuck until both men lowered their gazes to the floor. James Turner was still scowling from his seat beside his wife, but for once he kept his silence.

Brian turned toward the front of the room. He squeezed his wife's hand, knowing what being at the center of the conflict, not to mention seeing him knocked on his ass, must be doing to her nerves. But that hadn't stopped her. Nothing had stopped her the entire day, no matter how exhausted she must be. He'd never been prouder.

Kristen returned to the speaker's podium.

He could feel the weight of everyone's attention settle onto them as he and Sam and Chandler's assistant principal stared down the board and waited for someone to say something.

Julia Davis reached for one of the mics.

"Thank you," she said to all the parents standing in the center aisle, representatives in their own way of the families and lives that had been irreparably damaged by the shooting. Her gaze fell to Edna Wilmington, then swept to Mike Johnson, who sat mutely in his superintendent's spot. "I think the rest of the board would join me in thanking all of you, including Ms. Hemmings, for your honesty in sharing what you know of what happened the day of the shooting, as well as how it's affecting our town, our school, and our families."

Every member of the board nodded, each of them waiting for Julia to continue.

"I find myself agreeing with Brian Perry and Chuck Dickerson. While we do need to get to the bottom of the details of that day, so we can learn from our mistakes and better protect our children and staff, I don't see how assigning blame will accomplish any of that. An investigative task force has been formed to audit Chandler Elementary's student discipline and crisis procedures, and I've been appointed its chair. Until the time that we have a final report on whether all safety measures in place were appropriately followed, it's my recommendation that this board redirect its energies on moving our community forward in every way that we can. Including assisting our citizens who have been hurt so deeply, as well as preventing further tragedies like this one from taking place."

The audience began murmuring again.

The board members whispered among themselves, each of them nodding toward the superintendent.

"Then if there's no counter to Councilwoman Davis's recommendation"—Mike raised his gavel, as if to call the session to a close—"I hereby—"

"Wait." Keeping his wife by his side, Brian stepped to Kristen's podium and swiveled her microphone until he could speak into it. "I wanted to say one final thing before we leave tonight, to the council and everyone here. As I said, Sam and I have unfortunately been through something like this before . . ."

He felt Sam stiffen beside him. Her hand tried to pull free of his, but he held her close. He needed his wife to hear this most of all.

"And what we've learned from every mistake we've made since that experience is that the only way through trauma this horrible is to focus on healing. On healing ourselves and our families and the others who've been hurt in our community. Being honest. Talking. Leave the rest of it for the media and the politicians to sort out. But our school and our community's parents and kids and families have to start talking about this for real. We have to stop pointing fingers and stop blaming each other."

He glanced toward Chuck and Dan. Both men nodded, one after the other. Pete clapped a supportive hand on each of their shoulders.

"If we don't protect each other," Brian continued, "and listen to each other, and even let ourselves misbehave if we have to, and then give ourselves a safe place to come back to once we're done, our community will never recover. Nothing's going to take us back to a place where we thought school shootings couldn't happen in Chandlerville. So we have to let that Chandlerville go, and figure out what we want our town to be now. My wife's helping me realize that about my own family. It's taken me too long, but I'm finally starting to understand what she's been trying to tell me about our experience after 9/11—we can't go back, and we'll tear each other apart trying to. We can only go forward, from wherever we are now, trying to deal with what we have to . . . together."

He glanced down at Sam.

If you don't know how to break . . . she'd challenged him earlier that day.

Brian looked back at the board.

"We're broken," he confessed to his wife and his community. "Badly broken. As people, as families, and as a town. And if we can't face that and accept our responsibility for fixing it, Chandlerville doesn't have a chance in hell of becoming whole again."

Chapter Fourteen

"Wow," Sam said. She and Julia had slumped into a pair of the Davises' Ethan Allen kitchen chairs. "You've had a busy night of rescuing assistant principals and fighting for Chandlerville's soul."

Julia snorted. "Tell me it hasn't really been only six hours since I said almost the same thing to you."

The school board meeting had broken up almost as soon as Brian finished speaking, the room roaring with motion and talking and neighbors reaching out to neighbors and then to their community representatives—not to cast more blame, but trying to figure out what the next step should be.

Brian had pulled Sam's hand to his lips and given her a chaste kiss, admiration in his eyes, and love and . . . passion, before letting her go. She'd mumbled to Kristen that she'd be waiting in the parking lot and fled the auditorium and the panic of feeling the room shrinking around her and the air being sucked away by too many bodies.

It had taken an extra trip across town to deliver Kristen to her condo before Sam could return to the lane. She'd called Mallory to check on her boys, who'd been watching a video with Polly. Her friend had heard the exhaustion in Sam's voice and insisted that Sam head straight to Julia's and crawl into bed—Brian would pick up Cade and Joshua soon enough. Sam had made a brief stop at her own house first, though. She and Julia had pulled into the Davises' driveway at practically the same time, just after eight, with Julia looking as run-down as Sam felt.

"You and Brian were something else tonight." Julia massaged her temples, closing her eyes. "Kristen Hemmings, too. Roy'd better watch out. He's got competition for his job when his contract's up next year. My money's on Kristen being Chandler's next principal. She kept her cool, stuck to her guns, and handled every outlandish thing Mike threw at her. We couldn't be in better hands with her volunteering to serve on the task force on the school's behalf."

"She's pretty awesome." Sam sat up straighter. "That's why I went over to her place before the meeting to ask her for help."

Julia lowered her hands to the table. "With what?"

"A waiver from the county, so I can homeschool Cade for the rest of the semester while following Chandler's curriculum, so he can graduate with his class—assuming he'll do the work he has to do to pass."

"Really?" Julia's surprise morphed into a proud smile. "You're going to be a teacher again."

"I asked if Kristen could work it out so I could do the same for Nate."

"Really?" Her friend's reaction this time was so deadpan, Sam laughed. Julia reached for her hand and squeezed. She headed to the coffeemaker in the corner. "Good for you. But I wouldn't hold my breath waiting for the Turners to warm up to the idea. Not after tonight."

"I know." Sam's heart was breaking for Nate. He'd seemed so . . . lost after his and Cade's fight. "But I'm not giving up."

"James Turner has called someone on the board to rant every day since the shooting. Beverly might be your way in. I'm not certain what she thinks herself, versus what she's agreeing to in order to keep the peace at home."

"Yeah, but—"

Before Sam could tell her friend about the fight she and Brian had broken up between the boys that afternoon, the butler's door from the dining room swung inward and Walter staggered in. Sam glanced at the clock as he walked toward his wife. Walter had started early tonight. He usually waited until around nine to mix up the first of the several Jim Beam and Cokes he drank before he collapsed on the couch to sleep them off.

"It took you long enough to get home." He gave Julia's cheek a sloppy kiss that had Sam touching her own and remembering the firm softness of Brian's lips. "It's almost eight. Where you been all this time? I'm hungry."

Julia ignored him for the few seconds it took her to finish setting up the coffee. She rounded on Walter and shoved him to the side, opening the freezer to pull out what Sam could hardly believe was permitted in the Davis house. Julia handed her husband a frozen dinner and turned him in the direction of the microwave that sat on its own shelf, custom-built above the halogen stove top.

"I told you." She returned wearily to the chair beside Sam. "I had a board meeting tonight, the boys are out with friends, and I'm too tired to cook something for just the two of us."

Julia admitting she wasn't up to cooking something homemade for her husband was like Martha Stewart suggesting that they all eat on paper plates, because she didn't see the point in using china and silver when it meant you were going to have to wash everything when you were finished.

"Another meeting for what?" Walter held out the frozen box of what looked like fried chicken and mashed potatoes. "What's this crap?"

Sam's friend flinched.

No one used curse words in the Davises' home. Certainly not Walter. It was one of his pet peeves. At least, it had been, until his drinking had become a problem.

Sam remembered the hurtful, judgmental things she'd said to her friend earlier, to distract herself from her own mistakes with her own family. She took Julia's hand now in silent apology, wishing she knew what to do to make what Julia was going through easier. She suspected that at least at some point tonight, Walter had remembered that his sons and wife weren't going to be home for dinner, or he wouldn't have started cocktail hour so early. Which meant he'd gone out of his way to make sure he was good and drunk enough to worry Julia once she returned home.

Julia's emotionless glance, her eye roll, said she'd arrived at the same conclusion. She slammed her palms down on the table with enough force to make Sam jump. Her ceramic napkin holder crashed to the floor, the cute little kitten making the saddest, dull tinkle and breaking into too many pieces to be repaired. Julia pushed to her feet and rounded on her husband.

"The meeting was about the Chandler shooting," she said, "and the whole town was there. You should have been, too, instead of hunkering down here pickling your brain. You were Troy and Cade and Nate and Bubba's football and baseball coach for how many years? But you couldn't show up to support their families tonight, and maybe help the town figure out what to do to make sure that no more kids like Bubba and Nate get hurt."

She was as close to losing it as Sam had ever heard her.

"And that"—Julia pointed at the frozen dinner—"is all there is for dinner tonight, unless you forage in the fridge I made sure was fully stocked before I left, and make yourself something else."

Walter was breathing even harder than Julia, his glassy gaze growing more shocked with each hostile word his normally adoring wife shouted.

He turned and slammed the frozen box of food into their sink, the crash lifting Sam out of her chair and sending her edging toward the door to the backyard. It was way too early for the kind of night walking she liked to do. But Julia wouldn't want her there to witness her long-overdue confrontation with her husband. And Sam's nerves were too frayed to endure it.

"Well, maybe if you spent more of your time taking care of your own damn family," Walter raged, "instead of worrying about the whole damn town, thinking you can solve everybody else's problems at your stupid meetings, I wouldn't be left here, rattling around this place by myself, *pickling* my brain the way you hate."

"The meetings are important, not stupid," Julia fired back. "Thanks to Brian and Sam and Kristen Hemmings, we made real progress tonight. You'd have known that, if—"

"Progress?" Walter raged, a stranger to Sam and, she suspected, his wife. "You mean someone figured out how to go back and stop Dillon Wilmington from whaling on his wife and kid? Someone got to Troy and Bubba in time to help them and keep us all from becoming another national news exposé on how small towns like ours don't know jack about taking care of our own, any more than people in big cities do? Is that the kind of *progress* you're making? No? Then you're not doing shit, Julia. There's nothing anyone can do now to save either of those two boys or any of the rest of us from the mess we've made!"

Sam escaped into Julia's professionally landscaped, immaculately maintained backyard, horrified by what she'd just overheard, knowing Julia would be mortified, too—and likely Walter, if he remembered any of it tomorrow, or that Sam had even been there.

It was beautiful outside. Julia and Walter had lovingly cared for every part of their home and their boys. That was what made what was happening to the Davises' marriage now even harder to watch. If Julia and Walter couldn't make it after everything they'd done for Chandlerville and so many families like Sam and Brian's, it was easy to think that none of the rest of them had much of a chance, either.

She headed off, walking into the deepening twilight, thinking of Mallory and Pete's upcoming wedding this summer, and the new journey they were beginning together. When Sam and Brian had moved to the lane, Walter and Julia Davis and Pete and Emma Lombard had welcomed them with so much southern hospitality and charm, it had been more than a little overwhelming. But their neighbors hadn't batted an eyelash at Sam's peculiar need to keep mostly to herself and avoid group gatherings.

They'd made her feel at home. The Davis and Lombard families had become extensions of her own. Now so much had changed, with Emma's death and Julia's issues with Walter, and the hit the entire community had taken with the shooting. It felt as if it were all slipping away, a world that Sam had come to rely on more than she'd realized. A community that had strengthened her over the years, even when she wasn't aware of it, helping her to be ready when it was time to take her stand with Brian. Even going to Kristen's condo today, fueled by the determination to do something to help her son, had been partly because of the kick in the pants Julia had given her when they'd argued earlier that afternoon. And she and Brian had both found their separate ways to the meeting tonight, so they could stand in front of their town together and try to help.

Sam stopped in the middle of the road. The truth settled around her as softly and perfectly as the night. She'd be nowhere without these people, or this place. She and Brian owed them all so much for giving them the time and space to fall apart the way they had since moving here. And maybe, just maybe, to knit themselves back together again.

"A penny for them . . ." a deep voice said from the gathering shadows around her.

"Brian!"

Her heart beat faster at the sight of her husband, and it had absolutely nothing to do with him surprising her. She was remembering the feel of his lips against her fingers in the auditorium, his kiss on her cheek when he'd stopped to check on her before the meeting, and the raw urgency of his embrace during their walk earlier.

Her entire body felt alive as she watched the man of her dreams step closer to where she'd stopped at the curve in Mimosa Lane that ended their cul-de-sac and curled back onto the main road. She felt herself smiling at him, especially the shiner he was going to have tomorrow from Dan's punch.

"I didn't mean to startle you." His fingers curled into hers, where they'd always, always belonged, no matter how bad things got between them.

"You didn't," she assured him. "What are you doing here?"

"Stalking you." His grin turned sexy as hell. "It took Pete and me a while to get away from the meeting. I got home a few minutes ago and was on my way over to Mallory's to get the kids. I saw you slip out of Julia's, and I . . . I needed to see you. I got your note."

He held up the Post-it she'd left in the kitchen when she'd stopped by the house on her own way home.

I'm so proud of you!

And she was, for so many things. For everything he'd done today, opening himself up to Cade. For saying what he'd said at the meeting tonight, baring his heart to their friends and neighbors. And for helping Sam to be able to stand there with him.

"I'm proud of *you*," her husband said. "You've been a warrior all day, even when I was so angry at you early this morning. I . . . I needed to see you again tonight, Sam, for me. Not to check up on you, or to worry about you. I mean, I know how frazzled all this has left you, and you have every reason to feel whatever you need to. But it's been a hell of a day for me, too, and I . . ."

He sounded lost suddenly. Alone. Searching. Her unstoppable, unflappable husband. Empathy flooded her, and gratitude.

We're broken, he'd said in front of the school board.

And when he'd needed something he couldn't find for himself, he'd come searching for her.

"I hope you don't mind . . ." His smile was gone. He sounded so unsure of her, and himself. "But I was wondering if I could just walk with you a little tonight."

"No." She caught the flicker of regret in his eyes, the flinch of the muscles along his jawline. "No, I mean, it's fine. I don't mind. In fact . . ."

She brought his fingers to her lips, returning his earlier kiss goodbye, making it her welcome.

"I'm glad you're here," she said. "I'll walk with you as long as you want to."

***

Brian strolled with his wife down the lane that had become their home in ways Manhattan never had been.

They'd escaped to Georgia, yes. But they'd raised their boys in Chandlerville. Most of their memories with Cade, all of them with Joshua, were wrapped up in this place. In New York, he and Sam had been little more than kids themselves. Their circle of friends had been about fun and exploring the city and letting off steam on the weekends. On Mimosa Lane, they'd put down roots and nurtured deeper ties and found other families that, even if they hadn't shared the same beginnings, had been moving in the same direction with their lives and wanting the same things for their futures.

"I used to blame you, you know." He'd promised himself that the next chance he got to speak with Sam privately, he'd make it count. He wouldn't flub things the way he had when they'd walked this same road just a few hours ago.

Sam didn't answer at first. She didn't let go of his hand, but he could feel an invisible part of her move away from him—the trusting part that he'd won back, at least for a moment, during the board meeting. Then she nodded.

"About having to move here?" she asked.

"Yeah . . ." He'd been so blind. "It was stupid."

"You were entitled. You gave up a lot when we left the city."

"But I gained a lot more. An entirely new life. With you. I

think maybe . . ." He'd gone over and over it in his head on the way to city hall, and when he'd been half listening to the first part of the meeting, and then on the drive back to the lane. "I think maybe I was pushing you so hard to get better sometimes, because . . ."

"You thought that if I did, then maybe we could go back to New York and start our lives over where we left off?"

She'd known. Of course she'd known. His wife was, bar none, the smartest, most intuitive person he'd ever met. She'd known all along that he'd been giving the second chance they'd found in Chandlerville only half his attention. Half his passion. As if he'd somehow left the better part of himself behind in Manhattan.

"I've realized something else," he said, "after I listened to you talk with Cade and Nate. You helped them through what was happening, because you've been exactly where they are, and you've found your way back. And that's when I finally got it."

His wife looked at him for the first time since they'd started walking, a little startled, it seemed, by his shift in topics.

"What?" she asked. "What did you realize?"

"That you started getting better three months ago." It had floored him, even though it had taken his meltdown at work for the truth to finally penetrate his thick skull. "The moment you stood up for yourself and stopped letting me put words in your mouth that weren't true—that everything was fine or okay or whatever you hate so much when you hear me say it. That was the moment when you finally started getting better."

And at that point, the life in Chandlerville he'd taken so for granted had begun to unravel. Because Sam had pulled away from him in order to get better herself, and he'd lost the very best part of him. Without Sam beside him, for the first time since 9/11, he'd had only his own broken pieces to focus on.

She hadn't been the only one who'd been damaged by what had happened to them at either Ground Zero or Chandler Elementary. And it had been suddenly clear that Brian's wife was leaps and bounds ahead of him, dealing with both her problems and his denial.

"I . . ." She shrugged, her reaction so much like Cade's when their son couldn't quite say what he was trying to, it grabbed at Brian's heart. "I know it doesn't seem like it, the way I've acted a lot of the time today. But I feel stronger. A lot stronger. It's kind of sneaked up on me. I hadn't realized it. I expected to fall apart again at the school. Then arguing with you. Confronting Cade. Dealing with tonight's meeting. But—"

"You're stronger than either one of us gave you credit for. Yeah. Go figure, huh? I've always said you were more of a hero than I'd ever been, for what you've overcome. But I had no idea, Sam, how much you were still hurting while you managed to live the life we have here. Now look at you, at what you've been able to accomplish in a single day, after just a few months of focusing on what you really needed to."

They were approaching the playground, where Sam had met Nate so many times. She walked over to the swings where Brian had freaked after finding her pouring her heart out to their neighbor's son instead of him. She sat, sadness and worry overshadowing the beautiful picture she made in her jeans and soft sweater.

"He won't come tonight," she said. "Will he?"

"It's a good thing." Brian took the swing beside her. "He has his parents' attention now. Hopefully he won't need to roam anymore. He and Cade finally had it out. I'm worried about both of them, after how rough things got in the kitchen. But it's a good start. Today was a good start for a lot of people."

"Us, too?" She pushed off, swinging.

His chest squeezed at the wistfulness of her question.

She was opening the door that she'd slammed in his face three months ago. And, Lord, he didn't want to screw this up now that they seemed to have turned a corner. Which pretty much made it the worst possible time for him to come completely clean about everything that had happened to him today. But he was going to talk with his wife. No more holding back things he didn't want to upset her with.

"I've taken a leave of absence from the firm," he said. "Hell, I may have saved myself from getting canned. But for now, the partners have agreed to an indefinite leave while everyone reconsiders their options."

She came to a halt beside him so quickly, the toes of her favorite Converse sneakers, the ones she wore for gardening, dug into the dirt.

"What?" she asked.

"I told the partners that I needed some time." Nope. Strike that. No more dancing around the truth. "Actually, my memo said that you and the boys needed more of my time, and that I needed to be here with you, fully focused on you, for as long as it takes to sort out our problems. Which they'd pretty much figured out already, since I blew off another important meeting this morning to be at Chandler, and then stayed way too late talking with Kristen after you left with Julia."

"You . . ." Hope bloomed across Sam's features, transforming her into a vision of the beautiful, carefree girl who'd captured his attention at a long-ago dinner party he'd almost skipped. "You said that?"

"I meant it." Whatever he had to do, he was going to do it.

The right way. For the right reasons. "I've made a mess of things. Myself most of all. I've put all the responsibility to get better on you, while I've used my career as an excuse for not getting myself to a place where I can be what you and the boys need. That ends now, whatever the consequences at W&M. You and our family are my first priority from here on out, whatever . . ." He swallowed. The next part was harder to get out, but he'd promised himself he'd say it, too. "Whatever you decide you need to do about our marriage, I'll always be here for you."

Whatever you decide to do about our marriage . . .

He watched it settle over her—the reality of him giving in to her need for them to take their time and realistically figure out what was best for them and their boys. She shook her head, something not quite fear in her gaze, and seemed to be grappling for something, anything, to say in response.

"Consequences?" she finally settled on. "What do you think the partners will do?"

Brian kicked off, swinging and not allowing himself to push her for a definite answer about their future. "Whatever happens, I'll make it work. If it comes down to it, I've started over professionally before. I can do it again."

Sam caught his swing's chain, jerking him off balance. "But you can't do that. You've worked so hard to get where you are at the firm."

When he was once again sitting still beside her, he reached out and cupped her cheek, cherishing that one simple touch and her acceptance of it as much as he had the most intimate moments they'd known.

"It's done," he said. "I'm finished with everything I've been doing that's been taking me away from working as hard as I need to on our family. And I'm not going back to W&M until we've figured out where we're going next. Nothing's more important to me, Sam, than doing things right this time."

She launched herself into his arms, leaving him little time to react. He tumbled backward out of his swing, dragging his wife with him to the ground, cushioning her fall. And then he was staring up into her sparkling eyes, the full moon high in the April sky above them, setting her auburn hair on fire.

"Samantha . . ." he whispered, capturing her lips with his and praying he wasn't rushing her again.

"Brian," she whispered back, taking over the kiss, his heart, as she loved him with her mouth.

Her body settled against his, feeling better than every dream he'd had of her since she'd walked away. Letting his instincts lead, taking in all the incredible things Sam made him feel, he let his hands roam down her back, molding her lower belly to him as he massaged the base of her spine. She gasped, and then their tongues were dancing. They both groaned. They both held on tighter.

"Let me love you," he insisted, his fingers finding the hem of the soft pink sweater that had bewitched him earlier. "It's dark. There's no one around but us, and no one can see us this far back from the road. Everyone's eating dinner or cleaning up after it or out doing something for the night or settling into bed. Let me have you, Sam. Let me make you feel good again."

She nodded, kissing her way down his neck and back up to his ear, nibbling at the place she knew would drive him crazy.

"Hurry," she whispered.

He sat up, chuckling. "I'll remind you that you said that."

She settled against him perfectly, balancing in his lap, and raised her arms high while he peeled away the material that was in his way.

"You're supposed to be playing hard to get," he reminded her, burying his nose in the cleavage created by her powder pink bra.

"Maybe I want to get gotten," she said against his neck. She kissed her way down his throat. Her fingers unbuttoned his dress shirt.

The husky timber of her voice, the need in it, stopped him. He framed her face with his hands. She lifted her gaze until she was looking at him, looking into him, there with him while they both tried to catch their breath.

"I'm so sorry," he said. "For everything. For not fighting for this sooner. I let it slip away. I let us slip away. The closeness. The talking we used to do, and the dreams we had. The family we wanted, and knowing that no matter what, we could tackle anything together."

Sam bowed her head, the lightness that had been shimmering in her expression dulling.

"I wish . . ." she started to say.

"Don't!" His anger was for himself alone. "Don't you apologize, damn it, because I've been phoning it in, thinking I'm some kind of big-shot hero for doing all the heavy lifting since we moved here. When it's been you who's learned what you needed to and fought your way back. And now I'm . . ."

"Lost," she finished for him. "I know. I think we all are still. Maybe Cade most of all."

Brian kissed her with all the tenderness inside him, in no rush now, wanting to savor her all night if she'd let him. "But we won't let him stay lost. *You* won't. And I won't be in your way anymore. I'll do everything I can to help you and Cade both, and Joshua. I'm listening to whatever you think will help us, even if I don't want to hear it. No more holding back or avoiding difficult conversations or bad days or even breakdowns, if someone needs to have them. Even me. We can get through all of that, as long as we're really together from now on."

He realized he was holding his breath, as if he were waiting for something magical to happen. And then it was there—the sly, confident smile spreading across Sam's face as she reached behind her and worked the clasp of her bra, letting its straps ease down her arms in a slow arc. She went to work on his buttons again, her lips curling higher when she reached the waist of his pants and unfastened his belt.

"Tell me," she said, finding him beneath the material of his pants and underwear and reminding him what true torture felt like, "what are you hearing me say now?"

He kissed her, loving her sass and every other thing about her and the night deepening around them and the fresh start they were reaching for.

"That you're willing to take a chance with me again," he said. "I swear I'll be there for you from now on. All the way. Wherever we need to go, this time we'll be there together . . ."

Hope bloomed in every touch they shared. Trust. Acceptance. Forgiveness. She released him from his boxers, loving him with her delicate fingers. He made fast work of her jeans and rolled her beneath him. He was moving to cover her with his body when she stiffened in his arms, her palms plastered against his chest.

He bit back his denial and waited, watching her, knowing what was coming and wishing to God there were something he could do to make this moment easier.

"It's okay, sweetheart," he encouraged her. "Go ahead and say it. Whatever it is, it will be okay."

She stared up at him.

The hated word he couldn't seem to banish from his vocabulary echoed around them, but this time he was hoping she understood that anything, everything, would be okay between them from now on, no matter what.

"I can't . . ." She shook her head. "I don't want you to think that . . ."

"That this means you're coming home?" He settled against her, humbled by the rightness of having her in his arms again. "I know. I know you're not ready. And maybe I'm not, either. Cade for sure doesn't need more tension around him now. That's not what tonight is about, Sam. I swear. This is just about us. About now. I need you. I think you need me, too. Let me be there for you, at least in this. Let me love you and show you how good we can still be together."

She nodded.

"There's just one more thing," she said, arching into him until they were one, husband and wife, perfect together the way they always would be. Then she stilled, holding him tight inside her, her gaze filled with the trust he thought he might never earn back. "It might be taking on too much, but I've asked Kristen to help me do something for Cade, and maybe for Nate. I need . . . I'm going to need your help talking with the Turners."

"Help with what?" He was losing track of what they were saying. Of anything but the perfect feel of being with her, whole again.

"I want to start teaching, Brian."

"Teaching?"

After all this time.

"I can help our son and his friend deal with the school part of their problems, at least," she said, her excitement thrilling and terrifying him.

What if she *was* taking on too much? What if Cade didn't respond and disappointed her? She'd been through so much already, and today alone had exhausted her.

Brian made himself stop worrying, stop rushing to protect her, and curled his wife closer. If teaching again was what she thought was best for her and Cade, then that's what they'd do.

"You're amazing." He kissed her soft mouth, sinking deeper into her body. "My crusader . . ."

He'd dreamed so many times of the sound of her sighs as he loved her. The feel of her shuddering beneath his hands and his mouth. He laid Sam back on the soft grass. Shadows and gentle, spring night sounds caressed them as he lost himself in their need for each other.

It was stronger than ever, this drive to be one, to never be apart. Her lips claimed his as she grew demanding, her tongue teasing and soothing. His hands molded her against his body. His hips moved faster. He couldn't get enough of her arching into him, her desperation feeding his own need.

This was his home.

Sam was where he belonged.

Nothing could break the raw honesty of this bond they'd found only with each other. Nothing would make him consider giving up, not when it came to bringing her all the way back to their family. And nothing would ever again tempt him to distance any part of himself from the honest connection she'd always gifted him, each time he saw love in her eyes.

They pushed each other closer to the pinnacle, moving in an ageless rhythm that was both the same and infinitely different after months of being apart. And just as they were about to fall, he watched his wife's gaze grow brighter as it locked onto his the second before she shattered around him, clinging to him, calling his name and saying the words he knew would hurtle him over his own edge.

"I love you . . . Brian, I love you so much . . ."

DAY THREE

Chapter Fifteen

April 12, 2013

As spring slipped closer to summer in North Georgia, morning light became a swirl of pinks and yellows amidst an indigo dream. The last few minutes before the sun warmed the sky could produce the kind of magic that night only dreamed of being.

Sam headed out at six o'clock for her walk, finding the temperature chilly enough for her to need a jacket over her sweat suit. But in the breeze curling its way along Mimosa Lane, there was already a whisper of the pleasant day to come. Or could it be the smile of the man waiting at the end of the Davises' driveway that was making everything still sleepy inside her instantly alert, more alive, at just the sight of him?

"Hey," she said to her husband.

Surprise thrilled through her body. It was Friday, and they hadn't had more than a few moments alone together since the first of the week, when Brian had escorted her back to Julia and Walter's after they'd made love in the park.

"Can I take my girl for another walk?" He held out his hand, and the soft, muted colors in the sky became even brighter, closer, bursting into an answering smile that spread across Sam's face.

She glanced behind him at their house.

"The boys are fine," Brian said. "I just checked on them. They're sound asleep. I left a note in the kitchen, and Joshie doesn't have to be up for school for another hour. I'm still having to roll Cade out of bed so he's ready to work with you once the bus leaves, but we have some time. Come walk with me before you dive into breakfast and trying to cajole our firstborn out of his funk."

Brian had become an instant champion of her and Kristen's mission to make sure Cade and Nate finished sixth grade with their class. James Turner, unfortunately, had still been fuming after the school board meeting, when Sam and Brian had approached him and Beverly about Nate homeschooling with their son.

Beverly could keep helping Nate if their tutor wasn't a good fit, James had insisted Tuesday morning. They knew that the bruises on Nate's face were from a fight with Cade. Were Sam and Brian crazy, thinking that anything good would come from throwing their families together even more? Then the man had slammed his front door in their faces.

Sam took Brian's hand now. They walked out of the cul-de-sac, the feeling easy and simple, as if they did this sort of thing every morning. Maybe they were a little crazy, not yet living together again when they were feeling closer to each other now with each passing day.

"I know you're worried," he said. "I am, too. But Cade will come around. If anyone can get through to him, you can."

"You could . . ." She couldn't say it. She hadn't found a way to say it yesterday, either, or any other day since she'd started teaching their son.

Even though he'd taken a leave from his job at W&M, Brian still headed out in the mornings once she and Cade were settled in for the day. Brian and his briefcase simply disappeared to *somewhere*, and her curiosity to know where was killing her.

"Maybe I could stay and help?" He shook his head. "I talk with Cade in the afternoons when I come home. And I'm doing a better job listening to our kids at night, just being there in the evenings while Joshua plays and Cade reads or whatever, or the three of us watch a movie. This good cop/bad cop thing we're doing is working."

"No, it's not. Cade's hardly working at all. He's still hurting, and he's not talking about what's bothering him, not enough, no matter what I try."

"He's sleeping better now than he did the first part of the week. And he ate dinner with me and Joshie last night, instead of getting up with his plate still full, and snacking later, the way he has the last few days. He's relaxing again. Dr. Mueller said to give him a little more time, but to stay firm about needing to get his missing assignments done and turned in. I don't want him to think you and I are ganging up on him about his schoolwork. Try again today. I have a good feeling about it."

She peered at her husband out of the corner of her eye. Brian had been to see a therapist that week, too—later in the day Wednesday after they'd taken Cade for his session with Dr. Mueller. Brian hadn't been ready to talk about what he'd discussed with his own doctor, the same as their son was once more keeping his feelings to himself. And Sam had given them both their space, trusting that they'd share what they could when they were ready. But something must be working for her husband. He seemed lighter. More relaxed . . .

And she felt nervous around him now, the way she had when they'd first started going out in Manhattan and had been discovering new things about each other every day. There was . . . mystery between them again, not just the pain of the last few months, or the confusion and desperation of the last twelve years. There was the promise of a brighter future, even if she couldn't yet see it clearly.

I swear I'll be there for you from now on, he'd promised. *All the way. Wherever we need to go, this time we'll be there together . . .*

She wanted to ask him about his plans with W&M, and about what he was thinking about the two of them. But he was no longer pushing her for things when she wasn't ready. He deserved the same consideration from her.

Damn it.

They'd reached the bend in the road that would take them to the playground. She touched his arm and slowed. They stopped beneath a street lamp that glowed amidst one of the prettiest maple trees in Chandlerville. In the fall, its leaves turned a brilliant gold, making this same spot at night something an animator might paint into a fairy tale. Above them, bright leaves would be backlit by the street lamp. Below, a carpet of yellow would encircle their feet.

Brian looked up at the newly sprouted green overhead, then at Sam.

"So," he said, smiling. "This is as far as we go?"

"Today," she whispered, thinking again about Monday night and how perfect those moments in his arms had been. "This is as far as we go today."

"That sounds promising." He bent his head and placed a chaste peck on her nose.

"I . . ." She wanted to say something to reassure both of them that even though it had only been a few days, she was even more confident than she'd been on Monday that their marriage was going to survive all that they'd been through. "I think I want to start working in the yard again . . . Is that okay?"

He pulled her into a hug, cupping her head to his shoulder. "You feel so good in my arms. You know I'd do anything to keep you close for as long as I can have you. But . . ."

"I shouldn't have asked. I've been over almost all day, every day, and you've been more than reasonable about me staying the night at Julia's still."

He didn't know that she was maybe staying at the Davis place now more for her friend's sake than she was for herself. Julia and Walter were barely speaking since their blowup Monday. Walter wasn't drinking at home any longer, but he looked worse and worse by the day. Julia was beside herself with worry.

"It's not fair of me," Sam said, "to ask for even more time at the house without moving back home completely. I honestly haven't even thought about the garden before this morning, so—"

"You can ask me for anything you want." He sounded angry, but his touch as he pushed her away was as gentle as ever. "Don't apologize. I just . . . I wish you'd leave the garden alone for a while. Focus on Cade while you're there. I know you like to be outside. I'll walk with you anytime you want, every morning and night from now on if that will help us sort things out. But leave the yard be, okay?"

Was he still afraid of losing her? Of her disappearing again? She'd hidden in her gardens for years, finding comfort and nurturing there instead of with him and their boys.

"Okay," she promised. For emphasis, she pushed onto her toes and kissed him.

It went straight to her head, how the gentle caress expanded so quickly inside her into full-on need and desire and memories from a time when feeling this way each time they touched had been simple and easy. Brian seemed lost to it just as completely, his hands framing her face, his strong body trembling against hers. Their kiss ended, but neither of them pulled away. They stayed beneath that fairy-tale tree, gazing into each other's eyes, their foreheads touching, for what seemed like hours.

Lacing his fingers with hers, Brian steered her back toward the cul-de-sac. If felt as if they were returning from a date, instead of a quick stroll around the neighborhood. The sun peeked over the very tops of the trees lining the backyards of the houses on their right, sparkling and cheery and showing off, welcoming them home.

"Thank you." She leaned her head against her husband's shoulder and closed her eyes.

"For walking with you?"

"For bringing me here. To Chandlerville." He'd sacrificed everything he'd built in New York to make this life possible. "This is where we were meant to be. These are our friends and where we're supposed to raise our family. Mimosa Lane is where I needed to heal, and somehow you knew that. Even with the shooting at Chandler and the world coming unglued around us again, I can't imagine being anywhere else but here. Thank you."

They were back at Julia's. Brian winked, and then he let her go. He fished his keys from the pocket of the dress slacks he'd worn along with an oxford shirt that he'd left unbuttoned at the collar. No tie today. No briefcase. He looked like a sexy banker on holiday.

Where was he going?

She was dying to know.

"Have fun mixing up something outlandish for breakfast," he said. "What kind of muffins will it be this morning, I wonder? Banana and kiwi? Orange and peanut butter?"

"I'm making French toast." She slapped at his shoulder. "Why don't you . . ."

When he came back each afternoon now, just as she was finishing trying to work with Cade, right before Joshua was due home on the bus, she always asked whether he'd like to join them for breakfast the next day. He shook his head now, just as he had all week.

"Your time with the boys is special to them," he said. "Cade's still not completely on board with all of this. Dr. Mueller said structure will be important for him. I don't want to meddle with things until he's in a better place."

"You're right." Brian was being so slow and cautious with their new start, while she was the one feeling reckless. "We need to figure our relationship out and be sure, before we risk confusing the boys even more than we have."

"We need to stop confusing ourselves." Her husband's next smile wasn't as wide. His wink was gone. But there was love in his gaze. "We're at a crossroads. We can do anything we want from here, and we should."

"We should what?" Her heart stumbled at the thought of the limitless future he was describing.

"We should figure out what our next . . . *everything* will be, instead of being so careful all the time and settling the way we have been. I learned that about myself through all of this."

"From your therapist?" she asked.

He shook his head. "From you."

"What?" What had she taught him?

"We're not meant to settle. You're right. We belong here, on Mimosa Lane and in Chandlerville. But not like this. Not like we've been living. We've let so much slip away, Samantha. It's time for us to take the best parts back."

Samantha.

Us.

Sam nodded.

It was magic, hearing her husband talk about searching and wanting again—dreaming of who they'd become, instead of clinging desperately to the life they'd lost.

There might still be broken things between them, but it felt so real, standing with Brian at sunrise and talking about what could be. The numbness, the separateness that had protected Sam for so long from the fear of letting her family down, was gone.

"I . . ." *I love you*, she wanted to say.

She'd already told him that when they'd made love. She hadn't been able to hold the words in. They'd been so close, and it had felt so perfect, being in her husband's arms again. But this was a different kind of awakening. This morning, something beyond their physical reconnection was pressing to the front of her mind. A truth. A need. A realization that had been three months—maybe even twelve years—in the making.

"I miss you," she whispered instead. "I miss you and me so much."

"I know you do." He checked his watch. He dug his hand into his pocket, pulling out his smartphone and checking his appointment app. "I have to get on the road."

"Where are you going?" The question gushed out before she could swallow it.

He'd half turned already toward his car, which he'd left at the end of Julia's driveway. He pivoted back, a knowing gleam in his eyes, and he pulled her into a rib-crushing embrace. He kissed her, wet and wild with tongues mating, until she was clinging. She moaned when he set her away, his expression assessing and in control while she breathed too heavily to take in any real air.

"I'll tell you all about it tonight," he said. "Go mother our boys until they relent. I'll take care of dinner and homework this evening. Then meet me here at sundown. Be my girl again tonight, Samantha, and I'll tell you everything. I've been missing you, too."

***

Cade stopped outside his brother's door on the way down to breakfast.

Friday was usually the best day of the school week, only he wasn't going to real school today. He hadn't gone back since Monday. And that was great. It should have been great. Or at least it should have been better. Better than seeing the doctor Mom and Dad had taken him to on Wednesday, or going back to Chandler, where he didn't want to be—not without Nate on the bus again, or in Mrs. Baxter's class. He'd heard Nate wasn't coming back at all this school year. They might not see each other again now until junior high.

His mom and dad had been serious about Cade being able to work at home, too. Mom had lesson plans and everything, like a real teacher, which was what she used to be, they'd said, when she'd never, ever talked about teaching before. Wasn't that lucky?

Except . . . Cade didn't feel lucky. Dad seemed a little better.

And so did his mom. And Joshie was as happy as ever, even though he'd mostly stayed away from Cade all week. Because Cade was still mad . . . or something, and his brother wasn't stupid enough to mess with him right now.

Cade didn't know what he was. Which was okay, Dr. Mueller had said, as long as Cade figured out how he was feeling eventually, and then he figured out why. Only he didn't want to know why. He just wanted it to stop. He missed Nate. He knew that. He missed how he used to not worry about anything except his family. And how school didn't used to feel so scary. He missed how he didn't used to be a jerk to everyone whenever he was feeling so bad.

He missed it all, he'd told the lady doctor who'd only wanted *him* to talk, when he'd wished Dr. Mueller would just tell him what to do or what to think or what to say to make everything better again. Because staying home wasn't working, and Mom being there wasn't working, and not seeing Nate still *really* wasn't working, especially after their fight. Cade even missed pushing his little brother around, and then making Joshie laugh again, and then pushing him around some more.

It felt like he was missing everything, everyone. Only he didn't really want to do any of the things or be with any of the people he was missing. Which was weird. And it was making him more mad than sad. All completely normal, the doctor had said, which was even weirder, an adult telling him to be mad about the stuff he didn't want to feel mad about anymore.

Maybe Dr. Mueller was the one who needed to talk to someone.

She'd said feelings could be awful, but he had to feel them anyway and get them out. Otherwise, how was he ever going to make the worst of them leave him alone?

Cade knocked on his brother's door.

He pushed it open.

"Joshie?" he said when the door snagged on a pile of clothes on the carpet. "Are you up?"

Joshua was dressed for school and on the floor near the end of his bed playing with his LEGOS. The kid was obsessed—more than usual after Monday. Cade wished he hadn't been such a pain, and that his bratty brother wasn't so quiet around him now. Joshie mostly just played by himself and stayed out of Cade's way once he got home from school.

He was going to build big things for real one day, their dad always said. While Cade had always wanted to . . . write. Writing was what he used to do when he needed to think things through, the way his brother was doing more of his LEGOS this week than ever before.

Only writing didn't make Cade feel better the way it used to. He hadn't been able to write anything, even school stuff, since the shooting. Writing was his thing—his thing that he'd wanted to do big one day. It used to be his way to say how he felt. But even though Mom and Dad were acting like they were getting better, and they were saying that things with school would be better, too, and they said that things with him and Nate wouldn't always be so lame if Cade just gave it time . . . Cade would look at a piece of paper, feeling awful and wanting to get it out the way he used to, and he . . . couldn't.

And when he'd told the doctor that, all she'd done was ask if he thought he knew why.

Wasn't that what his parents were paying *her* to tell them?

The only thing Cade knew as he sat on the floor next to his kid brother, who didn't look up from the spaceship he'd been building and taking apart and then building again all week, was that he was sad all the time still. And mad. And lonely. And it wasn't getting better for him the way it was for everyone else.

"I'm sorry," he said, meaning it.

It made him feel a little better, getting that out. Then things felt a little more like a real Friday, when Joshie glanced up at him and smiled through the gap that used to be his front teeth.

"For being a butthead?" his buttheaded little brother asked.

"For scaring you on Monday." Cade looked at Joshua's half-finished spacecraft, guessing which piece from the pile of scraps around them the kid might want next. He handed it over.

He used to be good at being a big brother. His parents had said so, over and over. He wanted to be good at it again. He'd thought a lot about it, since talking to Dr. Mueller about how his brother had tried to break up the fight between him and Nate, and how Joshie had cried when he'd begged them to stop, and then how he'd run to their mom. Cade had thought a lot since Wednesday about how fixing things with Joshua might make some of the sad go away.

"I wasn't really scared," Joshua said, leaning against Cade's shoulder a little. "Not like when you almost got killed at school. That scared me more."

"You know what scares me a lot?" Cade asked, just realizing it for sure himself.

"What?"

"Thinking of how much I'd be missing my snot-nosed little brother if Mom hadn't stopped Troy from taking me and Nate out. I don't ever want to miss you like that, Joshie. I don't want any more weeks like this week, like we can't do anything together and stuff, because I'm being such a dork."

Joshua looked as sad now as Cade felt. "You'd have missed Mom and Dad, too, right? Even though you're still kinda being weird with them?

"Yeah. Them, too."

"But Mom *did* stop Troy." Joshua snapped the LEGO piece Cade had found onto his spaceship. "So there's no reason to be scared now. Mom stopped him."

"Yeah," Cade said. But some of the mad was coming back, just because they were talking about her. "Mom can be really cool about some things."

"She wants to come home."

"Except she's *not* home. Not all the way."

"She wants to help you with school."

"Except she's not. She's not helping me with the essay." He'd begged her to get Mrs. Baxter and Ms. Hemmings to give him another assignment.

"You're being mean to her about it."

"I know, all right!" he yelled, probably scaring his little brother all over again. Because it felt scary, not being able to write. And not being able to be with his mom like before, even though she was spending even more time with him and letting him be however he was and not acting like it was making her feel bad, even when he was a pain.

"Why don't you want to do Expressions?" Joshua asked, which made Cade feel lonely again, because no one in his family understood.

"I just . . . can't."

"Well, then I don't want to do the contest this year, either."

"You never want to do the contest."

"Well, this year, if you don't, I won't."

Cade laughed. "Thanks, but you should probably stop making Mom mad about that. Let me take the heat. You don't have to."

"You write all the time," his brother said.

"Not anymore." Not this essay.

"It's just a stupid contest."

"The topic is about *heroes*, okay?" Cade yelled at his brother. Why was it so hard for everyone, especially his mom, to understand why he didn't want to write about that. "What do you know?"

Instead of yelling back, Joshie picked away at the LEGO piece that hadn't worked on his spaceship after all.

"What do *I* know about heroes?" Cade said, a lot softer.

Joshie stared at him weird, scared, like he knew Cade was trying not to cry.

"You know Mom," his kid brother said. "And I think she knows a lot about heroes. People are talking all the time about what she did to save you and Nate and Sally. And about stuff from before the shooting, the stuff from before she and Dad moved here that they don't talk a lot about. The 9/11 stuff."

"Yeah."

The 9/11 stuff.

The hero stuff that made her mad and sad and scared, just like hero stuff made Cade now. Only she'd never talked to him or Joshua or anyone about it. At least not about what it had been like or why she was so messed up about it.

Every kid had studied 9/11 in school and watched the videos everyone else in the world had seen. But it wasn't something his parents ever wanted to talk about, except to say that they'd lived in New York then, and that Mom had worked near

Ground Zero, back when she had a job like so many of Cade's friends' moms.

But Cade had thought for years that 9/11 was what had made Mom so sad. And maybe even mad, too. Dad had slipped up once and said Mom had been a hero the day the Twin Towers fell, but then he wouldn't talk about it when Cade had asked what he meant. Dad had said that Mom would be upset if they ever brought it up, so they shouldn't. They should just leave it alone.

That was when Cade had known that something about being a hero that day was why she wasn't like the other moms on the lane. Like Cade knew it was part of why she'd been living next door since she'd been a hero with Troy. It was part of why she and Dad weren't getting along like before.

And she didn't want to talk about it. Like Cade didn't want to write about heroes. Only Mom didn't have to talk about anything she didn't want to, while he didn't get a choice about his essay. And every time he tried to write it, all that came out was stuff about Nate and Troy and Bubba and that day. And he really, *really* didn't want to think about that day, or write about that day, or feel anything from that day again—just like his mom and 9/11.

"Cade?" she called from downstairs. He'd heard her come in half an hour ago to make breakfast, after he'd heard Dad pull out of the driveway. "Joshua?"

"We'd better get down there," his brother said. Joshie headed for the door, stopping to look back when Cade wasn't right behind him. "You comin'? It's Friday. One more day and it's the weekend."

"Yeah." Cade followed. And for his little brother, he tried to sound like he wasn't about to hurl again. "It's Friday."

"Wahoo!" Joshua cheered, running ahead and down the stairs. "Friday!"

"Wahoo." Cade stared after him, getting madder and madder at their mom and the stupid essay she was going to hound him about doing all day.

Chapter Sixteen

Sam smiled down at the yellow piece of paper stuck on the counter beside the stove.

You're the best woman, wife, and mother I know.
It's time to make our dreams come true.
Now get to work, Teach!
Love, Brian

Lifting the oversize Post-it by its corner as if it were the most fragile of priceless possessions, she cupped her husband's words to her heart.

She'd almost missed it. She'd been busy setting up for breakfast, whisking eggs and milk and cinnamon, warming her favorite frying pan, pulling out the thick slices of bread she used for French toast. She'd been distracted by that morning's walk with

Brian, in a wonderful place she hadn't been in for so long. A better place, even, than after they'd made love Monday night.

The thought of walking with Brian again tonight was making everything brighter and lighter and exciting. She'd forgotten what it was like, being at the center of her husband's attention—beyond his drive to take care of her. He wanted to spend more time with her, talk with her, and tell her everything he hadn't about whatever he'd been doing this week. He was so proud of her sticking with their plans for Cade, even if their son was still struggling. He was encouraging her to do more, not less.

And he missed her, too. He still loved her. Despite everything they'd been through since January, if felt as if they were closer as a couple now than they'd been in years.

Love, Brian

He'd never, in their entire marriage, written her a note. Her husband knew numbers and dimensions, and he could create awe-inspiring buildings with them. But not so much with the putting words on paper, the way she'd put her heart on the line with each loving thought she'd scribbled to him. He'd bought her flowers and candy and precious little trinkets to show he cared, for important occasions and sometimes for no occasion at all. He'd always been thoughtful and kind and loving, in his own special way. But it was as if he'd wanted to speak *her* love language this morning.

Now get to work, Teach!

He was challenging her. But he was also fighting alongside her, leaving a part of himself there with her, his confidence filling her up until there was no room left for doubt. She patted his note against her heart. She was slipping his faith in her into the pocket of her sweats, determined to once again be that fearless teacher from her past, when she heard footsteps thundering down the kitchen stairs.

Joshua hurtled toward her, his arms wide for the hug he demanded every morning.

"You're making French toast!" He knocked her back a few feet with his enthusiasm, his arms wrapping around her waist. "With powdered sugar on top?"

"Is there any other way to eat it?"

"I'll get the syrup." And he was off to the fridge to dig out his bottle of maple, and the artificial blueberry concoction that Cade loved, though everyone else in the family thought it tasted like cough syrup.

"Ready for your test today, buddy?" She dropped the first slice of toast into the cast-iron skillet she'd bought at a tag sale, smiling down at the sizzling, bubbly goodness.

"I'm always ready for math." Joshua owned his father's confidence with all things numbers.

"How about your essay?"

As part of their overall grade, each student at Chandler, no matter the grade level, was expected to enter one of the categories for the national Expressions contest. It was actually a privately sponsored competition, but school districts all over the country challenged their kids and communities to participate. The goal was to express yourself as creatively as possible, to represent what was best about your community, and to compete for a spot in the digital "album" of award winners that was posted to the Internet each fall, which intermingled the work of entrants from all over.

A beautiful tapestry of sorts resulted—a feast for the eyes and ears that spotlighted the very best of what it meant to live in the United States, blending ages and regions and experiences and backgrounds until there were no barriers left. There were countless options to choose from, with each competition category linked to the arts in some way. And the least objectionable for both of Sam's boys had always turned out to be the essay contest.

"Have you decided what you're going to write about?" she pressed her youngest.

Joshie shook his head. He sat on his stool and looked down at the island, his playful excitement gone.

"Can you tell me what's wrong?" she asked, trying not to sound as if she were begging. "You seem to be having an even harder time with the competition this year. I really want to understand."

Both her boys were downright miserable about entering. Cade especially. Mrs. Baxter and Ms. Hemmings had both agreed that the score Mrs. Baxter gave him on his entry essay could be counted as his language arts grade for the entire semester. The class had been working on theirs for weeks, and it was already a big part of the overall semester grade. It was a perfect solution to Cade's situation.

Except, as it turned out, for the topic of this year's competition—which Cade had totally balked at. And his therapist had said not to let him off the hook writing the essay, unless he could tell Sam or Brian why he didn't want to do it. Which he hadn't yet. And Dr. Mueller had said it was important not to give him that out, no matter how much Sam wanted to spare him.

"You," Cade said from the bottom of the stairs. He'd come down so quietly, she hadn't noticed him there. "You're what's wrong, Mom."

She curled her hand into her pocket, around Brian's note. When she was sure of her voice, and that she could be a teacher in that moment instead of a worried parent, she said, "How am I your problem, when you're the one not doing your work?"

"You won't talk Mrs. Baxter into giving me another assignment."

"Because you won't give me a good reason why you won't do this one."

"I don't want to. That's the reason."

"Well, you don't have a choice."

She'd avoided talking about her own problems for too long. She wasn't going to make that same mistake with her son.

"Like you have a choice?" Cade trudged across the kitchen and practically threw himself onto his own stool. His face, like his father's had, still sported bruises from Monday. "You're an adult, so you get to never talk about what you don't want to talk about. But we're kids, right? So we have to do what we're told, no matter what."

Sam blinked, forcing back the sudden need to give him a smothering-mothering hug. But Cade needed both a mother *and* a teacher right now, and Sam wasn't giving up until she'd found a way to be both for him.

She glanced at Joshua, who was still looking down. She flipped the first slice of French toast over, added a second that had been soaking. Then she faced both boys and crossed her arms.

"I don't like to write," Joshie finally said.

"You never have." Sam flipped the new slice of toast and transferred the first onto a plate. She sprinkled it with powdered sugar from the shaker she'd grabbed from the pantry. She handed Joshie the plate, a napkin, and a fork from the silverware drawer. "That hasn't stopped you from doing Expressions in the past. What gives now? Besides the fact that your brother is refusing to do his work,

261

so the two of you are banding together in solidarity, or something like that."

Joshua doused everything in syrup, cut off a huge bite and shoved way too much food into his mouth.

"Soli-what?" he asked around the mess.

"Are you not writing your entry"—Sam smiled, holding the everyday moment close—"because your brother's not writing his?"

Joshua shrugged and swallowed. She stopped herself from saying how proud she was that he'd stick up for Cade that way, even though they'd been having a tough week with each other. Instead, she flipped the second piece of French toast onto a plate. She handed it and a napkin and fork over to Cade, who didn't like sugar on his.

"I don't care what he does," Cade said. "I'm not writing any stupid essay."

"You love to write." He'd been so proud of his entries in the past. Each year, he'd won the school competition for his grade. Once he'd even won at the county level, and his entry had earned him an honorable mention at state.

"Not this year."

"Why?" Sam turned back to the stove, soaking two more slices of bread in the mix and dropping them into the pan.

She was pretty sure she knew why. But the doctor was right. No matter how much Sam wanted to soften the blow, Cade needed to work his own way through what was troubling him.

"Why don't *you* ever talk about it?" Joshua asked over his next bite.

"Why don't I ever talk about what?" Sam flipped the last two slices.

When she turned back, Cade pulled something from his pocket. It was a crumpled, stained Post-it. The one she'd left Brian Monday morning after they'd argued in the park.

I'm so sorry.

"The 9/11 stuff," her son said, his voice quiet but fierce at the same time. "How about you talk about that? And then I'll do my essay."

"Wh-what?" Her hand curled around Brian's note in her pocket, holding on to her husband's confidence, his love. "Why do you need to hear about that now?"

Talk about it?

Share with her already traumatized son what it was like to be a 9/11 *survivor*, and how it had felt all these years as if parts of her had never really left Ground Zero or the students she'd refused to keep up with after that day?

Is my mom going to be there? little Krista asked again, over and over again in Sam's mind. *Please . . .*

Sam gripped the edge of the countertop to keep the memories and the panic that swooped in with them from dropping her to the floor.

"Why not?" Cade accused. "No one makes you talk about what you don't want to. Why are you making me?"

Her unattended toast was burning. She grabbed the handle of the iron skillet without thinking—without a pot holder protecting her skin. Searing pain made her yank her hand away. But not in time.

"Ah!" she gasped to the sound of the school bus pulling into the cul-de-sac.

"Gotta go!" Joshua bounded off his stool and hugged her good-bye as if it were any other morning. "See ya later."

He grabbed his backpack off the kitchen table and raced out the garage door, slamming it behind him in such an ordinary boy way. Sam wanted to rush after him and hug him again and not let go until he, too, reached his older brother's age and began asking difficult life questions that deserved answers.

Only would she be strong enough then to give her boys the answers they needed, without falling apart herself?

She scooped ice out of the tray in the freezer, twisted the cubes in a kitchen towel, and then wrapped it all around her hand. She glanced at Cade, picking up the pot holder and then the frying pan and walking to the sink to dispose of the burned toast.

She sighed as she scraped.

"What don't you want to talk about in your essay?" she asked, focusing on teaching him, while she felt like an absolute failure as a mother.

She remembered like it was yesterday, Cade recognizing her fear the morning of the bake sale and saying she didn't have to talk about it. That she never had to talk about it. She and Brian had done more than become pros at hiding from their own awful feelings. They'd taught their son how to hide as well.

"The hero stuff," Cade said over what sounded like a mouthful of syrup and toast. "Everyone says you're a hero, but you're scared all the time. Everyone's talking about Nate and me like we did something big just by not getting dead like Bubba . . . like we're not scared all the time now, either. And I don't want to talk about it, just like you don't."

The hero stuff.

The 9/11 stuff.

She dropped the frying pan with a thud. She braced her hands on her hips. The one she'd burned throbbed while she tried to think of something, anything, to say.

Now get to work, Teach!

"Mom?" Her eleven-year-old sounded as young as Joshie now.

"It's . . ." She turned to face him. She'd almost said it wasn't the same. But it was. She knew it was. She knew just how difficult a thing she was asking of him—and how important it was for Cade to get his feelings out, before keeping them in became a habit. "I just can't, Cade. What happened in New York, it was like . . ."

Dying.

Every time the memories came back, whether she wanted them close or not, it was as if another part of Sam died.

"Well, I can't either." He pushed his half-eaten breakfast away.

"That's not an option for you."

Her heart was breaking for him. But he needed to say it, write it, shout it, even if he was shouting at her while he did it— whatever it took to get his fear out there, instead of holding it in. Sam had spent too many years trying to ignore her panic into oblivion, instead of honestly dealing with it. And look at where that had gotten her. She dropped the dripping ice into the sink and used another towel to dry her burned hand.

"Don't make the same mistake I did, buddy. Don't let yourself off the hook with the stuff you and Dr. Mueller are talking about, or with your Expressions entry."

"Then you do it first." He stepped down from his stool and crossed his arms like she had earlier. "You do it, or I won't."

"Do what?"

"You write an essay about heroes, too. Anyone can enter Expressions. Mrs. Baxter said so. It's not just for schools and kids.

You write an essay about the stuff you don't want to talk about. And I'll write mine."

He was deadly serious.

"Cade—"

The doorbell interrupted them.

"Don't you move a muscle." She pointed a finger at her soon-to-be teenager. "We're going to finish this conversation, and then you're getting to work."

She left him to his French toast. She tried not to run away from her child like a coward as she stumbled across the living room to the front door.

She pulled it open, not bothering to plaster on a smile for whoever was there.

"May we come in?" Mallory Phillips stood on the porch, beside Beverly and Nate Turner. From the look of things, Mallory was the only one who really wanted to be there. Her companions didn't bother to make eye contact.

"Maybe," Sam said. "How can I help you?"

The question was for Beverly, who had been standing silently beside her husband Tuesday morning when James had slammed their door in Sam and Brian's faces. Beverly wasn't saying a word now either, while she kept a viselike grip on Nate's arm.

"Oh, for heaven's sake." Mallory gave Beverly's shoulder a gentle shove, and suddenly the three of them were in Sam's living room, and Sam was shutting the door and turning to face them.

Cade wandered in from the kitchen.

"This has gone on too long," Mallory said to the lot of them. "I'm late for school. Mrs. Turner and Nate turned up on my stoop this morning, and I've been talking with them for over half an hour. We're not getting anywhere. Your families have known each other since the boys were practically in diapers. Fix this. Together. Now."

Mallory headed out the door before Sam could respond, shutting it again, this time behind her. The oxygen in the room seemed to leave with her.

Sam and Beverly stared at each other. Cade stepped to Sam's side, surprising her when he kept walking until he and Nate were face-to-face.

"Hey," he said to his friend, sounding for all of his eleven years as if he were a hundred instead.

Nate looked at Beverly and Sam, and then at Cade and said, "Hey. Whatcha doin'?"

"Breakfast." Cade shrugged in the direction of the kitchen. "Mom burned it, but I think there's cereal. Do you . . . do ya want some?"

Both mothers watched and waited.

Nate pulled his arm away from Beverly's hold. "Sure. Why not?"

The boys walked away side by side, humbling Sam with the simplicity of the acceptance and healing they were giving each other after so much arguing and pain. She turned back to Beverly, wondering whether the grown-ups in Chandlerville would ever be as wise.

Sure. Why not?

"Would you like some coffee?" she asked.

Beverly shook her head. "No . . . I . . ." Her thin laugh made the last of Sam's anger melt away. "I should be getting to work. Nate . . . He's made it clear he doesn't want me to stay home with him. He doesn't want his tutor. He won't do his work, and he says he misses his teachers and his friends at school, even though we barely talked him into trying to go back on Monday. And his therapist doesn't want him to try Chandler again until they've had more sessions and Nate opens up about some of this. He has to complete his makeup work, though, and I'm tired of putting up with his attitude, even though I'm worried about what disciplining him might do. And . . ."

Another mother's confusion should have been overwhelming to hear, the way other people had overwhelmed Sam for so long. Except Beverly's issues were Sam's issues, and both of them were trying to understand the unexplainable.

Cade and Nate laughed, the familiar sound filtering into the living room from the kitchen. Beverly's answering smile made her look ten years younger.

"What were you going to work on with Cade today?" she asked.

"The Expressions essay. It's . . . not going well."

Beverly's eyes rolled. "I can't convince Nate to do it, either."

"I was about to resort to threatening when you rang the bell. Then maybe move on from there to extortion."

Beverly laughed again.

They fell into a strained silence.

"Does James know you're here?" Sam asked.

Beverly shook her head. "He's in New York through the weekend."

"Would he mind?" The last thing they needed was to throw the boys together, only to have James forbid Nate from coming over again.

"I don't really give a damn right now. I have to do what's best for our son, and that's clearly not me. I'm not a teacher. And another tutor he's never met is a bad fit right now, with the way he's feeling."

"But I'm not a teacher anymore either. Not really."

Sam hadn't even been able to agree to do the one thing her son had finally asked of her to do, so he'd get down to work himself. Mallory shouldn't have put her in this position with the Turners. Beverly shouldn't be looking at Sam as if she were the answer to all of Nate's problems.

"Of course I'm happy to talk with Nate," she said, "anytime he wants to. But I don't know why you think he'd respond to me any better than he does you."

"He told me . . . about you two meeting at night. He said it helped. Just like talking with you at school on Monday helped. You got him to be honest about what he needed. You got him talking with me, at least for a few hours. You're really good with kids still, Sam."

"Yes." Right up until they were depending on her to be brutally honest with herself.

Beverly blushed. "I can't believe I'm asking you this . . ."

"And it means a lot to me that you are, really, after how difficult things have been between our families. But—"

"I'm mortified about how we've behaved, Sam. How James and I forgot what you and Brian have been through. I know my husband feels just as bad as I do."

Sam wasn't so sure of that. But she nodded, accepting the apology for their boys' sake.

Another round of laughter reached them.

"Do you think . . ." Beverly asked. "Could Nate stay, at least for today? Can't we see how it goes?"

How it would go?

While her son was calling her out on how she was still too closed off to be helping him open up about his own feelings?

"Beverly, I don't think—" She never got the chance to finish.

"Mom!" Cade ran into the living room and right up to them, Nate sprinting behind him. Both boys had transformed. It was like seeing them again the way they'd been in early January—full of energy and enthusiasm and hope. "Mom, can Nate study with us today? Please?"

"Honey, I don't know—"

"You don't have to help me now. I promise I'll do my work. Nate and me, we're going to help each other write our Expressions essays. I won't have to do it alone, and you won't have to do it with me. Isn't that great? Please, Mom. Let Nate and me do it together . . ."

Chapter Seventeen

"My intention was never to take your business away from Whilleby & Marshal," Brian said to Jefferson Kelsey, across the table they were sharing at the Thanks a Latte, in historic downtown Chandlerville.

"You're not." Jeff added a packet of raw sugar to the chai tea he was drinking instead of coffee. "Whilleby gave the commission away when he took you off our account. I've decided I don't want to deal with another associate. I came to *you* when Ginger turned our plans for a nursery into creating the Taj Mahal in the middle of a three-story colonial. Because I knew I could count on you not to pick my pocket, while your designs blew my socks off."

Jeff's southern accent complemented his good-ol'-boy grin. But there was no mistaking the power he effortlessly exuded. He was a man who knew what he wanted, and always negotiated for whatever that was until he got it at a steal.

"I'm afraid I didn't give the partners much of a chance to change their minds when they pulled me from your project." Brian was still a little stunned by the proposal Jeff had made. And he refused to even consider it until they were clear on the circumstances surrounding his leave of absence from W&M. "I asked for time off. Not because of your project, though I was sorry to see it transferred to another associate. My family . . . needs me to be more available to them than I can be working the hours I have to at the firm. And clearly my attention has been distracted away from the work Jonathan Whilleby and the other partners need me to be doing."

"Both good reasons why you should start your own firm. Here, in Chandlerville. Make the work what *you* want it to be. Work only the time you can, and do it where you don't have to spend hours a day in the car, commuting." Jeff took a long drink, eyeing Brian the way Whilleby had a time or two, when the older man had been debating Brian's future in the firm his father's father had started seventy years ago. "Unless what you're saying is that you don't have what it takes to design and manage projects on your own. I'm betting you do."

Other than his wife and family, there was nothing Jeff Kelsey enjoyed more than a good bet.

He was legendary on Mimosa Lane for the boys-only gambling trips he sponsored to Vegas every year during the Super Bowl. He chartered a plane, arranged for big-roller comps at one of the casinos on the Strip, and invited a handful of his neighborhood friends to join him, at least the ones who could beg a weekend away from their own wives and families. What you lost and won was your own affair, but Jeff never made a secret of starting with $50,000 and not caring whether he came in under or over at the end of the trip.

He was usually over, and he'd promised Brian a time or two that he could make the same magic happen for him, if Brian was willing to risk the starter money. But since $50,000, if he had it to toss around, was what Brian imagined might be a drop in the bucket when it came to paying for his boys' college tuition one day, he'd always politely passed on the invitation to gamble away his savings.

Now Jeff was proposing something even riskier. Brian's reputation in the field of architecture. His security at Whilleby & Marshal. His family's already tattered peace of mind, if he threw a wrench in the works by going out on his own.

But wasn't that exactly what Brian had been thinking about every day and night since stepping away from the firm? He'd even talked about it with his new therapist, whom he'd seen again yesterday, not just the one time on Wednesday that Sam knew about. And the bulk of the time each day that he'd steered clear of the house to give Sam and Cade a chance to work, he'd been poring over small-business research material at the library, thinking and planning some more.

Even before Jeff's offer, Brian had been working on the beginnings of a business plan that had been feeling less hypothetical by the day. He'd been dreaming of taking on the kinds of projects he'd always wanted, with clients looking for the environmentally conscious designs he'd studied and begun challenging himself with before leaving New York.

It might be a selfish dream, given his and Sam's problems and Cade's struggles. It *was* selfish. But a little more every day, Brian was feeling like the man he'd once been. He was remembering a time when cutting-edge architecture had been so perfect a fit for him that he wouldn't haven't blinked before jumping at the crazy proposition his friend was making.

"Your own firm," Jeff said. "You in the driver's seat. I've got the seed money, Lord knows, with what my family's left me. My financial advisor's been at me to diversify by investing in some kind of small-business venture. But what I don't have is the play in my schedule to take on another time-intensive investment."

Jefferson was an entrepreneur and an independent financial advisor, with clients and connections all over the country. He knew money inside and out. He knew business. He knew people. He understood precisely what Brian would be giving up if he walked away from W&M. And he was an intuitive bastard who'd likely noticed from the start how Brian had been chomping at the bit to call his own shots on the Kelseys' remodel, rather than playing by Whilleby's rules. And now Jeff was moving in for the kill.

"My commission alone," he said, "would be the kind of start that'll attract other clients. Ginger's talked to several design magazine editors—in Atlanta and New York—who want to do before-and-after features. Make that happen, make her happy, and by this time next year you'll have more business than you know what to do with."

Brian had already admitted that he was excited by the prospect. The risk. The chance to build and be part of something where he controlled the vision and creative content. Jeff would make a solid partner. And this man who lived to take risks in life and in business was ready to roll the dice with him.

"I don't know what to say," he said for the third time since they'd sat down.

Jeff checked his Rolex. "I'm on a conference call for the rest of the morning. Then I'm taking clients to dinner tonight. How about we do this again tomorrow. I know it's Saturday, but I'll be around. Text me when you can get away from your family, and I'll meet you here. You can give me your answer then."

Brian had been surprised to get Jeff's call last night. He'd been dreading another long night without the wife who clearly still loved him but wasn't comfortable enough yet to come home. After a brief conversation about Jeff's idea and an agreement to talk more this morning, Brian had spent another sleepless night tossing and turning. Only this time, his mind had been spinning over exciting career possibilities and potential conflicts and the thrill of figuring out how to make it all work, rather than the state of his personal life.

Now he was facing a nuclear deadline that left him very little time to decide what direction he wanted that life to take next. His shock must have shown.

Jeff chuckled as he stood, taking his chai with him. "Have you talked it over with Sam?"

"I wanted to this morning . . ."

Brian had met her for the walk he knew she took every morning, intending to ask her what she thought. He'd left her a note in the kitchen, thinking that by the time she'd read it, they'd already have discussed the outrageous gamble he wanted to take with Jeff. He'd hoped for her support, her understanding. But all he could think about after he'd taken her hand outside Julia and Walter's place had been Sam and the boys and their marriage and their family. They had so much up in the air still. How did he add even more confusion to the mix?

"I'll make sure Sam and I get together about it tonight . . . somehow," he said. "I'll have an answer for you in the morning."

Jeff held out his hand, his expression sympathetic. "I know you guys are in a tough place. But refocusing at least some of your energy on something in the future while you deal with the rest would be a good distraction. And I don't see you at Whilleby & Marshal forever. We could take one hell of a ride together, Brian, if you're willing."

Willing?

Brian was aching to do this. It was taking every scrap of professionalism he still possessed not to jump at Jeff's offer, before he'd figured out whether he and his family could actually deal with the reality of it.

"It's an exciting opportunity, Jeff. I appreciate your confidence in my ability."

"This is about more than ability, boy."

Jeff slapped him on the shoulder as they headed outside toward their cars—Brian's a dependable Nissan, and Jeff's a jet-black Ferrari. The man's ride would have better fit a rock star than a Southern aristocrat whose wife's family fortune was reported to have once upon a time stayed buried for five years beneath an occupied grave, to keep it out of the hands of the damn Yankees who'd burned their plantation down.

Jeff wasn't what the rest of country had in mind when they thought of a good ol' boy. There were more families like the Kelseys sprinkled about the South than people realized. Around Atlanta, it wasn't all that uncommon to run across old-money families entrenched in everyday, upper-middle-class neighborhoods. They could afford a more upscale zip code, and there would always be talk about why they didn't. But couples like the Kelseys didn't really care what people thought about their choices. They enjoyed their money, but they didn't let it define everything about how they lived their lives.

Jeff was eccentric. But he seemed just as satisfied to spend time with his and Ginger's Mimosa Lane friends as he would being with whatever social connections he'd made in New York or Los Angeles.

"This is about character," he said. "I was at the school board meeting Monday night, where you collected all that color on your face. You've got balls of steel, my friend, and the integrity to say what you think. I'm looking for a business partner I can trust. I could find a good architect anywhere. What I want is someone who's lookin' to shake things up. Whatever you decide, the commission for Ginger's and my extension is yours if you want it. And I'll put my lawyers on whatever noncompete agreement you signed with W&M when they hired you. Though I doubt they'll fight my decision to stick with your expertise privately. I'm negotiating several corporate projects with the firm that I doubt they're going to want to punt, just to bully you around over a home remodel. You let me know tomorrow if you're ready to saddle up for the rest of what we've discussed."

***

Kristen stopped by Mallory's office, aware that her school nurse had arrived close to an hour late for work.

"How are things on Mimosa Lane?" she asked, cutting to the chase.

You either got to the point during a school day at Chandler, or the point left you behind in a big fat hurry.

Mallory glanced up from the stack of papers she was working with—student records that needed to be continuously updated with contact and health details they tracked from various sources, the most unreliable of which often seemed to be parental communication. The school was due for a county audit soon, and the clinic's information for each child was most definitely on the list of things to be pored over by people looking for a reason to find Kristen's team lacking.

There were still so many unanswered questions about how no one had identified the depth of Troy Wilmington's issues, the bullying he and some of the other kids endured at school each day, and how much pressure he was being subjected to at home. Terrified, hurting parents wanted reassurances about the safety of their children. And even after their community's progress at Monday night's school board meeting, there were those who would continue to look for someone to blame.

One bright spot had been the news that Nate Turner's parents were backing off their demands for a formal investigation into Edna Baxter's "mishandling" of her classroom, and their call for her forced retirement. But even so, Chandler had a bullying problem to deal with. Kristen was on a personal mission to make sure that none of her kids suffered in silence the way Troy had. And to make sure that children prone to pick on those they saw as weaker students, the way Bubba had, would learn to handle their insecurities and aggression more constructively. That's why she'd volunteered to be the school's liaison to the board of ed's new task force.

Meanwhile, the county would continue to analyze every move Chandler's administration made, looking for lapses in judgment or unmet regulations, starting with the medical records kept for the students. Mallory was usually the most dependable of Kristen's staff, a calm voice amidst any difficulty. Her assistance and expertise since the Wilmington shooting had been invaluable—creating a support network on the fly for dealing with the trauma and psychological aftereffects. But this morning, Chandler's nurse was clearly running on empty.

"The lane seems to be having a collective nervous break-down." Mallory blew her bangs out of her eyes, tossing her pen on top of the papers and pushing her computer's keyboard away. "I can't reach anyone in Chandlerville over the phone to update their records. Practically no one's showing up yet for the family support group I've e-mailed parents about. But that doesn't stop them from asking me for advice and help every time I turn around. Because things are going from bad to worse and no one's working on their own solutions yet—no matter how hard they think they're trying, or how much good Brian's speech Monday night might have done. Beverly and Nate Turner showed up at my front door this morning."

"Really?"

Kristen waited, in case the other woman didn't want to talk about it. Mallory's scrubs that morning were covered in smiling puppies showing a lot of teeth. Given her present mood, all that happy came off more menacing than soothing.

"Right there in front of her son," Mallory said, "Beverly started telling me all over again how much difficulty they were having getting Nate to concentrate on his schoolwork. She asked if there were any meds I could suggest that their pediatrician might give him to help Nate get over what he's been through, enough to at least get to the summer without flunking out of sixth grade."

"Poor Nate. What did you say?" Kristen knew her friend had very definite opinions on the subject of medicating a child, in-stead of actually figuring out whatever else a student needed to feel better.

Mallory folded her hands together, sitting back in the creaky desk chair someone had found for her when she'd first started at

Chandler and realized that the former nurse hadn't kept a desk at all. Mallory had been all business then, even though she'd doted on the kids from the start. And she was all business now.

She studied Kristen from head to toe and back up again. Kristen knew just how bloodshot her eyes were, and how much more makeup she needed these days to cover the fact that she looked almost as bad as she felt. She hadn't taken the time to press her suit that morning. And even though the wrinkles weren't that noticeable, she felt certain Mallory had catalogued every one.

So what if she still wasn't sleeping, despite how well Monday's meeting had gone? They were talking about Nate, not her.

"What did you do with Beverly?" she insisted.

"I sat and listened, while the woman talked to me about personal things she thinks she and her husband are dealing with, except they're not. Which is exactly the sort of thing a parents' support group would help her figure out. Not that the Turners plan to attend a group meeting. Which is when it dawned on me . . ."

"What?"

"That I've been enabling the woman and the other well-meaning parents who keep calling me for advice, except they aren't taking the steps they need to help themselves or each other."

"And?"

Kristen could empathize with the Turners.

She'd received a flood of offers of support from the local education community. She'd carefully thanked each person, but had backed away from everyone, before people had had to distance themselves from her situation—because no one in their right mind really wanted to tangle with the board or superintendent in such a high-profile way. And Kristen would rather proactively decline each well-meaning but empty offer of support before it disappeared on its own. She'd learned from experience that her self-esteem took less of a beating that way, when in the end she still wound up facing what she had to alone.

Accepting help, trusting people when they offered it, left you in a vulnerable place that evidently a lot of people in Chandlerville were steering clear of.

"*And*," Mallory said, "I marched Beverly across the cul-de-sac to Sam's house, where Sam's still having trouble getting Cade to work, and I pretty much threw them at each other. And then I got in my car and drove to my day job—you know, the one where I get to relax for a few hours doing my nails and gabbing with the girls."

Kristen smiled at the image of Chandler's clinic nurse stomping to her perky, yellow VW Beetle and tearing down Mimosa Lane in a huff.

"Have you called to check up on them?" Kristen asked.

Mallory glared at the phone, back at Kristen, and then down at her paperwork.

"No." She sighed. "I was going to wait until after lunch. I have to finish all of this first."

Kristen chuckled and collected the student records.

"You're officially on lunch break," she said, thrilled at the thought of the Perry and Turner families making progress with their boys, and loving how much Mallory cared right along with the rest of Kristen's staff. "Go ahead and call." She plopped herself down in the guest chair beside the desk. "Gab away. You're dying to hear what happened. I know I am."

Chapter Eighteen

"I need your help," Julia said, when Sam answered the door for the second time that day.

"What's wrong?" Sam asked, not that she really wanted to know.

Though her son's enthusiasm had led her to relent to Nate staying, neither boy had wanted to do much more than goof around. They'd gotten very little work done, but their happiness at once more being friends had been a promising start. Plus Cade had laid off Sam for the rest of the morning and early afternoon, allowing her nerves to settle a bit—though she still felt guilty for not being able to give her son the only thing he'd asked her for since the shooting.

Nate was gone now. She'd just seen him and Beverly off—agreeing, mostly because of the pep talk she'd received earlier when Mallory had called to check in, to give the boys working together one more shot tomorrow—*if* James Perry signed off on the arrangements, and only if the boys agreed to buckle down and focus on their assignments, in particular their essays.

Cade and Joshua were having their after-school snack of homemade oatmeal cookies in the kitchen. Brian still wasn't home from wherever he'd spent the day. And Sam's ability to cope was frayed beyond the point of holding herself together through yet another demand for her attention.

"It's Walter." The fear and outright panic in Julia's voice vaporized Sam's self-pity.

She stepped back. Her friend rushed inside. Julia paced a few feet away, came back, and shook her head while staring through Sam. And then she paced some more, repeating the entire process. Before she could get away again, Sam took her hands and squeezed.

Julia's customary forced cheer had disappeared over the last week. So had the smile that had told the world since January that nothing whatsoever was wrong in the Davis house. And as many times as Sam had wished her friend would deal more realistically with the state of her own family instead of focusing so much energy on Sam's problems, why did this epiphany have to be happening today?

"What's going on with Walter?" she made herself ask.

Because she *did* want to know. And she did want to help. Really, she did. They hadn't spoken about Monday night. Julia hadn't wanted to before now, and Sam had been worried about her all week.

"I told him after that awful scene he made in front of you," Julia said, "that he was done drinking at home. I wasn't having any more of it. And he said he was sorry. He said he'd stop, that he'd never meant to say those horrible things." She walked to the kitchen and peeked around the corner at the boys. When she came back, she was wringing her hands. "I really thought he'd stopped."

Sam checked her watch. It was a little after four. Surely Walter wasn't over at Julia's now, tying one on.

"All day," her friend said. "He's been at it all day, from the sound of it. All week, ever since Tuesday morning. I don't know if he's quit his job, or gotten himself fired, or if he's pickled his brain until *he* doesn't know. Just that he's managed to be sober enough when he gets home to lie his ass off to me about where he's been and what he's been doing."

Hearing Mimosa Lane's moral compass saying the words "lie his ass off" got to Sam more than her friend's agitation. Julia took off pacing again, her knee-length, Ralph Lauren print skirt swishing about her in pleated perfection. The sleeves of her purple silk blouse floated around her arms. Her leather shoes were just right, their kitten heels giving her enough lift to show off her legs without looking as if that was what she wanted them to do.

Julia looked utterly cool and capable. And devastated.

"All day?" Sam repeated, treading carefully. "He's been . . ."

"Drinking down at McCradey's. All week. They open for early lunch, he settles in at the bar for a sandwich, and he doesn't move until it's time to come home for dinner, or so Law Beaumont says. He's their regular day bartender now. He was one of my volunteers at Chandler when I ran the PTA. He only worked nights back then, and his days were almost always free. With him and Sheila split up now, he's paying alimony and child support and only sees Chloe on the weekends. So he's pulling double shifts every weekday he can, and he thought I should know that Walter was there again. That he was there *every day now*, he said.

Because my husband's evidently been doing this since the shooting, off and on, only *now* it's every day, and Law says today's been the worst of all . . ."

Sam's head was pounding as Julia's frantic explanation wound down. She'd felt shell-shocked all day, a low-level panic persisting ever since Cade had let her off the hook about the essay.

I won't have to do it alone, and you won't have to do it with me. Isn't that great?

Yeah, it was great.

She was a coward, just like Brian had said. And no matter how much she talked about wanting to change for herself and her family, she hadn't been there for her son that morning. How many more chances was she going to get before Cade stopped expecting her to be there for him at all?

"What are we doing, Julia?" She gazed at her friend, who'd been agonizing for months over how to help her husband, while Julia hadn't really done much of anything at all except worry. "How did everything get so messed up?"

They'd been leaning on each other since January, but neither one of them had wanted to face the harsh reality that it was time to start leaning on their own families again, before it was too late.

Julia swallowed, as if she were afraid to answer. "We're living our lives the best way we know how."

Lonely . . . But never alone.

"We've been hiding from the people we love for so long, they think we don't want to be there for them." Sam had been so determined to see her stay at Julia and Walter's as moving forward. Brian was proud of the stand she'd made. But she'd kept seeing other things all day, over and over in her mind.

Cade curled up on the patio swing at the house the morning of the shooting, waiting for her to come home from the night walking that had kept her at such an emotional distance from her family. He'd known how upset she was, and he'd wanted to be with her and help her somehow. But now that he was struggling, even when he'd told her exactly what he needed her to do to help him—the same way she'd been trying to get Brian to understand what *she* needed—what had Sam done? She'd totally bailed on helping her child.

So Cade had gone and found a friend to help him, the same way she had when she'd left their family to stay with Julia. The same way Julia was here now, instead of confronting her husband.

"We're both cowards," she said.

Her friend looked hurt and confused, but concerned, too. "What happened? What's wrong?"

"Beverly Turner came over with Mallory this morning. Nate and Cade worked together today. They may finish their home-schooling for the rest of the school year together."

"How wonderful!" Julia's typical enthusiasm was the final straw.

"As wonderful as your life with Walter?"

Julia raised a hand to her throat. "Th-that . . . That's not fair."

"Relationships seldom are."

"What's gotten into you, Sam?"

"Life. Love. Not being able to handle either one like an adult, the same as you."

She'd been relieved when Cade had begged to let Nate stay. She'd been *relieved*—grateful beyond words—to not have to talk with her sensitive, loving child about something only she could explain to him. Shame had been eating away at her ever since.

But had that led her to take Cade aside and talk with him, once he stopped demanding her attention? Of course not.

"I love Brian and my boys with all my heart. You love Walter and Justin and Austin. So why do we keep doing this?"

"Doing what?"

"Everything we can to avoid the only thing that will make any real progress in our families."

"I'm not avoiding anything. I came here thinking my friend would help me deal with my husband, before the rest of the town knows what he's been up to."

"We're the biggest hypocrites on the block. You rock every-one's else's world, including those people at the school board meeting, with the way you take charge of whatever needs to be done. But you can't face the decisions you have to make for your own family. I take a stand against my husband and tell him we have to face some tough choices so our family can heal, he turns himself inside out so that can happen, only *I'm* the one who can't do my part. I never could."

"Oh, please—you're one of the strongest women I know."

Sam laughed. "Beverly's strong. She's creating even more trouble between herself and James, bringing Nate over to me, but she did it anyway. Kristen's strong for standing up to Roy and the school board. Even though she loves this community and des-perately wants her contract renewed for next year, she's fighting for the truth about the shooting to come out, so the right choices will be made for the school and the kids. The Dickerson family is strong, dealing with every parent's nightmare—losing their child—but they showed up at that meeting to make their voices heard. They're still trying to understand. They're not giving up. But you and me . . . Your husband drinks until you and your boys are half afraid of him, then apologizes the next morning and all is forgiven, because you don't want to deal with the alternative. So he's still drinking. I've been telling myself that I can't come home until Brian deals with what he has to, only . . ."

"Only what?" Julia sounded more furious than Sam had ever heard her, even during Julia's argument with Walter Monday night. "Speak for yourself, Sam. If you want to spiral into a permanent pity party no matter how many good things you still have going for you, be my guest. But don't drag me down with you. I needed a friend, not a lecture. If you can't be there for me with Walter, I understand. I'll simply—"

"Take him back and pretend this isn't happening either, just like all the other nights it hasn't happened since January?" Sam heard herself attacking her friend for the very same kind of avoidance she and Brian had perfected. But she couldn't seem to hold the words back. She'd been holding in too much all day.

"My life may not be as perfect as it seems on the outside," Julia said. "But I'm doing the best I can to keep what's important to me. And what's important to me is having my family together, including my husband, whatever I have to do and however long I have to keep taking him back. Most people don't get over a decade off to figure out what they're going to do about the mistakes they've made. The rest of us have to find a way to do the best we can with the crappy hand we've been dealt. Otherwise nothing gets done. We hurt and deal with things badly and we paste on whatever Band-Aid we have to, to just hold on for another day. Even if it means never getting to the bottom of what's wrong, or never fixing everything completely, or never making some grand gesture to prove just how honest or strong or courageous we are. Wake up, Sam, and be grateful for what *you* have—a husband who loves you more than life itself, and two fine boys who don't need you to be a hero for them as much as they need their mother back. Knock this shit off, before you throw away more than our friendship."

Sam felt as if she were melting beneath her friend's glare.

God, what had she done?

She'd never heard Julia talk this way. And she'd caused it. She'd meant well, but she sounded like a judgmental shrew who'd needed her best friend to feel as bad as she did, so she wouldn't feel so terribly alone.

That wasn't true.

It couldn't be true.

You're the best woman, wife, and mother I know . . .

"I care about you, Julia," she said, because her friend had to know that. Now. Before it was too late to fix this. "I'm so sorry I—"

"I need to get to McCradey's." Julia turned to leave.

Sam rushed to her side. "Let me go with you. I'm worried about you. I swear that's all I've been trying to say."

"Is that what 'you're a hypocrite' means in New York?"

"No. I'm so sorry I said that to you. And I—"

"What's happened?" a voice said from behind them.

Brian was in the doorway leading in from the garage. Neither Sam nor Julia had heard him come up the driveway.

"Oh, thank God you're here." Julia ran to him and away from Sam. "I need your help," she said, the same as she had when Sam first answered the door. "Please, Brian. I don't know anyone else I can turn to. It's Walter. Please help me get him home."

"Of course." Brian pulled her into the gentlest of hugs, no questions asked. No hesitation. "What can we do?"

Chapter Nineteen

McCradey's was a local dive. The first time Brian had stepped inside the corner pub just a mile down the road from the northern end of Mimosa Lane, it had felt just right to him.

His favorite joints in Manhattan had had the same lived-in feel. The seedier, the better had been his mantra in college and the early years of his marriage and fledgling career. You wanted to relax in a bar and forget your world for a while. Comfort and no stress and blending in were what mattered, so the rest of the day could slip away. Atmosphere was more important in a place like Chandlerville, where a man's wife or his girl would want to know where he'd be hanging out for ball games and prizefights and whatever else he'd have more fun watching with the guys instead of at home alone.

Not that McC's was a place where the local ladies cared to make regular appearances—an added bonus for their men. The food was basic, but good. The beer was reasonably priced, with enough variety on tap and bottled in the fridge to mix things up. The flat-panel TVs overhead were always set to sports channels, and positioned so at least one of them could be viewed from each end of the bar and from every table.

It had been longer than Brian had realized since he'd been there. He pushed open the bar's oak door, Julia and Sam close behind him, trying to remember the last night he'd ventured out alone on a Saturday to cut loose. He'd never been one to stop for a beer on the way home from work, though he'd known for years that some of the other dads on the lane were five-day-a-week regulars. A few more, rumor had it, since the shooting at Chandler.

Folks were handling the fallout in their own ways, many struggling in private, the way Sam and Brian had. Others preferred gathering with friends in public places like McC's, trying to reclaim a flicker of what the world had felt like before the security of thinking their kids were unconditionally safe had been forever ripped away.

Walter had evidently been even more private than Sam and Brian as he'd dealt with his demons. He and Julia had always been hyperaware of their standing in the community. It wasn't as if they were prudes—they'd always served beer and wine when they'd hosted parties in their home. But Brian, like everyone else, had pegged Walter as a responsible, conservative neighbor, a sought-after CPA for a private Atlanta firm and a dedicated family man. So what if he had a few beers on the weekends?

Now there his neighbor was at five o'clock in the afternoon, elbows spread on the bar with a beer and a shot in front of him, tossing back peanuts and staring at ESPN2 on one of the flat-panels.

And evidently this was exactly where he'd been all week. The man Brian had coached club basketball and football teams with was sucking down booze in the middle of the afternoon like it was just another day in Margaritaville. He was half falling off his stool, actually, with one hand holding on to the bar as if the room were spinning, while with the other he lifted his beer mug for a swallow that didn't end until he'd drained most of it.

"Oh my God," Julia whispered.

Sam stood silent and still as stone near the doorway. She hadn't said a word since Brian had ushered her and Julia to the car after making sure the boys were settled and Mallory was available if either of them needed anything. Something was definitely off between Sam and Julia, not that either one of them was talking about it.

"Let me see what I can do," Brian said. Julia was staring mutely at her husband. At this rate, she might still be there at closing time and not have managed a word.

"I'll stay with her." Sam tugged Julia toward the door. "See if you can get Walter to come outside and talk."

Brian nodded. His wife led a shell-shocked Julia to the parking lot. He approached Walter, catching Law Beaumont's gaze. The hulk of a man was filling a pitcher from the taps at the other end of the bar. Law, easily six foot five and 320 pounds, glanced at Walter, shrugged, and went about his business with a sigh.

Brian took the stool beside his friend, raised a finger for Law to bring him a draft, and asked, "Long day?"

Walter grunted, chewed his peanuts, and never looked away from the color commentary on a top NFL rookie who'd been suspended because his drug arrests and pending IRS tax audit were distracting him from grinding bones on the playing field.

Brian shelled a few peanuts and took a sip of the beer Law set in front of him, not certain what he was doing there. But he'd had to do something. Feeling Julia's desperate trembling after she'd literally thrown herself into his arms, he'd jumped at the chance to fix something, anything, when his own life felt as if it were still teetering on the brink, no matter how much progress he and Sam had made.

"I got an interesting job offer today," he said. "It's the offer of a lifetime, you know? But . . ."

"But everything's so screwed up, how the hell will you get away with taking it?" Walter kept chewing. He drained his beer, threw back the shot, and signaled for another round for himself and Brian.

"Something like that." Brian waved Law away before the man could pull him a second draft. He took another sip of the first. "I don't know. These days, nothing I do to help my family seems to be the right thing. Making a huge change in the middle of the mess Sam and I have made would be reckless."

Walter grunted again. After Law refreshed his drinks—tequila turned out to be Walter's poison—Walter cast a bleary glance at Brian. "I always pegged you for a secretly reckless sort of fellow, Yankee."

Brian chuckled at the nickname. He didn't mind it a bit. No one in Chandlerville ever completely forgot that he and Sam weren't from the South. But none of the people who'd taken the time to get to know them really cared, either.

"I used to be, Walter. A long time ago, I used to be."

"Yeah." His neighbor let out a sigh and downed his Patrón. "Me, too."

Brian did the grunting this time. "You? A rebel accountant without a cause?"

Picturing slightly balding, slightly paunchy Walter as James Dean had Brian grinning from ear to ear. His friend was smiling, too, staring down at the fresh beer he hadn't touched.

"I was a semipro bowler," Walter said. "Did you know that? Back before grad school and the kids and making partners and clients happy, because that kept the bonuses rolling in and everyone in town looking at me like I'm the man you want to handle your money, because I'm as solid as they come."

Bowling?

Brian had heard once that Walter and Julia used to be on a bowling team, before everything else they did for the community and their family had eaten up their free time. But he'd bet Jeff Kelsey's kind of money that jonesing for the good old days wasn't why he and Walter were sitting there.

"You give up things," he said, carefully feeling his way. "It's worth it, what you get in return."

"It's for shit," Walter sneered, when Brian had never once, in five years of coaching together, heard the man swear. "You have to give up yourself to get the people in your life to want you? To keep 'em safe and happy? What the fuck good does that do? We've got kids killing each other in our schools. Babies—the babies we've coached and tried to teach to do right. We've got wives who are unhappy and hiding it, and kids who just want the hell out of our houses—at least mine do. They're never home anymore, after all the time I've put into being there for them whenever they needed me, whatever they wanted. We live on one of the nicest streets in Chandlerville, and it might as well be the ghetto to them."

Brian had wondered about that last part—why the Davis boys had been so scarce lately. Watching Walter once more down half his beer in a single gulp was like a punch to Brian's gut.

"Is this about your boys?" he asked.

"Nah." His friend wiped his mouth on the wrinkled sleeve of his dress shirt. "It's . . ."

"It's what, Walter? What the hell? You're scaring Julia to death, even though she's right outside, still trying to understand. What, you've decided out of the blue to throw your marriage away, because you think becoming a drunk would be a better use of your time? I know everyone's had it tough since the shooting. But whatever's going on with you, don't make the same mistake I did and wait too long to ask your wife to help you deal with it."

"Deal with it?" Walter half yelled, half sobbed, his pain suddenly off the charts in a way Brian didn't want to witness but couldn't turn his back on. "Deal with what Troy did, when I could have stopped it?"

"How could you have stopped it? What makes you think you could have stopped Troy, when we haven't coached the kid in two years?"

"Because . . ." His friend sighed and wiped at his eyes. He stared at the ceiling, as if he were praying. "Because two years ago I caught Dillon Wilmington slapping his son around after practice one night, after you and everyone else had gone home. I'd circled back to the playing field because I'd left my clipboard, and there they were—Troy trying not to cry while his old man called him every name in the book for being afraid of being tackled, and Dillon slapping his kid across the face, raging that he'd show him what it was like to really be scared . . ."

Silence fell between them. Brian took a long drink, empathy nailing his ass to the bar stool for as long as Walter stayed. His son's heartbreaking guilt had sounded equally out of context. And for months Cade's secret had fueled his assumption that he was to blame for Bubba's death.

"Did you . . ." he started to ask, but he didn't want to sound as if he believed for a second that his friend was any more at fault than the rest of their community.

"Did I say anything to the son of a bitch?" Easygoing Walter clenched his fists and pounded them on the bar. "I wanted to take the man apart. Right there in front of his kid, I told him if I ever saw anything like that again, I'd report him to the county. I told Troy he didn't have to take that kind of abuse . . ." Walter covered his eyes with his hands, all of him shaking now. "But what did I do when Wilmington pulled his boy from the team before the next practice, so I never had to deal with him or Troy again? Nothing. Not a damn thing. I was busy with my own shit and with the other boys, and I didn't want to get involved, right? Maybe I'd just caught the bastard on a bad night. After all, if he were really knocking his kid and maybe even his wife around that badly, wouldn't someone else know? Someone at school or at their church? Who was I to pry into his life?"

Brian didn't know what to say, other than, "I'd probably have done the same thing . . ."

He didn't like to think that he wouldn't have been there for Troy. But since the chaos in his own personal life had always been a struggle to handle, it was a good bet that he wouldn't have involved himself in another family's problems, unless he'd felt he had no other choice.

The question was, why hadn't *anyone* in Chandlerville or on Mimosa Lane done anything on Troy's behalf before it was too late? Had everyone else been blind to the warning signs Cade and Walter thought they alone had seen? Or had the entire community let down an abused little boy, and Bubba, because they hadn't wanted to see what had been going on right in front of them all this time?

He put a hand on his Walter's arm and squeezed.

"It's not your fault," he said again. "We all should have known. We all should have gotten involved—with Bubba, too.

He'd been ganging up on other kids for years. Everyone saw it on the ball field. You and I even talked about it a few times. But it hadn't gotten bad enough to do anything about. At least, we thought it hadn't . . ."

His friend yanked his arm away, mumbling something unintelligible that, had it come from anyone else, Brian would have thought sounded like *fuck off.*

Minutes that felt like hours passed in silence, except for the soft drone of the TVs overhead.

"So . . ." Brian cleared his throat.

He drank more of his beer while he thought about how genuinely Walter and Julia had always loved Chandlerville. They'd given so much of their time to the community. And here Walter was, feeling the Wilmingtons' and the Dickersons' tragedies as if they were his own—to the point that his grief and guilt were ripping at all that was most precious to him in his own life.

Brian's neighbors were remarkable people.

"So, you were a good bowler?" he asked, sounding like an idiot. But he was desperate to say something, anything, that wouldn't set his friend off again.

Walter turned his head to stare, his eyes bloodshot and glassy.

"Had plans to go pro for a while," he said, his attention returning to the nearest TV. "But I'd have had to drop out of college, and my old man wasn't having any of it. Then Julia and I made plans of our own . . . Still, opening my own place coulda happened, if I'd pushed my wife for it hard enough."

"A bowling alley?" Brian wouldn't have been any more surprised if his friend had said he'd wanted to build a spaceship and fly to the moon.

"Bowling *center*. A family joint, where the community could come and hang out. Kids' leagues. Adults. Church groups. Even the biker types who want to hoot and holler a bit. A place for everyone. A good-time place . . ."

And instead, Walter had been sitting behind a desk in a corporate office much like W&M for going on twenty years now.

"Wow," was all Brian could say to that, staring down at his mug and at the gauntlet of his own life choices.

Walter nodded. "Sometimes I wonder . . ."

"What?"

"If it would have made a difference."

Brian felt the world settle a little heavier on his friend's shoulders.

"At home?" he asked, genuinely curious.

"With my boys and Julia. With Troy and Bubba and their families and the rest of us. Everyone's so busy . . . Everyone's got so much on their plates, and we're all just winding tighter and tighter until there's nothing but the busy, and we forget who we were when we all started, and something just . . . unravels."

Like Beverly and James Turner. And even though Brian didn't know the Dickersons well, he knew for certain after witnessing the man's heartbreak at the school board meeting that Chuck had never intended to set his boy on the path of bullying and hurting others, until it had cost Bubba his life.

"So, bowling's the answer?" Brian asked, only half kidding.

Another grunt from Walter.

He drained the rest of his beer.

"Nah," he said. "But maybe liking what you do is. Liking your life, and spending time doing what you like. Work. Family. Your kids. Friends and the community. Julia and I, we thought we were all about the community, but I haven't made the time to speak one-on-one with Chuck Dickerson since Bubba aged up to another football team. And, well, you know just how relieved I was to not see Troy and Dillon Wilmington any longer. What kind of coach lets something like being worried about a kid's safety slide like that, just because you're busy and have a new team of players to coach who won't be nearly as much of a hassle?"

"It's *not* your fault. It's nobody's fault."

"It's all of our faults. These are our kids. This is our community. And we've given all that security up. We want more for ourselves and families than we had growing up, sure. But working for *more* has taken over everything, until we don't see each other anymore. Until our kids are turning on each other, because we don't see how much they're hurting."

"You didn't do any of this," Brian said, trying and failing to understand his neighbor's inebriated logic.

"Then why can't I go home and spend time with my boys anymore? Not after what I knew about the Wilmingtons. Not after I did nothing. I hate being with my wife and my own kids. I hate being at work. I want to be somewhere else all the time. I want my family to be something else, and we never will be." Walter signaled for Law to set him up again.

"And you think drinking is going to fix that?"

"I yelled at her, man," Walter sobbed into his empty mug. "Came home early from another nothing day where I cared about numbers and other people's money more than I did anything important, and my boys were gone as usual. Julia was gone. Nothing to eat in the place, when she used to make it smell so good and keep the boys close because they'd always be home for her dinner if nothing else. Now I don't know them anymore. They don't want to know me. And I got so pissed I started drinking early, to keep from smashing something with my bare hands. Then what did I do when my wife finally did come back—from the school board meeting I'd promised her I'd be at but didn't show for? I started screaming at her right in front of Sam, because that's what I am."

"What?"

Brian tried to imagine the scene his gentle neighbor was describing. Walter had never so much as raised his voice to any of the kids they'd coached together, no matter how frustrating a game or practice got. And Sam had witnessed his meltdown in person, without ever letting on.

"What are you?" Brian pressed.

"A lousy bastard who's gotno business takingcareof nobody anymore—not my wife and kids or anybody else's." Walter dropped his head into his hands, having an honest-to-God crying jag, his words more slurred by the second. "I don't wantany ofit. None of the worthlessstuff we've got. What good isanyofit? Our families are falling apart, and there's no fixing them."

He went to throw back the latest shot Law had poured. Brian put his hand over Walter's and slid the tequila out of reach, until his friend finally let go.

"We don't have *nothing*," Brian said. "We have our families still, even if we've messed things up for too long. Our kids are still here. We can fix this, Walter. Every family in Chandlerville has a chance now to see what's been slipping away and fix it. But drinking's not going to get it done. You know that. What are you doing here like this, worrying your wife? She loves you, no matter how bad it's gotten, no matter what you've done. Don't keep doing this to Julia. The two of you can make it work together. Tell her what's wrong."

The way Brian had never been completely honest with Sam until now. And even though he'd promised himself and his wife that he'd changed, he was fighting daily not to fall into feeling the same panic as his friend—that maybe it was too late, and there was no going back to what they should have been from the start.

"I quitmy job," Walter mopped at his face again with his wrecked dress shirt. "Couldn'tbethere anymore. Couldn'tkeep being whatIdidn'twant to be, where there was no pointanymore. I couldn'tbe home neither. So I've been here with my buddy Law sinceTuesday."

For four days? Walter had quit his job Tuesday, and had been going on all-day benders ever since. Brian looked over at McC's bartender, who nodded in silent confirmation, shaking his head while he dried off the mugs he'd pulled from the steaming dishwasher beneath the counter.

"You need to be home, Walter," Brian said. "With Julia, no matter how hard that's going to be for a while. Just like Sam needs to be home with me, if I can convince her that I'll work on our problems the way I haven't before. No one's going anywhere, not my kids or yours. But we can't help them until we get ourselves together. If . . ."

If what?

What had Sam said to Nate at Chandler? Something about not coming back to school if that's what he needed. Not forcing himself to do what didn't fit, when doing something else was going to make the difference between him continuing to hurt or getting better.

"If you're not happy, change things," Brian said to his distraught friend, thinking as he had been all afternoon about the decision he owed Jeff in the morning. "Talk to your wife and figure something else out. Anything but just sitting here and throwing away everything you two have built. If the old stuff isn't working anymore, find a new dream together. What about the bowling alley you said you wanted to build?"

Walter harrumphed or hiccupped or both. "Whatabout it?

"You've got the connections to finance it. And I hear tell you've got a neighbor who's a fair to middling architect, if you're in the market for one."

Walter's red-rimmed eyes were brimming with tears and confusion. "I can'tletyou do that."

"You can't let me help you, the way you and Julia have been there for my family? If I've learned anything from the last three months, it's that we need our friends when we're dealing with hard stuff like this. And sometimes we need to *push* each other to get better, instead of watching everyone make the best out of staying hurt. So, I'm pushing. You think neighbors and community don't mean anything in Chandlerville anymore? Let's prove you wrong. And if you think a bowling center is what we need to change things, I'm in. Whatever it takes to make this work for you and Julia."

Walter chuckled again, as if they were both nuts. And maybe they were. But Brian was thinking of Jeff's offer again, and the other man's seemingly sincere interest in making the opportunity of a lifetime possible for him. There were worse things in life, than to go out on a limb for a friend who wasn't quite ready to stand out there on his own.

"But first," he told Walter, "we've got to dry you out."

"'Cause that's gonnamake everything feel better?"

"Nope." Brian pushed his own beer away, resisting the urge to drain the rest of it.

"'Cause I'vegotta face my wife and figure out how much of a marriage I've got left to make work?"

"Yep." Brian clapped a hand on his friend's shoulder, the way Pete had for Brian so often this last week. "The same way I've got to maneuver Sam back under my roof, before I end up being Law's next good-time buddy."

***

"I'm sorry," Sam said, hoping for her friend's forgiveness for what she'd said back at the house, and knowing she'd likely have to wait a long time to get it.

She and Julia were waiting in Brian's Altima. Standing outside the car, outside McC's, with the community driving by soon on their way home from work, had been a nonstarter. Julia had taken the backseat again. Sam was once more in the passenger side, front. And the silence between them since they'd left her house had to stop.

Sam couldn't stand it.

She turned sideways, looking over the headrest. Julia was staring out her window, as if the empty Waffle House across the street held the answers to all her problems.

"Sorry for what?" Julia asked. "Finally saying what you've clearly needed to say since you moved in with Walter and me?"

"No. For pointing my finger at you and your difficult choices, so I could ignore my own colossal mistakes for as long as possible. You've been the best friend I could have hoped for. Both you and Walter have been. I'm a louse for not being supportive when you needed me."

"Best friends tell the truth, even when it hurts." Julia went from gazing out the window to staring at her clenched hands. "That's the kind of support that really matters. And you're right. I don't know what we've been doing, you and I. But we're not helping our families. Maybe the only people we've helped are ourselves—making it as easy as we could *not* to deal with things."

Sam nodded—to herself.

"I'm moving back home tonight," she said. "Brian and I are going to handle our family and our problems together, no matter how hard that's going to be."

"And I'm talking my husband into dealing with whatever he's going through instead of drinking until he's unconscious, or he's not welcome back in our house."

"I'm not sure I can be the kind of woman Brian wants for his wife." Sam's hands were fists now, too. "He deserves someone who believes in the good things in life, and someone who trusts the bright future stretching out ahead of us. And some days I do. A lot more days now, thanks to the time you and Walter have given me. But then . . ."

"I'm not sure Walter knows what he wants anymore, except to push away me and his sons and our life . . ." Julia patted Sam's shoulder and managed a brave smile. "I'm ready to push back, though."

Sam covered her friend's hand with her own, their connection solid and more priceless to Sam than ever. Julia stiffened. She was looking out the windshield, where the front door to McCradey's had swung open. Walter and Brian left together. Brian had his arm around Walter, keeping him on his feet.

"I'm right here if you need me," Sam said, determined to never again let her friend down. "Always."

Julia nodded. "You, too, darlin'. We've got to take care of our own business, but we'll never be alone, you and I. Never. Right?"

Sam smiled, feeling better and worse that they'd come full circle.

"You bet your southern butt," she said.

Chapter Twenty

Brian pulled onto their cul-de-sac with Sam beside him and Walter and Julia in the backseat, silent and as far apart as they could get—connected only by their clasped hands.

Julia had reached out for her husband when he and Brian had made it to the car. "We need to talk when we get home," was all she said. To which Walter had hung his head and nearly collapsed at her feet, saying only, "I'm ready."

Brian stopped the car at the Davises' driveway. Julia unhooked her seat belt first. After several failed attempts by Walter, she helped her husband with his. In the rearview mirror, Brian watched them gaze at each other for several weighted seconds.

"Are the boys home?" Walter said, near tears again.

Julia nodded. "They've been part of this all along. You owe them an explanation, the same as you do me. And they need to be part of whatever decision we make next."

Walter swiped at his eyes with the heel of his free hand. He nodded once.

"Thank you both," Julia said to Brian's reflection. "I don't know what I would have done if you—"

"Don't finish that sentence," Brian said over the lump in his throat. "You never have to worry about finishing a sentence like that with us. We're here. After what you've done for our family and our community, all the lives on Mimosa Lane and in Chandlerville that you've touched . . . We'll always be here."

Julia smiled. She opened her door.

"And Walter?" Brian said. When his friend's gaze met Brian's in the mirror, Brian said, "Call me about that venture we discussed. Whenever you're ready, I'll do whatever I can to help."

Walter shook his head, trying and failing twice before he got the door handle to work. He and Julia stepped out of the car, shutting the doors behind them and heading up the driveway.

Brian wasn't certain Walter was sober enough to remember anything they'd talked about. But that was fine. Brian wouldn't forget. And he had his money on Julia convincing her husband to get the help Walter needed, so that one day soon Brian could remind him about the dream he'd shared, and Brian's commitment to help make it a reality.

Sam watched their friends disappear inside their home.

"Is this your stop, too?" he asked, prepared to fight this time, this night, to keep her from slipping away from him.

When she didn't immediately say yes, his heart soared. Then her gaze dropped to where he'd been holding her hand since the bar, her grip tightening. Whatever had been upsetting her since he'd gotten home that afternoon wasn't passing, even though she and Julia seemed to be in a better place. The weight of all the things they needed to talk about felt like a third passenger in the front seat, lodged between them.

He thought about taking her on the walk they'd discussed that morning. It had been such a romantic idea. But it wasn't dark yet, and Sam liked to walk at night. And romance wasn't what they needed right now, even though it would be a welcome distraction.

Turning the wheel, he made the decision for both of them and headed into their driveway. He stopped halfway down. He didn't push the button to open the automatic door on the garage. Instead, he turned the engine off, excited suddenly, like one of their kids on Christmas morning.

"Come on," he said. "I want to show you something."

Sam nodded, curious and surprised and maybe a little excited, too.

They stepped out of the car, the cool, clean evening feeling amazing around them as they smiled at each other. This was one of those moments, Brian realized, that you rarely saw for what it was when it was happening.

It was almost as if they were young again, free again, happy where they were, knowing they where right where they belonged. Or maybe it was just Brian, sensing that they were back where they'd started so many years ago in New York, discovering themselves and each other and looking toward the future as an adventure instead of a struggle that they'd have to fight their way through day by day.

He rounded the front of the car. He drew his wife around the side of the house toward the back. He was desperate for her to love the surprise he and Joshua and Cade had created for her over the last two evenings after she'd retreated once more to Julia and Walter's.

"Where are we going?" Sam asked.

"You'll see, love."

She was his inspiration.

She was his miracle.

There was nothing she couldn't do, no matter how fragile she seemed or how much help she might have needed to get them all to where they were now. She was a source of relentless strength that Brian hadn't valued enough, until she hadn't been there, and life had become unbearable.

Never again.

He'd never again take what they had for granted. He'd never again help her hold herself back. He was going to be there for his wife—and himself—from now on. No matter how difficult their journey, they would find a way to be honest with each other about what they needed. Including him coming clean about deciding at McC's to take Jeff up on his offer and follow his career dreams, the way Brian had encouraged Walter to.

He stopped just before they would have turned the corner to the backyard, amid the overgrown bushes and flower beds along the side of the house that no one had touched in months. He curled his wife into his arms and pecked a kiss on the tip of her nose.

"Ready?" he asked.

Her kiss back, on his cheek, arrowed straight to his soul. "For what?"

"For a glimpse of how I see our future," he hedged. "The boys are so excited. And they've done such a great job of not spoiling your surprise. Particularly Cade. He's been like a drill sergeant, telling Joshie and me what you'd want, and how you'd want it, even though I know you two aren't making as much progress as you'd like during the day. You have to promise to act surprised later, when they drag you out here once I say it's time."

"Okay . . . I promise."

Her eyes sparkled, the way they always did when he teased her. He made a mental note to tease her more often. Every day, for the rest of their lives.

"Come with me, Samantha," he said, leading her around the corner.

***

Sam stopped walking, staring at the beauty before them.

The garden that had sprung to life again in their backyard wasn't perfect. It wasn't what she herself would have done. Her family had gone for abundance of color, rather than texture and sustainability, since many of the bedding plants and flowers they'd chosen would bloom just once before needing to be replaced. But her husband and sons had clearly poured their hearts into her surprise. Their love for her was a living, shining feast for her eyes that she knew she'd see again every night in her dreams. And they'd done it all since she and Brian had walked in on Cade and Nate's fight Monday afternoon.

"It's . . . it's beautiful," she whispered, afraid of speaking too loudly and risking the boys overhearing, wherever they were inside. "Oh, Brian. It's the most beautiful thing I've ever seen."

. . . a glimpse of how I see our future . . .

Her backyard was thriving once more, overflowing with love. They'd tried so hard, creating a special place for her to be outside, where she could feel safe and calm enough to want to come back to them. And despite his anger at her that morning, Cade had been part of this?

She brought her hands to her mouth, taking everything in, until she was once more gazing at her smiling husband.

"Oh, Brian," she whispered again, and promptly burst into tears, burying her head against his strong shoulder and crying for all the hurt and worry and heartache she'd caused her family. "I'm so sorry," she said. "I'm so sorry . . ."

"Hey." He pushed her away and swept back her damp bangs. He kissed the tears at the corners of her eyes. "Hey, what's wrong? This is supposed to be a good thing. We wanted to show you how much we missed you. I wanted to show you how sorry I am for not paying attention to what you've needed to feel good here. We wanted to make you . . ."

"Want to come home." She sobbed, hiccupping to try to keep from crying even harder. "I know. You thought you had to make a place for me that was separate from everyone and everything else, or I'd never come back. I'm sorry, Brian. Really. I'm so sorry you guys thought it was the only way I could be happy here again. I never meant to do that. I don't know how I've let this go on for so long. But I swear, Julia and I talked while we were waiting in the car, after we've fought about it more than once this week. And I think I was even realizing it at the school board meeting on Monday. And then when Beverly brought Nate over this morning, and after Cade asked me to write my own essay, and I let our son let me off the hook so I wouldn't have to open up to him the way he needs me to . . . I'd already decided not to do this anymore. Not this way. I swear this isn't what I want, no matter how beautiful you've made my garden again. I don't want it like this anymore. Not alone, with me hiding from the rest of you like I was before . . ."

She was babbling and reaching for her husband, wrapping her arms around him and holding on and hoping he'd understand even though she knew she wasn't making any sense. Not yet. But she wasn't going to let him go, or let herself go back to

Julia's or even inside her own house to see her sons, especially Cade, until she'd asked her husband for the help she needed to do the right thing.

Not until she'd begged Brian to hold her to the commitment she knew she needed to make for herself first, and then for all of them.

Brian guided her to the wooden swing beside the back door, sitting with her on the plush green cushions and giving her a few seconds to quiet down.

"Talk to me," he said. "Whatever it is, let it out and talk to me, until we both understand what you need. And then . . . There's something I need to tell you, too, Sam. I've made a decision, and it's got me spinning as much as all of this has you."

He looked around their backyard—*their* garden now, hers and Brian's and their boys. He wrapped his arm around her and waited. No telling her it was going to be okay. No trying to get her to stop crying before she was ready. Her husband was waiting for her to take the lead. And he was saying he needed her to make sense out of something that was bothering him.

The last time it had felt this way—calm and close and safe— had been the night they'd decided to move to Atlanta and take the job offer at Whilleby & Marshal and start their life over.

"Could you . . ." She loved this place. She loved *them* in this place. And she was terrified of messing it up. "Do you think you could start? Saying whatever you wanted to, I mean. I promise I won't wimp out of telling you what happened today with Nate and Cade. I want you to hear it all. I want to know what you think. But . . ."

"You need me to go first?"

She nodded, holding her breath.

"Okay." He held her hand in both of his.

"Thank you."

He brushed his thumb across her palm and back. "I'm not going back to W&M. I have a better offer. A riskier offer that will take a bit more of my time up front. But it will free me up in the long run to be at home more to help you out with the boys, so you can do more for yourself when you're ready. There's no guarantee that it'll work, not like staying where I am would keep paying the bills for as long as we need it to. But I have a chance to do the kind of designs and projects I've always dreamed of. I'll be happier with my work, I think. And I'll . . . I'll be able to help all of us be happier with staying here. It'll be . . ."

He squeezed her hand, struggling.

"It'll be a good change?" She remembered him saying the exact same thing about their move south.

"Yeah." He let out a breath, sounding as if he'd been holding it in for twelve years. "I think it's exactly the change I need."

"Then that makes it exactly what we all need."

Her husband had never been indestructible or perfect or incapable of feeling the damaged, scary things she did. He'd simply thought he'd needed to hold it together, and hold everything inside, so she and their boys wouldn't know. Now Brian was trusting her to be strong enough to accept what he needed to get better, even after she'd just blubbered all over him.

Surprise at her instant agreement made funny little wrinkles in the space between his eyebrows. "You don't even know what I want to do yet."

"I know *you*. And I want to hear everything. But whatever you decide to do, I know we'll be just fine, as long as we have each other."

He'd said that to her, too, that night in their tiny apartment kitchen in New York, when she'd been too messed up to stay, but terrified of leaving behind everything and everyone they knew in Manhattan to begin again. Now they had Chandlerville and Mimosa Lane and their friends and their family. They had each other, and the long journey they'd taken to this moment, where they could finally see what they'd moved here to see.

"We're ready, Brian. You've made sure of that. You've given me so much. You've given me time and love and a new life. Now let's take care of what you need. I'm ready. I promise I am. I won't let you or the boys down this time. We're in this together. I won't ever walk away again."

At some point while she'd been babbling once more, her husband had started crying. Softly, so slightly, but he was crying and pulling her close, and kissing her the way he had the day he'd finally found her after she'd walked her students out of Manhattan, and he'd fought his way through the traffic and people and panic to reach her.

"I love you like dark chocolate," she said, when he finally let her breathe. "I love you so much, Brian."

"Thank God," he murmured against her lips.

And then he was laughing and kissing her again.

"What?" she asked, inching back and loving the happy sound of him chuckling. "What's so funny?"

"Will you still love me so much if I tell you I may have promised Walter that I'd back him if he decided to open his own bowling alley? He might not remember a word of our conversation. But if he does, I'm on the hook for helping him design his dream business. It might not be a very lucrative way to begin my own firm."

"A bowling alley?" Walter Davis?

"A community center," Brian corrected himself. "Where families and neighbors and all kinds of different people and teams could come together and spend time getting to know one another better and having fun. It's his dream. It's a good dream. I'd like to be a part of making it happen for him."

Sam was laughing now, too, at the thought of Walter and Julia running a local bowling joint. "Okay, then. If that's what our friends need, that's what we'll do."

Whatever it took. Whatever kept her husband behaving as if the world had been lifted off his shoulders.

"Okay then." He nodded, still looking at her as if she'd grown a second head.

She stopped giggling, feeling the questions before he could ask them. Her reprieve was dwindling fast, as night closed in and crickets began to cast their spell, along with the frogs and other night creatures that added to the symphony she loved so much during a Mimosa Lane sunset.

"Are you okay?" he asked.

His gaze held hers, as the love and concern behind his question washed over her. He wasn't assuming that she would be okay. He wasn't pressuring her to *be* anything at all. She didn't need to hide what she was feeling. She never would again. No more faking. No more pretending or walking away from the truths they both needed to face.

"I'm not sure," she admitted. "I think I will be, but I'm going to need your help. Cade asked me to do something today. Actually, he demanded it, and I brushed him off. I could let it drop, now that he has. But I won't. Please don't let me."

"I won't," Brian promised, letting the silence gather around them again. Then he prompted, "Beverly and Nate came over?"

She nodded. "She's going to talk with James. Nate's going to work with Cade again tomorrow, and maybe through the end of the school year. The boys are friends again. They spent most of today talking and goofing around. But if they'll get down to work, I think they're both maybe ready now to finish what they need to, so Kristen and Mrs. Baxter can promote them to junior high. I think they can do together what Cade hasn't been able to on his own."

"Even the essay?"

She nodded again, feeling the words rising inside her.

All the words and the images and the stories she'd never shared with anyone, not even Brian. The things she'd learned that day and every day since, because of the community she'd been a part of in New York and the new friends and family she'd made in Chandlerville. There'd been heartbreak and loss, but there'd also been love—the forever kind—and rebirth and courage and hope.

And it was those final lessons she couldn't teach her son, not the way a mother should, the way *she* should, until she put all the other words out there for him to read and understand and ask questions about. He clearly needed that, to help him make sense of what he'd been through with Nate and Troy and Bubba and the rest of the kids at Chandler that day. And she needed to do this for him—she needed to do this for herself and her entire family.

"Like I said, I need you to help me do something," she said to Brian. "Actually, I need you to do something *with* me."

"Anything," he promised her.

She laughed again at his eagerness.

"You're going to regret that, big guy. I know just how much you hated writing essays in school . . ."

Epilogue

September 1, 2013

"Everyone ready?" Brian asked.

Sam smoothed her hands down her summer-weight cotton dress. It wasn't yet nine o'clock in the morning, but the day's heat had already taken an enthusiastic turn toward broiling. But that wasn't why she was feeling light-headed, or why her palms were sweating, or why she was hanging back in the kitchen while the rest of her family headed toward the patio door.

"Mom?" Cade asked. He opened the door.

"Wahoo, a picnic!" Joshie yelled as he sprinted into the garden.

Beyond Cade, she could see the crimson blooms of her roses, swaying with the breeze.

"Sam?" Brian stepped closer again—he'd stayed close all morning, ever since they'd gone for a walk at dawn, the way they had most mornings since she'd moved back home in April. "You okay?"

She threw her arms around his strong shoulders, loving the word she'd once hated so much. He was making certain she knew that she could still back out of their plans, and he'd be fine with it. There'd been no forced cheer that morning. And breakfast had already been on the counter when she'd come down from her shower to cook. Brian had scooted out for doughnuts, so she wouldn't have to bake anything for the boys.

And on top of the box had been a bar of her favorite dark chocolate. And a Post-it, its message repeating the most important thing the last eight months, and the last twelve years, had taught them.

We're together,
wherever you need to be today.
Love, Brian

Whether she made it out of the house or stayed home, he'd be fine. They'd be fine, the two of them and the boys and the extended family of best friends and neighbors they'd grown closer to since the last school board meeting.

"I'm wonderful," she whispered in her husband's ear. And she meant it. She leaned away, his blond good looks swimming into focus through happy tears. "I know I've been a little nuts, thinking about this morning. But I feel . . . so lucky to have you all with me. To have all of this back. I'm . . . It's wonderful. I can't wait to get there."

He kissed her, sweetly, like the love they'd made that morning before their walk, and after, while their boys slept and the world came to life around them and the future opened up for all the new dreams they were fighting together to make come true: Brian's plans for his new venture with Jefferson, not to mention managing the Kelseys' remodel; Sam's goal to get more in-volved in their son's and their community's worlds. He rested his forehead against hers in silent understanding of how far they'd come. Then with a wink, her husband headed out the door after Joshua, leaving Sam smiling at her eldest son, her fingers pressed to her lips.

"A little nuts?" Cade asked. "Mom, it's just a few people at the park."

She nodded, and maybe in the past she would have tried to shrug the moment away, without letting him see too much of her fear. But they'd agreed to talk with each other about what was going on from now on, especially if one of them was having a hard time. And Sam's new therapist, a PTSD specialist who was helping her minimize the severity and frequency of her panic at-tacks, had said talking before doing things she knew would make her tense would go a long way toward lessening their potential impact.

"It's not the people . . ." she said. "It's . . ."

"The essays," her son finished.

In a matter of minutes, they would be reading their Expres-sions essays to their friends and neighbors.

"I know," he said. "I don't really want to read mine, either. But I do, in a way. Like Dr. Mueller says, talking about it gets it out there, and then it's not so crowded inside. That's when you get to think about and feel other things."

Cade's therapist had turned out to be a godsend. So had the couple's counselor Sam and Brian were talking with every other week. And so had writing their essays—she and Brian doing one together about their 9/11 experience, and Cade and Nate writing one about the Chandler shooting. They'd all worked through so much.

But one of the things that had done the most good for their family had been sitting outside in the garden the night both essays were finished, and sharing what they'd written with the whole family. *That* had been scary for everyone, and there'd been a lot of questions and a few tears. But since then, there seemed to have been nothing that they didn't feel safe talking through together.

"How did we get roped into doing this?" she asked.

"I know, right?" Her son shoved one hand into the new khakis they'd had to buy for today, because he'd already outgrown the ones he'd needed for his Chandler graduation ceremony. "My stomach feels kinda like . . ."

"You're going to lose your doughnuts? Yeah, me too." Sam stepped a little closer to her twelve-year-old and the day ahead of them. "The Turners are probably waiting for us at the park. That's part of what makes this so nice, how close you and Nate have gotten again."

"It's cool how his parents aren't mad at you and Dad anymore."

A lot more of the uproar from the shooting had died down. Kristen's contract had been renewed. Roy's might not be, when it expired at the end of the just-started new school year. And Sam—she was actually considering substitute teaching a little at Chandler.

"It's been a crazy summer," she agreed. "It's been a good summer."

Cade nodded. He was looking more like his father by the day. But he was talking now about maybe wanting to be a teacher when he grew up—like Sam.

"I can't believe we're doing this," he said.

"It takes a lot of courage to write about your fears."

"It takes more to know other people are going to read about them, too."

It had been a shock, the call from Kristen saying that both essays had won national awards and were to be included in a slide show that had been e-published on the Fourth of July. The local news had picked up the story. A few networks had called about special-interest features tying in Bubba's death and Troy's upcoming trial. Both their family and the Turners had declined to go on the record talking about the shooting again.

But when Julia had suggested they share what they'd written in person at the Mimosa Lane Labor Day picnic . . . it had seemed right to everyone, even Sam.

"I'm so glad," she said, "that your dad and I got to share our story with you and Joshua first. You guys will be who your dad and I are thinking about today when we're reading for everyone else. Having you and your brother has changed our lives. You've given us a new dream to make come true, that we could never have dreamed on our own."

Cade and Joshua, and all the children who learned how to love and care about one another despite how harsh their world might be, were the heroes Sam and Brian had written about. Sam's children in New York. Her and Brian's boys. Nate and Sally, and the other kids from Mrs. Baxter's class who were thriving now, many of them peer counselors in their new junior high school. And all the children in the world fighting to grow up and make it a better place, instead of tearing things and people down.

"I'll be thinking about Bubba and Troy," Cade said.

"I know, buddy."

Bubba and Troy had been who Cade and Nate had written about. They'd rewritten that entire day at Chandler, only they'd shown Bubba and Troy making different choices, and Cade and

Nate making different choices, so that no one was hurt, and Troy got the help he needed, and Bubba realized how much he needed to stop being, as the essay said, such a *butthead* to everyone.

"You and Nate did a wonderful job," she said. "But I know how hard it will be for you to read it out loud. It will probably be hard for some people to hear."

There was no telling how many of their neighbors from the lane would be there. Julia and Walter were coming for certain. They were pouring their free time these days into making Walter's dream of a community bowling center a reality. Meanwhile Walter was doing freelance work for a local accounting firm, and he hadn't taken a drink since that day at McCradey's. Mallory and Pete and Polly would be there. Mallory and Pete had married in June, with Polly as their flower girl and Sam as Mallory's matron of honor. And at the picnic, Polly would be announcing that she'd be getting a new baby brother or sister come next April.

As for the rest of their audience . . .

"You know," Sam said. "I heard that Chuck and Charlotte Dickerson might be coming. Are you going to be okay if they're there?"

Cade shrugged.

The Dickersons had stopped by one night a few weeks ago, and they'd asked to talk to Cade. Chuck and Charlotte had wanted to say they didn't blame him for what happened to Bubba. They didn't even blame Troy anymore. They'd dropped their lawsuit against the Wilmingtons and were moving soon. If they came today, this would be their last Mimosa Lane event. They were starting over somewhere else, the way Sam and Brian once had. They hadn't wanted to leave any bad feelings behind, though. They'd visited with the Turners, too.

"I guess it would be okay," her son said. "I mean, we give Bubba a chance to do the right thing in what we wrote. We're giving him a chance to teach other kids how to do the right thing, Mrs. Baxter said when she read our essay. And I guess we must have done something right if it won the Courage Award in the competition. But . . ." Cade shrugged again. "It still makes me afraid sometimes, to talk about it."

"I know it does." Sam checked her watch.

It was getting close to the time Julia had set for Kristen to present their award certificates in front of the neighborhood. But Sam didn't want to rush this moment. It was too important.

"You might always feel that way a little," she said. "But you and Nate are already doing such inspirational things because of what you've learned. Don't stop now. Keep feeling and making that count, even if it's scary. You'll never be alone as long as you keep sharing what's going on inside you."

As a writer.

Or a teacher.

Or whatever else this amazing kid decided he wanted to be.

Her son and his friends had started antibullying support groups at their junior high school. Cade was talking about running for student council his eighth-grade year, on a platform of tolerance and acceptance. Who knew? Maybe he'd decide to be a counselor himself, or a politician.

"I'm proud of you."

Sam blinked at her son's words. She'd been about to say the same thing to him. And suddenly she lost her battle to stay cool. She closed the distance between them, smothering Cade in a hug.

"I'm so proud of you, too," she said, chuckling as he hugged her back, tight, and then shoved her away with the kind of enthusiasm possessed only by almost-teenage boys being hugged by their mothers. "I owe your father five dollars. He bet me I wouldn't make it out of the house without doing that."

"Well, Joshie owes me doing dishes tonight when we get home. He bet me you wouldn't embarrass yourself until we got to the picnic."

Sam looped an arm around Cade's shoulder and steered him toward the open door to the garden.

"How about we go embarrass ourselves together?" she challenged.

Her son grinned, half hugging her back. And then they walked out into Mimosa Lane's beautiful sunlight together.

Acknowledgments

Thank you to my mother-in-law, Jo DeStefano, for first telling me the story of the brave teachers working in the schools surrounding Ground Zero.

Though this novel is in all ways a work of fiction, it is my genuine attempt to imagine a heroic and happy ending for the untold sacrifices made that traumatic day twelve years ago.

About the Author

ANNA DESTEFANO

Anna DeStefano is the award-winning, nationally best-selling author of twenty novels, including *Christmas on Mimosa Lane*, *Secret Legacy*, *Dark Legacy*, and the Atlanta Heroes series. Born in Charleston, South Carolina, she has lived in the South her entire life. Her background as a care provider and adult educator in the world of crisis and grief recovery lends itself to the deeper psychological themes of every story she writes.

With a rich blend of realism and fantasy, DeStefano invites readers to see each of life's moments with emotional honesty and clarity. Her writing has been recognized with numerous awards, including twice winning the Romantic Times Reviewer's Choice Award, the Holt Medallion, the Golden Heart, and the Maggie Award for excellence. She has also been a finalist in the National Reader's Choice and Book Seller's Best awards.

Join Anna each week on her blog: www.annawrites.com/blog.

**Don't miss the next
Seasons of the Heart novel!
Kristen Hemmings finds her own
happily ever after . . .**

Love on Mimosa Lane
Coming early 2014

For a man who'd sworn off women, Law Beaumont was fixated. He was mesmerized. He was staring at the assistant principal who'd requested a meeting with him at his daughter's elementary school, the way he hadn't taken in the sight of a woman since he'd divorced.

But Kristen Hemmings was what songs were made of. She was poetry. She was tall and curvy and so clearly confident in her own skin. And her smile as she knelt in front of his anxious child was pure sunshine—her gentle intensity soaking into Chloe.

"Am I in trouble?" the third-grader asked, gutting Law with her worry and the scared look she shot him while he finished crossing the playground.

"Of course not," the assistant principal said. Kristen had called his daughter over when she'd noticed Law.

"But my dad is here." Chloe stared at the ground as he stopped beside them. "My mom won't like it if—"

"You're not in trouble, sweetie." Kristen stood. Her gaze slid over Law, challenging the indifference he was determined to maintain, no matter what new hassle his ex had stirred up.

"Then why am I here?" he asked. He was over being questioned every damn time he turned around about how he lived his life.

Bright green eyes narrowed, a second before the assistant principal reached out her hand. Chloe's attention zinged back and forth between them.

"Dad?" Chloe asked.

"It's okay, darlin'." Instead of shaking Kristen's hand, he gently cupped the back of his daughter's head.

"I need your help, Mr. Beaumont." The assistant principal dropped her arm to her side. "You and your daughter's."

***

Her dad being at school meant something bad, no matter what Ms. Hemmings said. Chloe knew it.

The one school day a week she stayed with her dad, he always went back to sleep after she left on the bus. When she got home in the afternoon, he was usually still tired. But he'd be up by then, making her laugh and taking her out for hamburgers and milkshakes for dinner—even on days like today when he'd come home late last night, and he'd stayed up even later arguing with her mom over the phone.

Mom had probably been mad that he'd worked the closing shift at the bar again. *What's the point of him asking the judge for more time with my daughter,* she kept saying to everyone, *if he isn't ever home when Chloe's there?* And people would nod and agree with her. Except Chloe knew her mom didn't really want her all the time—Mom just didn't want Chloe with her dad.

Now her dad was at school instead of sleeping the way he should be today. And he looked a little sick, only he didn't smell like he was drinking again—not like Mom told people he was. He looked . . . weird, so Chloe hadn't run to him when she'd first seen him.

It had been stupid, how she'd thought right off that maybe he'd come to check her out early, so they could do something together all day, before he had to drop her off at her mom's after dinner. Maybe they'd go to the zoo in Atlanta, she'd thought. He took her there a lot, even though she'd been going since she was a little girl. She loved it, and he loved her, and the Atlanta Zoo had the best milkshakes, so he always took her when she asked. They'd go every week if she wanted, he'd promised—until the animals got sick of them and the zoo threw them out.

Her dad was the best, no matter what anyone said.

But when he'd stepped outside the school just now, she'd gotten scared for some reason, like she did when her parents fought. He'd been looking at Ms. Hemmings weird, and Chloe had suddenly been afraid of what he might do, or what Ms. Hemmings would say.

"How can I possibly help you?" he asked the assistant principal. He dug his hands into his jeans pockets. He did that when he was upset, and he wanted to look like he wasn't feeling anything at all.

"Can I go now?" Hanging with her dad and the assistant principal in front of her whole class was *so* not cool.

He'd never come to school before, and Ms. Hemmings didn't want *help*. She probably wanted to talk about the divorce. Again.

And who cared? Like half the kids in Chloe's grade had parents who'd split.

No one thought it was a big deal that hers had too—except for Ms. Hemmings and Chloe's dad and her mom. All that mattered to the kids at Chandler was who they hung out with at school and on weekends, and who they talked to at night about what had happened that day. And the most popular girls in third grade talked to Chloe all the time. Which made everything okay still, no matter what had changed.

But Brooke and Summer had been watching from the swings since Ms. Hemmings called Chloe away. They were talking to each other now and laughing and kept looking over at Chloe like she was the joke.

"Can I go?" She put more *pleeaaaase* into the way she smiled up at her dad. That usually worked with him.

Without checking with Ms. Hemmings, he nodded, giving in like he always did these days, because he felt so guilty most of the time. Chloe ran before he could change his mind . . .